# SHANNON HOLMES
## INTRODUCES

SHANNON HOLMES • KEVIN WIGGINS
ANGEL MITCHELL • Da'NEEN HALE
GENA GARRISON • JOSIE N. BRADLEY
NICOLE "JAHZARA" BRADLEY • KIA DuPREE
DWAYNE BYFIELD •MICHAEL A. GONZALES
RHONICA WESLEY • ERIC WHITE
RUSSELL LITTLE & OTHERS

Copyright © 2008 by Shannon Holmes

Published by Shannon Holmes Communications Media
shannonholmes1050@hotmail.com

This is a work of fiction. All of the characters, organizations
and events portrayed in this novel are either products of the
authors imaginations or are used fictitiously.

Editor: Kia DuPree, kiadupree@yahoo.com

Cover Artist: Keith Saunders, info@mariondesigns.com
www.mariondesigns.com

Typesetting: Shawna A. Grundy, sag@shawnagrundy.com
www.shawnagrundy.com/typesetmybook

ISBN: 978-0-9814978-0-8

# SHANNON HOLMES
## INTRODUCES

KEVIN WIGGINS
ANGEL MITCHELL
Da'NEEN HALE
GENA GARRISON
JOSIE N. BRADLEY
NICOLE "JAHZARA" BRADLEY
KIA DuPREE
DWAYNE BYFIELD
MICHAEL A. GONZALES
RHONICA WESLEY
ERIC WHITE
RUSSELL LITTLE
& OTHERS

*Yolanda "Girlie" Whiteside*
*and*
*Roberta "Robbie" McNair*

Thank you so much for your help and support.

*Kia DuPree,* Editor

*Keith Saunders,* Graphic Designer

and

*Shawna A. Grundy,* Typographer

Thank you for helping me to bring this project
together:

This book is dedicated to my cousin,

**Shamel Moore**
*"Hold your head—be safe"*

# Also by Shannon Holmes

*B-More Careful*
*Bad Girlz*
*Never Go Home Again*
*Dirty Game*
*Bad Girlz 4 Life*

# TRAP-STAR

*Shannon Holmes*
Charlotte, NC

## Lucky Me

A beautiful, shiny new 2008 black Cadillac Escalade came to a smooth stop and parked perfectly in the parking spot. The vehicle was one of the trappings of success, a symbol of luxury. Behind the wheel was a young gorgeous African American female named Brianna Campbell. Through her Dolce & Gabanna shades, she glanced down at the platinum Rolex watch on her wrist. It read one o'clock. She was right on time for her hair appointment.

As soon as she entered the hair salon, Brianna noticed all eyes were on her. Still she remained cool behind her dark tinted shades. It would take more than a few envious eyes to unnerve her. Although Hera by Him, was an upscale hair salon, it wasn't free from the catty gossip that plagued every other hood salon. When Brianna strolled pass, almost immediately, the whispers and speculation began.

Because of all the high-priced designer accessories and clothes that Brianna wore, and the expensive toy she pulled up in, the majority of the women assumed that she was some ball player's girlfriend, mistress or wife. The large six carat yellow diamond did little to dispel those rumors. There was no denying that she was well kept. Every time she walked through those doors, she was immaculately dressed in some new hot European designer, from head to toe. Her outfits and designer bags caused some insecure women to fall back into obscurity when they saw her. They knew all her designer accessories were real, while most of theirs were bootleg, cheap knock offs. It was no comparison.

Usually all clients were required to wait in the sitting area until they were called by their stylist. Not Brianna. She strolled right pass the receptionist, heading straight to the back to her stylist. The receptionist merely glanced at Brianna, but she didn't attempt to stop her. She recognized Brianna as a regular. But besides that, Brianna had a swagger about her that suggested, don't mess with her. She wasn't for play.

Her stylist seemed to light up when she saw Brianna coming towards her. And it wasn't because she was happy to see her or liked doing her hair either. Brianna tipped well, it was as simple as that. The stylist knew that she wouldn't have to do another head today. When Brianna was done paying for her new hairdo and tipping her, she was going to be straight.

"Hey, Bri." The stylist happily said. "I can set my watch to you girl, you always on time. I wish all my clients were like you."

*Yeah, right. Whatever Bitch!* she thought to herself.

No matter how friendly her stylist was to her, Brianna was always the same, nonchalant. She always gave her the cold shoulder, spurring any attempts at them becoming too friendly. All the idle chit-chat that went on between stylist and client didn't exist when Brianna took her seat in the stylist's chair. Brianna guarded her privacy like a celebrity. What she did before and after she left the shop was nobody's business. She knew how loose stylists lips could be.

Besides these days, she knew nobody could keep a secret. It was almost as if a secret wasn't a secret unless one person told somebody else. Unfortunately, the secrets Brianna possessed had to go to the grave with her. If they got out they could get her in serious trouble, like indicted or murdered. Neither option was too appealing to her.

Outwardly, Brianna simply smiled in response to the comment.

After taking off her shades, placing them inside her bag, she handed her personal items to her stylist, who put the bag on the counter. Then they were set to begin.

In the mirror the stylist smiled as she examined different parts of Brianna's weave. She knew that her client was watching her too. She went from the front to the back inspecting her hair, when she reached the back, she grimaced slightly. Thankfully, Brianna didn't catch it.

A large scar on the back of Brianna's head, had caused this sour reaction. What in the world was a woman of Brianna's stature doing with such an ungodly scar on her head was beyond her. Matter fact it was the subject of debate whenever Brianna left the salon. To her credit the stylist never asked and Brianna never offered an explanation.

Brianna's scar betrayed her pampered appearance. Her stylist could tell she had been through some shit, exactly what, she didn't know. But she was dying to find out.

Quickly pushing those thoughts out her mind, the stylist went to work. She busied herself with the task at hand. Meanwhile, Brianna casually looked around. While her stylist moved about the booth Brianna took notice of her attire. She was dressed in black from head to toe, slacks and a t-shirt. Brianna looked down to see what she had on her feet and instantly she got pissed off.

Fuckin' Jordan's! she cursed to herself. Those sneakers triggered a horrific memory for her at a critical juncture in her life. As bad as she tried to control them, suddenly her thoughts began to run wild.

\*\*\*\*\*

The halogen headlights shone brightly from the four door European sedan, illuminating the entire garage. With a touch of a button, the garage door quickly closed. Calmly the two occupants of the car made their exit from it. Tre led the way inside the house. After placing his key into the lock, he entered the house and punched in his security code, deactivating the alarm. His girlfriend Brianna followed closely behind.

When the couple entered their townhouse they found nothing out of the ordinary to suggest that anything might be wrong. Everything was just like they left it. They had done this a thousand times, exited and reentered their residence safely. Always without any problems, to Brianna it was a given. But Tre would never get that comfortable with his own safety. His mind frame was totally different from Brianna. He never saw the world through rose colored glasses. Life was a bitch to him, always had and always would be.

In Tre's line of work, one could never be too careful. Drug dealers didn't have a long life expectancy. Most were here today and gone tomorrow, either to prison or the graveyard. It was simple his goal was the same everyday he stepped outside those doors, to return home in one piece. If he accomplished that feat then that day was a good day. See, he knew the game well, nothing was certain and anything was possible. The unpredictability of the drug game had drove Tre to take some extreme measures insulate himself from the streets.

"Stay on point. Keep your eyes open," he always said. Time and time again, he had warned his young girlfriend about the flip side of the drug game. He told her about the stick-up boys who would stop at nothing to rob him. He warned her about coming straight home and about taking a different route, not to be so predictable. He knew he could be the most security-conscious person in the world and one mistake by his live-in girlfriend could undo everything. Tre knew one mistake by either of them could possibly cost them their lives.

Such was the life of a drug kingpin and his loved ones. They always had to beware of that unseen threat that was lurking in the shadows.

Nowadays the streets of Charlotte were like a jungle, there were both predators and prey. They both seemed to balance each other out. But by no means was Tre anybody's prey. On the contrary, he was just as dangerous as they come. He was a killer in every sense of the word.

Still it was hard to fight an invisible foe, one who wouldn't tip his hand until it was too late. One who Tre would never see coming.

After a rare night out eating, finally they were home. Inside the luxurious confines of his townhouse, Tre breathed a sigh of relief. He began to let his guard down. Now he felt somewhat safe.

"Umm, that steak was good as shit!" Tre suddenly announced. "I'm full like a motherfucker. I got niggeritis."

Tre flopped down on couch, kicked back and relaxed. Reaching for the television remote, he turned on the big screen TV. Quickly he became captivated by a new video by rapper TI that was currently airing on BET. He was feeling extremely sluggish since the big meal he had eaten had begun to take effect.

Meanwhile, in the hallway Brianna began to get comfortable herself. She slipped off her high heel shoes, loosened the buttons on her blouse and made her way toward the living room.

"Hold on Big Poppa," Brianna said. "Don't go to sleep on me yet. I got something way better than that steak!"

To Tre that could only mean one thing, oral sex. Like the old saying went, 'The way to a man's heart may have been through a man's stomach'. But for Tre it was his penis. He went fool over some good head. And nobody did it better, that he knew of, than Brianna.

Immediately, Brianna sat down beside her boyfriend and went to work. Quickly, she unzipped Tre's jeans, reaching inside his pants she gripped his penis, pulling it out and took it into her mouth. Brianna's mouth was warm and wet. She feverishly performed oral sex on Tre. And he loved every second of it.

Suddenly, Tre became actively involved, pushing her head further and further down into his crotch area. Again and again, he thrust his hips to meet her hungry mouth. With his eyes closed, he enjoyed the moment.

"Suck dat dick bitch!" he cursed. "Yeah, do dat shit."

Tre cursing at her, didn't even bother Brianna. She was pretty thick skinned when it came to things of that nature. She knew he didn't really mean it. He only said it because it was in the heat of the moment. Brianna was with whatever it took to get him off. She knew if she didn't, there were plenty other hoes out in the streets who would jump at the opportunity. She felt if he was going to stray, it wasn't going to be because of anything she did or didn't do.

"Cum in my mouth daddy!" Brianna demanded.

The commandment drove Tre crazy. He quickly obliged. A hot jolt of semen shot from his testicles to the head of his penis, to Brianna's warm and waiting mouth. As soon as it came out, she gobbled it up and swallowed it down. Brianna drank Tre dry. When she drained every last drop of semen, she continued to suck on his penis. Unable to take any more, Tre finally was able to pry her off of him.

"Alright, God damn!" he exclaimed. "Brianna, that's enough."

From the floor, Brianna glanced up at her man. A sinister smile spread across Brianna's face. She knew this was a job well done.

Getting up off her knees, Brianna proudly stood above

her sexual partner, satisfied that she just put in work. She had bomb head and she knew it.

"Nigger, git up," she joked. "It wasn't all like that."

Tre lay on the couch in the fetal position, trying to regain the little bit of energy, he had just lost.

"Shiiitttttt!!!" was all he managed to say.

Brianna insisted. "C'mon, Tre stop playin'. Git up and come wit me upstairs to the shower. Let's get ready for bed."

"You ga'head," he told her. "I'll be up there in a minute."

"Promise."

"Promise!" he replied. "I'll be right up there as soon as I get myself tagether."

"Alright, hurry up!" she suggested. "We ain't finished. We got one more round to go."

Reluctantly, Brianna began to walk away to prepare for their romp in the shower. She hurried along in anticipation of what was to come. She had just bent the corner, taking only a few steps out of the living room when suddenly two masked gunmen appeared.

With the barrel of a semi-automatic weapon pointed directly at her forehead, Brianna didn't utter a word. Instinctively, she backed up as the gunmen moved silently toward her. The TV successfully drowned out any noise they made.

Quickly, the two masked gunmen burst into the living room, brandishing their weapons on both Tre and Brianna. Caught completely off guard, Tre just starred in disbelief, wondering how in the hell had these two armed bandits gotten into his house without setting off the alarm system.

At the time it was unknown to both Tre and Brianna, but the gunmen had circumvented the alarm system by climbing a nearby telephone pole and cutting the wires.

One gunman barked. "Nigger, you move and I'll blow ya fuckin' head off."

Immediately, one gunman snatched up Brianna, while the other converged on Tre. In these frantic few minutes, everything seemed surreal. It was like none of this was happening. Everything appeared to be moving in slow motion.

Brianna was violently shoved on the couch. This was a traumatic moment for her. Suddenly she began fearing for her life. Even with a gun pointed in her face, she couldn't do anything but stare. The gunman and his weapon were oblivious to her. Brianna's eyes focused on the man's hand. In cursive writing he had the name 'Smalls' tattooed. It was plain as day.

Though the robbers may have thought they covered all their tracks, this was a serious oversight.

"Bitch, don't look at me!" One gunman growled. "Turn ya fuckin' head!"

Either Brianna moved too slow or wasn't fast enough. Whatever the case maybe, as soon as the order was given, the gunman, viciously slapped Brianna. Her head recoiled violently from the blow. She fell back onto the couch with the taste of blood quickly filling her mouth.

"Ok, you know what it is. Don't make this a homicide. Just give us what we came for." He announced. "Now where the stash at?"

"Nigger ain't nuttin' here!" Tre snapped. "I don't eat where I shit at."

Unfortunately, the gunmen didn't buy a word he was saying. The room quickly erupted in violence. Without warning one gunman, began to pistol whip Tre unmercifully. He was pummeled to the floor where he was kicked and beaten some more. Blood began to flow freely from a gash in his head.

"Nigger, you think this a muthafuckin' game huh?" he yelled. "Now, I'ma ask you one more time. Where is it at?"

By now Brianna was in a state of shock. After watching

her man take such a savage beating she began to fear for her own safety. In her mind she wondered why Tre didn't just give them what they wanted so they could leave. She thought it was just that simple. She couldn't understand why he was lying to them.

Brianna didn't understand the game. She didn't understand what it was like to be hood rich, a symbol of success and a target. She didn't understand what it was like to be both loved and feared, to be revered and despised in the neighborhood that you grew up in. She didn't understand what it was like to be a dope boy.

"Look, I already told you. Ain't nuttin' here," Tre muttered through a pair of swollen lips.

One gunman quickly motioned to the other, nodding with his head. His partner reacted by reaching down, grabbing a handful of Brianna's hair, and snatching her up off the couch. He placed one arm around her neck, the other hand clutched the gun that was pressed to her temple.

"Nigger, you better tell us what we wanna hear and fast," one gunman spat. "The next muthafuckin' lie you tell, your girlfriend is dead! Now, where's the stash at?"

Though he was more than a little woozy, Tre was still defiant. He glared angrily at his two assailants. An evil thought ran through his mind. *If I can get to one of my guns. I'm going to kill these motherfuckers. Make them die slow.*

Amongst all the commotion, the shouting, the threats and the violence, the videos playing on the television, a tomb-like silence suddenly enveloped the room. The threat of death hung in the air.

For what seemed like an eternity no one said a word. Brianna's eyes suddenly locked with Tre's. They seemed to sing a sad song. They pleaded with Tre to give up the goods. Still he stood his ground, refusing to say a thing.

Seeing this, Brianna knew she would be forced to take

matters into her own hands. She felt it was the only way to remedy the situation, since her boyfriend wasn't talking. There was a sense of urgency and despair. Things didn't look too good. She had to say something to reverse their fate.

"It's upstairs in the master bedroom." She blurted out. "The money is upstairs in the master bedroom in a suitcase."

Damn! Tre cursed to himself. He shot her an ice cold stare.

Tre would rather Brianna had given up the location of the dope than the money. Money was too hard to come by. Now he had to take some more pen chances to recoup his cash. While if he was robbed of some drugs, he could go to his drug connection and get more on consignment.

The gunmen released his grip on Brianna, who stood there holding her throat trying to recover from the chokehold she had been in. Taking two steps away from her, suddenly the gunmen turned back around and viciously struck her with the butt of his gun. Caught off guard, Brianna went crashing face first to the floor. She was knocked unconscious by a blow to her temple.

Previously, Tre had been the recipient of most of the gunman's violent acts. He had been the target of most of their venomous speeches. He didn't know what provoked the man to do what he did. Tre just looked on helplessly at his battered girlfriend, while his blood boiled.

The other gunman laughed heartily, signaling his approval. "Damn, you knocked that bitch out cold," he commented. "Now go upstairs and get the money."

Doing as he was told, the second gunman fled the living room, and went to retrieve the money.

The gunman announced, "Nigger, ya girl smarter than you. You lucky she told us when she did. I thought we was gonna have to kill her ass, just for you to talk. Just for that we gonna let y'all live."

Tre really didn't believe a word the man had said. His mouth said one thing, but their actions suggested something totally different. Before Tre could give it any real thought or get himself together to mount an attack, he heard the other gunman come running down the steps. It was then that Tre realized that he may have blown his only chance of survival.

"You got it?"

"Yeah, I got it! It was right where she said it was," he said laughing.

Tre watched as the other gunman entered the room and dropped the bag. At this point, he sensed that something was up, though no more words were exchanged between the men. It was as if he knew what was about to happen next.

With two large caliber firearms trained on him, Tre watched as the men inched closer and closer, until they were upon him, within pointblank range. Now that he was on the wrong end of the gun, a strange thing happened to Tre. Something came over him and it was fear. Though he had personally sent countless individuals to the hereafter, now that it was his turn, suddenly Tre realized he didn't want to go. He wasn't ready to leave this earth, not at the ripe age of twenty-five-years-old. He had so much more living to do and things to see. He couldn't believe it was ending like this. Most drug dealers never consider this part of the drug business, until it's too late.

Tre wasn't no chump but he knew he didn't want to die. At least not like this. At least not right now. Unfortunately for him, there were no do-overs in life. Though there were second chances, but he wouldn't get one. He was about to become a statistic.

With the finality of the situation close at hand, Tre finally backed down off his defiant stance, his slumped shoulders now suggested he had gone into submission. A pitiful look appeared on his face, one that invited any act of divine intervention. Tre's look invited any act of mercy, so that his life and that of his girlfriend might be spared.

His would-be killers shot him a cold look of indifference, one that seemed to suggest that they would not deviate from their plan. Their hard core looks seemed to condemn him and his girlfriend to their fate, which was death.

Suddenly without warning, Tre lunged for one of the gunmen's firearms. If he was going to die, it wasn't going down without a fight. Too bad he wasn't quite fast enough to execute his plans. Gunshots exploded through the room, two bullets found their mark. When the smoke cleared Tre was slumped on the floor, dead.

"Now, finish the bitch! And let's get the fuck outta here!"

The first gunmen could have easily, walked over and killed Brianna. It would have been nothing again. He didn't need a potential state's witness to his crime, he needed a co-defendant.

Though gunmen number two wasn't a killer. He had no choice but to follow orders. Now he was in too deep. Standing above Brianna, he fired two shots. One missed badly and the other drew blood, but it only grazed her head.

Now Brianna was wide awake and she knew what was going on. An attempt had been made on her life. Lying motionless, the gunmen thought he had successfully executed her. Just like his partner had done her boyfriend. Grabbing the money, the two gunmen fled the scene, leaving behind a trail of death and destruction.

Long after the gunmen were gone, Brianna continued to lie on the floor, playing dead. She wanted to be sure no one was going to double back to finish the job. As she looked around, she saw Tre's lifeless body lying in a pool of blood. For a long time, she lay there thinking about Tre. It was heartbreaking to see him end up like that. Though he was certainly no angel, Tre didn't deserve to go out like this.

Brianna began to cry.

As far as she was concerned, this wasn't a random act. She couldn't quite understand why she had been shot. She couldn't understand why an attempt was made on her life. After all she was just a female, the so-called weaker sex. She wasn't a threat to anybody. She was just a hustler's wife.

To the killer's, she was a potential witness. They had nothing against her, this was business. She just happened to be at the wrong place at the wrong time, so she had to go, too.

*****

That night at the hospital, a weeping Brianna sat for hours answering every question that the police threw at her. Cleverly, she sprinkled lies in with the truth. Though she might have escaped death, she couldn't escape the empty feeling that had overcome her. Her man was gone. She suffered one of the greatest losses of her life.

When the police left, Brianna was alone with her thoughts to relive that night's fatal events over and over again. She couldn't bring herself to the realization that Tre was dead and he wasn't coming back. Tre wasn't there to take care of her any more. It was almost as if she was in denial or in a state of shock. Suddenly she began to worry about how she would make it without him. Tre had spoiled her. She was like a pretty little girl who was used to getting her way. Now she was about to see again that the world was a cold place.

Something clicked in Brianna's head. It dawned on her that the gunmen didn't take everything. Tre had a stash of dope buried in their backyard. She knew she had to get out of the hospital fast and back to the house. She was scared that someone else might find it first.

Late that night Brianna checked herself out the hospital. She didn't have a clue what she was going to do with all that dope after she dug it up. But one thing she knew, once she started down that path, there was no turning back.

*****

That was the most traumatic experience of Brianna's young life. She still winces whenever she reflected on the tragedy. Brianna Campbell stills sees the two pair of retro Air Jordan's, as the gunmen fled the house. Looking up from the floor as she clung to life, that's all she could see. Fortunately, Brianna survived by playing dead. Ever since then, she hated Jordan sneakers. She vowed never to buy another pair in her life.

*****

After her stylist put the finishing touches on her hair, Brianna gathered her things up, tipped her and walked out the door. Even to those who knew her, it may have seemed as if Brianna Campbell always had her eyes on hustling. But actually, she hadn't.

## Hard Knock Life

Brianna Campbell always had been a dreamer. She loved fairytales with happy endings. Ever since she was a child,she loved to pretend. Brianna was a latchkey child, raised on unhealthy doses of television and movies. She idolized black actors and actresses to the point she could quote and re-enact some of the most famous parts from a movie, line for line.

Her room was like a sanctuary. Life in the Campbell household wasn't the same for Brianna as it was for her two other younger siblings, Jonathan and Charisse. Almost from day one, she sensed that there was preferential treatment shown to her younger sister and brother. It wasn't until she was about to turn nine years old did she find out the why. At Brianna's ninth birthday party, things finally came to a head.

*****

"...how old are you now? How old are you now?..." the partygoers chanted.

In the darkened kitchen, the nine candles on the store-bought chocolate birthday cake, illuminated the room. Brianna hovered dangerously close to the cake, staring into the candle lights as if she were hypnotized. She enjoyed being the birthday girl, the center of attention. Sadly, she knew her moment in the spotlight would fade quickly. Still she lived in the moment. Like any good actress, Brianna played her part well. Outwardly, she grinned ear to ear at her adoring guests. Inwardly, she hurt badly.

As she scanned the room, looking at each familiar face, one was noticeably absent, her Dad's. For some strange reason, he never participated in anything dealing with her. By now it was routine, still it didn't hurt any less. She noticed that he always shied away from her. Often Brianna wondered just what she had done to deserve this?

"Brianna blow out the candles baby and make a wish!" her mother urged her.

"Ok."

Inhaling deeply, Brianna summoned all the air her tiny lungs could hold and blew out the candles. Momentarily, the kitchen went pitch black, the partygoers began to cheer loudly. When the lights came back on tears could be seen running down Brianna's rosy cheeks. Despite how it appeared, these weren't tears of joy.

"Oh, look at her. She's so happy she's crying," one parent suggested.

But Loraine Campbell knew otherwise. If there was one thing she knew, it was her children. She knew their temperaments and tendencies. And this was completely out of character for Brianna. She wasn't emotional at all. Loraine sensed that something was very wrong.

Gently, her mother took Brianna by the hand, and whisked her away from her guests. She led her straight to the bathroom.

"What's wrong with you?" she asked. "Why are you crying for?"

Though she tried her best to keep her composure, Brianna couldn't. Her tears continued to flow freely, now her body was racked by long hard sobs. Young Brianna merely stood in front of her mother unsure of what to say or do.

Her mother said, "Don't just stand there looking all sorry. Say something! How else will I know what's the matter with you?"

After shedding a few more tears, finally Brianna mustered up the courage to tell her mother exactly what was bothering her. "Where my Daddy?" she began. "How come he never comes to my birthday parties, huh? He always here for

Jonathan's and Charise's."

Her question caught Loraine off guard. She hadn't expect-ed this at all. But in the back of her mind she knew this day would come.

Now it was Loraine's turn to be dumbfounded. She didn't know where to begin. Though she knew that she had some explaining to do and fast.

"Brianna," she began. "the man you know as your father, is not your father. He's your sister's father and your brother's father. But he's not your father."

"Huh? I don't believe you. You're a liar mommy!" Brianna yelled.

At that point Brianna began to have a temper tantrum. She flailed her arms wildly at her mother. Dozens of light blows rained down on her mother's mid-section.

Unable to control her daughter's violent outburst, Loraine reached down and viciously slapped Brianna across her face. This seemed to bring her back to reality. Pain exploded across her cheek. She stopped her antics and clutched the side of her face.

Through clenched teeth her mother spoke, "Listen Miss and listen good. Herman is not your father. He is nothing to you. You and him have no blood relations. And that's that!"

Though Brianna couldn't comprehend everything her mother had said. She understood enough. She got the message loud and clear. From that moment on, Brianna was forced to grow up fast. She didn't like her mother's explanation, but she had to accept. For now it would be the only one she would get. It would be years before she knew the whole story.

Her mother and her stepfather Herman were high school sweethearts. When Herman went off to the army, following graduation, Loraine had gotten weak and had a one-night stand. Brianna was the product of that affair. But since Herman came home on leave around the same time she had gotten pregnant, and they too had intercourse, she chose to name Herman for the paternity of the unborn child. The other guy was a local thug who had nothing going for himself other than being cute. While Herman, on the other hand, had plans and goals he was working toward. He was merely using the military as a stepping stone.

Some years later, unable to deal with her guilty conscious any more, Loraine admitted her mistake to her husband. She received a severe beating as reward for her honesty. Still Herman couldn't bring himself to leave his family. Against his better judgment, he stayed. Herman, too, was the product of a broken home. To his credit he wouldn't let one act of infidelity break up his happy home.

Though Herman had forgiven Loraine, he could never forget. He was reminded of her infidelity every time he looked at Brianna. He grew to despise her. As the years went, he became abusive towards her. Not physically but mentally. Sometimes that was just as bad. His harsh words stung Brianna.

"You ain't cute. I don't know what you stay in the mirror for all day?" he commented.

Another degrading remark he was fond of saying was "You ain't shit! And you ain't never gonna be shit! Your Momma ain't shit!"

Brianna was a B-minus student, passing her classes with flying colors. But one marking period, she hadn't done so well. She received two C's. And her stepfather seized the opportunity to criticize and degrade her.

He spat, "Look at this shit here! You so stupid. How you gonna fail gym?"

Herman had degraded her time and time again, right in front of her mother. When Brianna looked to her mother for support, she got none. Not once did her mother come to her aid and defend her. She did what she always did, Loraine pretended not to hear it. Because of this, Brianna began to have animosity towards her mother.

Since Herman had money, he got away with murder around the house. Loraine tolerated his cruelty towards her daughter because he was a provider. A local businessman, Herman owned a string of soul food restaurants throughout Charlotte. While on the other hand, Loraine was just a homemaker with no income to speak of. She was just as much a dependent as her children on her husband. She dared not voice her opinion, in any way, shape or form or incur the wrath of Herman. Loraine knew when Herman got mad, he got even financially—by withholding funds from the children.

Brianna could do no right in her stepfather's eyes. Even though her younger sister and brother weren't nearly as bright as her, they always seemed to get the benefit of the doubt. When they failed a class, they failed because the teacher didn't like them. When Brianna failed, it was because she was just too dumb. There was a double standard in the Campbell household that Brianna would never measure up to.

Over the course of time, her stepfather succeeded in slowly stripping Brianna of her self-esteem. Brianna's grades began to suffer. She became a prisoner in her own home. She chose only to leave her room for one of three things: to go to school, use the bathroom and to eat. She avoided her stepfather as if he had an infectious disease.

Loraine felt her daughter's pain, but truthfully she was powerless to stop the abuse. With her husband's blessing, she decided to seek out Brianna's father. Secretly, her husband hoped that the girl's father would take her to live with him. That he would take Brianna off his hands.

One day Loraine walked into her daughter's room and surprised Brianna, telling her to hurry up and get dressed, that her father was coming over to meet her. Instantly Brianna's face lit up. She felt reinvigorated as if a burden had been lifted off her.

Brianna got dressed in her best clothes. She raced downstairs and sat on the front porch, eagerly awaiting her dad. Each passing car carried Brianna's hopes for as better life. And with each passing car, she was devastated more and more. Hours went by with no sign of her father. Still Brianna didn't move from that spot and she never gave up hope. She sat there till the sun began to set. Finally her mother had seen enough, she summoned Brianna in the house. Loraine was just as disappointed or as heart broken as Brianna.

"C'mon in the house Bri. That nigger ain't coming!" she cursed.

"Don't worry about it baby. He missed out on a good thing. Not you. It's gonna be alright! I promise, it's gonna be alright!"

Her mother's reassuring words did nothing for Brianna. If anything, they contributed to her ill feelings. Silently, she cursed the day she was born. All she ever wanted was a mother and a father. Was that too much to ask for?

Tears began to well up in Brianna's eyes. Suddenly, she took off like a rocket, racing up the stairs. When she reached the second floor, she spotted her stepfather exiting the bathroom. He had a shit- eating grin pasted to his face. Herman found a great deal of amusement in her pain.

Brianna continued to run, racing pass him to her room. She slammed the door and locked it. Throwing herself on the bed, she cried herself to sleep.

All throughout her formative years, Brianna had to endure this treatment. She became a stranger in her own house. So many things happened to Brianna that stagnated her growth, and killed her dreams, which took away from her be-all-you-can-be-attitude. She began to believe her stepfather. Maybe she wasn't going to be shit after all.

\*\*\*\*\*

The Westside of Charlotte has long been a breeding ground for top flight hustlers as well as ruthless killers. This was where Treshaun Smith, aka Tre, hailed from, LaSalle Street, the Betty's Ford section to be specific.

Almost from the time he was born, his life revolved around the streets. Both Tre's parents were hustlers. His father Wally was a low-level drug dealer. And his mother Marva was a booster who stole clothes for the entire neighborhood to buy. At one point or another, one or both of Tre's parents were in prison serving time for their parts in some botched crime. Subsequently, young Tre was raised by his maternal grandmother, on and off.

A day young Tre would never forget, was the day his parents got killed. Fresh out of prison, Marva was looking extremely good, so Wally concocted a scheme to make money. He sent her out into the night clubs of Charlotte, with form-fitting clothes, in search of hustlers. Marva would then bed the hustlers, sexing them on a regular basis. As she did so, she gathered information on them like where they lived, what kind of guns they had or how much money was in their house.

Marva and Wally's plan met success the first few times. Wally and his friend had successfully robbed a few weak hustlers. With each conquest, the couple grew hungrier for more. Ultimately their greed would be their undoing. Word had quickly spread on the street about the duo. They went to the well, one too many times. After robbing one big-time hustler, a hit was placed on them. Shortly after the order was given, Wally and Marva were found dead in the trunk of a car. They were both shot execution style in the back of the head. There were no witnesses to the crime and police never captured the triggerman.

Death seemed to further complicate Tre's already nomadic life. It left a void in it. The murder of his parent's left him feeling more vulnerable and broke than ever. He grew up thinking life wasn't fair. From that point on, young Tre knew there would be no happy endings in life. That life would only be what he made of it. With both sources of income gone, slowly he began to gravitate towards the street. Tre's neighborhood was filled with negativity. Eventually he felt obliged to engage in it.

Originally, Tre got into the game to provide for not only himself, but his grandmother too. He saw her struggling for the basic necessities, food, clothing and shelter. And he didn't want to become another added burden.

Around this time, Tre began to have a strange fascination with the streets. With negativity all around him, he began to look up to the local drug dealers. They had money, the finer things in life, jewelry, pretty women and expensive rides that they flaunted on a regular basis. It was one drug dealer in particular that Tre idolized, his name was Petey. He worshipped the ground Petey walked on since he was a ghetto superstar. To Petey, life came down to dollars and cents either you had money, or you didn't. It was as simple as that. He, on the other hand, was prepared to hustle to get it.

Only five years older than Tre, Petey carried himself like he was much older. Just like Tre, he came from a family of hustlers. His daddy ran a speakeasy and his older brother was a dope boy. Petey's entire family was involved in the game, in some form or another. It was almost expected that he would follow suit. And when he did, no one even raised an eyebrow. Out of all the kids in the neighborhood, Petey took a liking to Tre. Probably because Tre would do anything he asked of him. Petey was no fool, he knew a soldier when he saw one. For the disenfranchised black youth like Tre, he was a godsend.

Petey was a smooth dude. He was a lover and a fighter, a gangster and a gentleman, all rolled up into one. He was everything Tre wanted to be. But most of all he was a character who had game for days. There was always a reason behind everything he did.

"Nigger, you got some money in ya pockets?" he would always ask.

"No," Tre replied. "I ain't got nothin'."

"Here's a lil sumthin' sumthin'!" From a thick wad of bills, Petey peeled off a crisp twenty dollar bill and handed it to Tre. His eyes lit up like it was Christmas. At no point in time in his life had anyone just given him something without expecting something in return. That random act of kindness went a long way with Tre. It instilled a sense of loyalty in him for Petey. From that day forward, no one could ever say anything bad about Petey, not around him. Talking bad about Petey was like talking bad about his late mother.

Petey became like a big brother or mentor of sorts. Soon Tre became his sidekick, his 'little partner' as Petey referred to him. Before Tre knew it, he was running errands for him. Half the time he didn't know the danger he was in. Tre became a drug courier, helping to distribute Petey's poison all over town.

For his efforts, Tre received little or no money. Petey gave him just enough where Tre would always need him. It was more of an honor to be in Petey's company, receiving heavy doses of the game. When it came to the drug game Petey passed along whatever wisdom he could impart and Tre soaked it all up like a sponge. Like so many other young black males, in the neighborhood, Tre viewed the drug game as his ticket out the ghetto. He immersed himself in the murky, shark infested waters. Sink or swim, Tre was all in.

"Look nigga, you gotta always make sure you got at least

three broads on ya team. The first broad, she ain't a hood chick. She should either work or go to school, getting' an education. She wants somethin' out of life. That's your future wife. The second broad is ya soldier; she holds the money and the work at her crib. She gotta be trustworthy. That's your vice president, if somethin should happen to you, then she can take over.

"And the third broad, she just a hood rat, somebody from the neighborhood. You can keep the product at her house. Even turn her house into a dope house if necessary," Petey explained.

These were rules to the game that Tre would always remember. They were tried and true. He watched Petey implement them everyday. As time went on, Tre became more valuable to Petey. He carefully played his position while patiently waiting his turn.

Sadly, just like everyone else Tre ever loved, Petey died tragically, but not by an assassin's bullet. The word on the street was Petey was poisoned. Though there was no medical evidence to substantiate such a claim, Tre had his suspicions though. Women were Petey's Achilles heel. He was never good with them. So Tre tried to find the killer to avenge Petey, but it was like finding a needle in a haystack. Petey had that many women.

It was Tre who found Petey and rushed him to the hospital. He was there at the hospital along with a few members of Petey's family, when in the predawn stillness Petey took his last labored breathe, and then he was gone.

The mournful sounds of his mother's cries along with the steady bleeps and hisses of the life support machines could be heard throughout the room. It shattered the eerie silence of death. Unable to bear it, Tre exited the room to mourn his mentor's passing.

Petey's death would prove to be bittersweet to Tre, now he

was thrust into the role of the man, in the hood. His only wish was Petey was still alive to see it.

As a result of Petey's passing, a bloody drug war ensued. The death toll seemed to mount daily. Dealers were scrambling to takeover the turf that once belonged to him. Quickly, Tre had organized a team that took on all comers. When the smoke cleared Tre had emerged victorious. But he would forever be a marked man.

Just like Petey had controlled the neighborhood drug traffic for years, now so did Tre. He ruled the neighborhood drug game with an iron fist. His reign of terror enabled him to hold it down for several years by instilling the fear of God in his rivals. Murder was his favorite weapon of intimidation. Whenever there was a problem, he made examples.

*****

Seeking to getaway from the house, on the way home from school Brianna made a short diversion to Eastland Mall. It was a trip that would forever change her life. For hours Brianna window shopped, browsing every store from Foot Locker, the Downtown Locker Room to Marshall's. She dreamed of owning all the name brand stuff that she saw in these stores.

Her stepfather treated her like a stepchild in every sense of the word. When it came time to buying her school clothes, he made sure she got little or no money. Most times, Brianna's mother would have to take money from the other children's shopping allowance.

Standing outside of one store, Brianna stared at the mannequin that was modeling a cute pink Rocawear tennis skirt with a matching shirt. Unbeknownst to her, a pair of guys had slid up behind and began admiring her body. Even though she was shabbily dressed there was no denying her body or her beauty. The moment Tre laid eyes on her, it was clear that he was attracted to Brianna. He was smart enough to look pass her less-than-up-to-par apparel. He saw what her stepfather would never see. What he saw was potential. Tre was awestruck by her beauty. Tre knew he had to have her.

"You'd look good in that," he said with a playful smirk. "Girl, I can see you now."

Brianna simply smiled, she didn't know what else to do. Even at seventeen, she wasn't used to boys approaching her.

"You want that?" Tre asked. "Say the word and it yours."

Brianna shot the handsome stranger a perplexed look that seemed to say, "You can't be serious." Still she felt she had nothing to lose and everything to gain.

"Well, if you gonna buy it for me, I'll take it," she said meekly.

He replied, "C'mon beautiful, let's go get it."

This chance meeting turned into a makeshift shopping spree. Brianna entered the store with intentions on only getting an outfit, but she came out with a wardrobe.

After they finished shopping, Tre took her out to eat. It was there that they learned more about each other. Instantly, Tre knew that this was one of the chicks he needed in his life that his mentor Petey had talked about. He felt Brianna was wifey material. She was green to the streets, so he felt that he could easy manipulate and mold her. Her good looks were just icing on the cake.

On this day, fate had finally smiled on Brianna. It had brought someone in her life that could not only care for her, but supported her emotionally. She didn't have that type of support at home. Tre would become her mother and her father. Someone she could turn to in times of need. With Tre in the picture, suddenly living became worthwhile.

Brianna had entered Tre's life just as his drug dealing career had begun to flourish. He believed that fate had played a role in whatever success he had. It was fate that got him involved in the drug game and it was fate that paired him with the love of his life. And it would also be fate that would end his young life so tragically.

*****

After a year of courtship, when Brianna graduated from high school, she moved in with Tre. When she left home, her mother didn't so much as protest Brianna's move. Things had gone from bad to worse. Her husband and her daughter couldn't stand the sight of each other. Besides she had two other children to worry about.

Silently, she wished her daughter well.

## Where's da love?

Death never comes at a good time. For Brianna its timing couldn't have been worst. Her boyfriend had left so many loose ends behind it was ridiculous. Most people don't plan for their death, especially not drug dealers. When one lives on the outside of the law, one tends to live in the moment, so there are no wills. There is no paper trail to trace money owed out to them or assets hidden.

Since Tre was in the upper echelon of drug dealing, this only compounded the problem. After his passing, immediately everyone assumed Brianna was sitting on some dough, especially Tre's relatives. Their inquiries about his finances and assets led her to believe they were more interested in that, than finding the people who were responsible for his death.

Fortunately, Brianna was able to collect enough money off the streets to give Tre a proper burial. She managed to have a little left over for the bare necessities. After that, she was hard pressed to crap up another dime. Some dealers who had owed Tre large amounts of money for drug packages given to them on consignment, balked at paying, giving Brianna the runaround, claiming they had already paid or they just didn't answer their phones. However bad they felt about Tre's death, they weren't about to take a step backwards. This was the ultimate come up, one that had put many of them on their feet. They were not about to blow this once-in-a-lifetime opportunity by showing some sense of moral responsibility. Any thoughts they had of doing a good deed, like handing over the money, were an afterthought.

Brianna was left to bear the brunt of this burden. Right after the funeral, everyone started showing their true colors. Now it was clear to her that all the love she had enjoyed while Tre was alive was long gone. Everybody was in flip mode.

For days after the funeral Brianna did a combination of two things, moped and mourned around the house, she once shared with her boyfriend, unsure of exactly what was in store for her in the future. One thing about being alone in the house Brianna enjoyed was how alive it was with memories of Tre. All around the house there were various photos of him, riding in his big boy truck, the Infiniti QX56 SUV with 24" inch chrome rims. And some photos of him and her, spending a night out on the town. Others showed him posing for pictures at the club with his boys, with his trademark dreadlocks hanging everywhere.

Tons of images seemed to flash through Brianna's head as she relived the lasting memories that they shared. One image that would be forever etched in her memory bank was Tre lying on the floor next to her, dead. According to the coroner's report, the official cause of Tre's death was a gunshot wound to the back of the head. But Brianna knew the real cause of death. The cause he gave his life to so tragically was the streets.

She stared at the pictures for hours on end. They became therapeutic to her, a way for Brianna to cope with his death. They reminded her of a time in the not so distant past, when it was all good. It made her realize how quickly sugar can turn to shit. One could work a lifetime to acquire material things, or a good relationship for that matter, and lose it in the blink of an eye.

Brianna loved the past, the good old days. She wished she could turn back the hands of time and bring Tre back. If she could change fate, she would. There would be no more involvement in the drug game, none of this street stuff. They could just be the average working class couple, struggling to make ends meet. If?

Now more than ever, Brianna felt this way, especially since she didn't know what the future held. Still it was her present situation that disturbed her, life without her man. She wondered, what was she going to do without him?

There was no doubt that Tre was her nigger. She always felt to know him was to love him. Sure Tre may have been many things like a hardcore street nigger. But he also had a tender side to him. They shared some very special moments. Only a select few people ever had the privilege to see that side of him. Tre had guarded the tender side of himself as well as he stashed his dope. On the streets, Tre's alter ego was always on display: the killer/hustler. He always figured that his best offense was a good defense. So he had to shoot first to avoid getting shot.

As Brianna reflected on how complex Tre was, unbeknownst to her, her peace and tranquility was about to be interrupted.

*****

Ding, Dong! Ding Dong! The bell sounded.

Even in her sleep, Brianna had heard the bell. She thought she was dreaming though.

Ding Dong! Ding Dong! It went again, shattering the silence through the house. Now Brianna knew this wasn't a dream. Someone was at her front door. She wondered who it was? She hoped it wasn't the police coming to interrogate her again.

Slowly Brianna rose from her bed, gathering her bearings. She slipped on a large fluffy white bathrobe and a pair of Nike slippers, which formally belonged to Tre, and headed downstairs to answer the door.

Ding Dong! Ding Dong! Ding Dong! The doorbell began to go berserk. Just a few feet away from the door, Brianna feeling over whelmed was suddenly over taken by anger. She wanted to know who the hell was ringing her doorbell like that.

"Who?" she barked.

There was no answer.

"Who?" she screamed again.

Now Brianna was on fire. Somebody was at her front door playing games and she was not in the mood for it with all things considered.

Without thinking Brianna unbolted a series of locks and snatched open the door. To her surprise stood, Tre's aunt Angie and her daughter Yvette. She froze at the sight of them.

Suddenly, Brianna's mood went from bad to worse. Instantly she knew that their appearance at her front door wasn't a goodwill mission. They weren't there to offer their condolences.

"Good morning?" Angie greeted her. "You mind if we come in?"

Not waiting for a reply the two women barged right passed Brianna.

"Come on in!" Brianna said sarcastically.

As soon as they entered the house, the two women began scanning the premises for valuables as if this was an auction. No matter how hard they tried, their eyes couldn't hide their intentions. They were like vultures on a dead carcass, they were there to pick the body clean.

To her credit Brianna already knew what it was. She knew what they were there for. She had felt their vibe a few days ago at the funeral and every day thereafter. She expected them to show up. The only question was, what had taken them so long?

"Damn! Y'all was ballin' fa real," Yvette exclaimed, as she looked around the state of the art living room.

Brianna just stared at her blankly. She wasn't even going to dignify her with a response.

Brianna never liked Yvette from day one. She had it out for her ever since Yvette tried and kept trying to put her girlfriends on to Tre. Over the years they had dozens of verbal altercations over the matter. Each side issued threats but never once did they come to fisticuffs, because Tre wouldn't allow it. Now that the peacemaker was gone, it was open season on Brianna.

Angie suddenly announced, "Look, Bri I'm goin' to cut right to the chase. The reason we're here is to pick up some things that my nephew Tre had promised me. He always told me if anything ever happened to him that I could come over and take anything I wanted…"

Brianna replied, "Funny, he told me the same thing."

Brianna shot her a look that seemed to say, 'You-can't-be serious.'

She knew that Angie was lying through her teeth. Because Tre wasn't really close to anyone in his family accept his grandmother. He felt like his family was nothing but a bunch of leeches. No matter how much he gave them, they were never satisfied. They always had their hands out.

In spite of that, he took care of them out of a sense of loyalty.

"Yeah, anyway!" Angie countered. "Since I was his favorite Auntie and everything, he said he would feel better if I had it."

"Oh yeah?" Brianna shot back with her arms folded across her breasts.

"Yeah!" Angie said with emphasis.

In the background Brianna could see Yvette posturing with her hands on her hips. This provided Brianna only a hint of their collective foul mood. The sinister smirk that had spread across her lips seemed to tell it all.

The tension in the house was thick. At any minute violence could explode. Both parties took defiant stances, glaring at one another. Quickly Brianna weighted her odds, she ruled out striking Tre's aunt. She knew that if she fought one, then she would have to fight them both. And that they would most definitely jump her. With these two ghetto dwellers, there was no telling just how far they would go. They were the type to go all out in a fight, they'd probably bite her in the face.

"Look, this shit don't mean nuttin to me. Take whatever you want," She told them. "I'm in love with Tre! Not none of his possessions."

"Whatever Bitch!" Yvette snapped, trying to instigate a fight.

Brianna shook her head in disgust, she took pity on these two savages. One of Tre's famous sayings suddenly came to mind. "Don't become too attached to this shit. The drug game and life is so funny. What takes you years to get, can take you less than twenty minutes to lose."

Brianna was in an awkward situation. On one hand she felt that she was entitled to everything. On the other she felt indebted to Tre's family, but not these two. After all, blood was thicker than water. She had only known him a few short years and they knew him for a lifetime.

A concession had to be made. Out of respect for Tre, Brianna decided not to make a big deal of it. The material items in the house could be gotten again, more expensive items at that. Still that notion didn't stop her ill feelings toward them. In her book, they were just grimy. There was no other way to explain their actions.

Tre must be rolling over in his grave. She mused.

Spurred by disappointment, Brianna went upstairs to her bedroom and locked the door. In silence, she listened as the duo pillaged the house.

"Ohh, Mommy lemme have the microwave. You already got the blender," Yvette said.

Brianna listened intently as the two scavengers fought over who would get what. It was sad to see just how petty, two human beings could be. It was also disheartening to see just how death bought out the worst in people.

Upstairs in her bedroom, Brianna paced the spacious room, back and forth like a caged animal. She had to do something to rid herself of this nervous energy. She had to do something to keep herself from going back downstairs and jumping on somebody. Impatiently she bided her time in her bedroom, for what seemed like an eternity. Suddenly just as quickly as the commotion started, it came to an end. The quietness that engulfed the house was a sign to Brianna that the intruders were gone.

Quickly, Brianna went into her closet and opened a storage bin hidden way in the back. She pulled out a pair of old blue jeans and a bleached stained red T-shirt. In a hurried fashion, she put the clothes on. Then Brianna raced down stairs, through the house, into the backyard. It was time to dig up Tre's drug stash.

Tre wasn't too big on telling Brianna everything. Or any woman for that matter, he thought women were weak. If enough pressure was applied by law enforcement authorities, then women would break. Tre didn't want to tempt fate. He always said "what you don't know, you can't tell."

Over the years, he had grown comfortable with Brianna. He began to trust her. He began to let her in on some of his secrets. Just in case anything ever happened to him. As it turned out, this would be the most crucial one of all.

As soon as Brianna entered the backyard, she stood still. A puzzled look masked her face, as if she was trying to recall something. Scanning the yard she looked for a tool to assist her task. She spotted a garden hoe leaning against the house. After taking the tool into her possession, she went about her business. Retracing her steps, Brianna began her expedition at the back door. Slowly she took eight paces straight ahead, then made a sharp right and took four more paces. Where she stood, supposedly, x marked the spot. The dope was literally beneath her feet, buried in a shallow hole in the soft earth.

Burying this stash of dope was totally Tre's idea. He used to do this as a youth when he sold drugs out of a dope house. To avoid being robbed or caught by the police with large packages of drugs, he buried them in a nearby wooded area, taking only what he thought he could sell. This was a brilliant stroke of genius, not once did Tre lose a single gram adhering to this system.

Brianna was sure this was the spot. With all her might, she bought the hoe down tearing away at the patches of grass. Powerful strokes from the hoe, began to tear huge chunks of earth and grass. Soon Brianna began to break a sweat. She kicked away all the debris and fell to her knees. With her bare hands she began digging away like a dog. At a feverish pace, she attacked the earth as if it were a bitter enemy.

Brianna was glad it was still early, her neighbors most likely were at work, so no prying eyes would witness the extraction of drugs from the earth.

"God Damn!" she cursed. "Where the fuck is it?"

Just as Brianna was about to lose hope, her hands unearthed some plastic. She breathed easy. She knew this was it. She watched Tre when he prepared the dope for burial. The sight of the package of dope spurred her on. She began digging with a renewed vigor.

Finally Brianna excavated the package of dope, it was taped and double tapped, then wrapped in plastic to protect it from the elements. She didn't even bother to brush off the leftover particles of dirt. She merely clutched the package to her chest and rushed inside her house.

Now that Brianna had the drugs in her hand, she was overcome by a sense of urgency. She didn't know who was going to come knocking at her door, demanding what. One thing for sure though, Aunt Angie and Cousin Yvette would be back. So it was time to leave.

Immediately, Brianna raced upstairs, changed clothes and began to pack up her things. She decided against trying to remove anything of real value like televisions, furniture and appliances. She had other plans for those things. Since she was in a rush, Brianna just took all her clothing and a car that was in her name.

Making repeated trips, up and down the stairs, Brianna managed to load up her clothing and the dope. The interior of the car and the trunk was jam packed with clothing and shoes. If the vehicle hadn't been a BMWX5, then Brianna might have been mistaken for a can or junk collector. When she finished placing her things inside the car, she went back into the house to take care of some unfinished business.

First Brianna began to smash every appliance and television in sight. Since she couldn't take them with her, Brianna would be damned if she let Aunt Angie and cousin Yvette have it.

"Fuck them hoes!"

Brianna proceeded to trash the whole house. She gathered all of Tre's expensive clothes, put them in a pile and poured a gallon of bleach over them, thus ruining everything. Brianna didn't want anyone wearing Tre's clothes. She had a sentimental reason for that. Then Brianna proceeded to relieve herself on the King-size, pillow-top mattress. She broke bottles of nail polish on top of the rest of the bedroom set. She did a number on the living room, kicking a hole in the big screen television and throwing hot grease all over the living room set. Then Brianna entered the kitchen and broke every dish, glass and cup in the cabinet.

Wait till them bitches see this. They're gonna have a fuckin' heart attack.

The mere thought of their facial expressions caused Brianna to laugh as she exited the house. She only wished she could be there to see it.

With a push of a button, Brianna opened up the garage

door and fled the house. She left behind a trail of destruction in her wake. The message was clear, "Fuck you, too!"

# LOST ONE

## *Kia DuPree*
## Washington, DC

Filthy Timberland footprints tracked through Yum's Chinese Take-Out, evidence of all the hungry people who had waited for their number to be called. Meche stared at the sticky, sludge-stained tiles, dried ketchup splatters and the bones of fried chicken wings lying by the Pac-Man arcade. He thought about canceling his order.

"I just know they frying cats in this dirty ass muhfucka," Rahmel fumed. "I can't see how you eating from outta here."

"Man, go 'head. Wendy's ain't no fuckin' better. You eat that shit all the time." Meche knocked on the inch-thick bulletproof window separating the customers from the staff and said, "I'm hungry as shit. Mamasan, what's up with my order? When you gonna call 232?"

"It coming one minute," the Chinese woman said.

Meche nodded. "And don't be asking for none of my food either, nigga," he said turning to Rahmel.

"Me no want no MSG cat legs," Rahmel said shaking his head, walking back toward the glass door. He stared out into the dark street. They were in a part of town he rarely visited, and he was cautious about the neighborhood. Meche was an Uptown dude, but Rahmel was from the Southside. They only happened to know each other because Meche's grandparents lived in Southeast, too. They knew each other since they were young kids catching tadpoles in the creek behind his apartment building.

Rahmel didn't like the vibe at all Uptown. The last time he'd been on Georgia Avenue was for Georgia Avenue Day—the day in mid-August that attracted large crowds, lots of vendors selling fried fish and crab cakes and the celebrity or two. It had been four years since the last one and he'd only gone because his favorite Go Go band, Backyard, was performing. He heard Nas was going to rock the mic with them. But before Back could even hit the stage on Bannekar High School field, those Uptown boys started shooting as usual and the overcrowded avenue became chaotic—girls screaming, mothers running frantic pushing strollers with wailing babies, police sirens howling, bodies running in every direction through the streets. When it was over, two people were shot dead and the city had finally decided to cancel plans for any future Georgia Avenue Days.

The only reason Rahmel was Uptown again was for some pussy. One of Meche's girlfriends lived across the street from Yum's and she had just introduced him to her fine ass cousin Asia who lived down the street. Rahmel talked to Asia twice on the phone before they met earlier that night. The two couples had spent the entire night cracking jokes, getting high and watching a bootleg Kat Williams DVD.

"Number 232," the Chinese woman said putting a plastic bag with a Styrofoam container in a rotating glass cylinder, passing the food through the window.

"You put Mumbo sauce on my wings Mamasan?" Meche asked.

"It in there. Want more?"

"Nah. I'm good," he said walking to the door. "You gonna call Asia tonight?"

They walked out into the cold air. Rahmel pulled the hood up on his North Face and smiled, even though the bitter air chilled his mouth. "What you think? You see that *ass* nigga?" he asked raising an eyebrow.

"Fuck yeah. She got a bubble on her for real. I told you I had you." Meche clicked the alarm on his 2001 blue Impala and slid into the driver's seat. "You want to stay by my people's or you want me to take you back home?"

"Take me back in the morning. I wanna whip your ass in some Madden at least one good time."

"Man, please," he said before starting the car. "In your dreams."

*****

Meche woke up to snow piled as high as the front steps and a headache that thumped like a drum section.

"I told you about that MSG those Chinese people use in that food," Rahmel said. "You gonna fuck around and get cancer."

"Dawg, please just shut up," he said covering his face with a pillow. They had stayed up drinking Patron and playing Play Station into the wee hours of the morning. Rahmel was still up when the first flakes had hit the window since he was busy looking at the pictures of Asia he took with his cell phone. Her heart-shaped face and juicy lip-glossed lips filled the screen on one shot. On the other, she posed in the hallway against the wall, her brown Senegalese twists dangling down her shoulders. He had thought about calling her, but didn't want to appear too anxious. But something happened that he did not intend. His thumb hit the talk button while he scrolled through his other saved pictures. And it was too late, his phone was dialing the number that matched the picture he had been staring at for minutes. Instead of hanging up and having to face her reaction later, he let the phone ring, deciding to leave a voice message.

"I know you done lost your ever-loving mind calling me at four-thirty in the morning," her sexy voice scowled into the phone.

"Girl, you know you couldn't stop thinking about me," Rahmel had said sinking into the couch, surprised that she'd answered the phone on the second ring.

"Apparently, it's the other way around," she said letting a yawn escape her throat. "What you want this early in the morning? Calling me like the police or something."

"You," he said thinking about the way her hips looked in the tight jeans she had on earlier.

"Is that right?"

"What you got on? You sleep naked?"

"Boy please!" she said sounding more awake than she wanted to lead on.

"You know you want me to know."

"No, I don't!"

"You don't think I'm cute?"

She was quiet then. He could hear her thoughts. Most girls thought he was cute, always comparing him to the singer Chris Brown. He could even see the slight resemblance, although he had a five-inch long scar etched into his forehead. He usually wore a wavecap with a hat on top to hide it, especially whenever he met someone new, looking to avoid explaining how it got there. Rahmel walked toward the window to peer outside. Snow had begun to fall, covering the hoods of parked cars and grass in the front yard. "Why you get so quiet?" he asked.

"Look Rahmel, you don't know nothing about me and you already trying to get into my panties. You just like the rest," she said.

"Nah, don't say that. What's wrong with wanting to be close to you? You right. I wanna be in those panties," he whispered. "It's probably the warmest place to be right now. You know how cold it is outside and—it's snowing right now."

She giggled and just as quickly said, "Goodnight."

"Goodnight? Just tell me what color they are so I can have sweet dreams tonight."

"Goodnight Rahmel," she said again in a voice as sweet as syrup.

"Well, at least blow me a kiss, something."

She giggled again.

"Come on," Rahmel asked in his most alluring voice. "Just one."

The phone grew quiet for a long moment and then he heard her wet lips smack together, followed by the words, "Goodnight Rahmel."

"Mmmm. Goodnight Miss Asia. I'll call you in the morning."

"It is morning."

"Well, later then. Get some sleep."

With the sunlight now shining through the Venetian blinds, Rahmel sat on the love seat with his long legs dangling off the armrest. The mere thought of Asia's phone kiss had left him rock hard. He had only gotten a few hours sleep, but he stood up and stretched anyway. Rahmel was ready to head back to the Southside, but he didn't want to wait for Meche to wake all the way up or for him to get over his hangover. The car needed to be dug out of the frozen cave that surrounded it. Taylor Street needed to be scraped and probably wouldn't get done until after the bigger and busier streets had been plowed first. Rahmel was as good as stuck.

He leaned out the window and saw Meche's father shoveling the steps. "That's a start," he whispered.

After Rahmel went to the bathroom, he threw his clothes on and headed out the den.

"Hey Mama J," he said to Meche's mother who sat at the kitchen table reading a magazine and drinking coffee.

She looked up. "Rahmel, I know you're not planning to go out in that snow today. Do you see how much is out there?"

"Yes Ma'am. I know, but I need to go home."

She sighed. "Well, it'll probably take you a long time. The trains may be running slow and I know Ameche Kamau Jamison isn't going to move his precious car today."

"I know, you're right. But I'm just gonna take my chances with the train. I got some things to do."

"You sure it can't wait? It's so cold out there. I would hate for you to go trudging through all that just to end up with pneumonia."

"I promise I'll be all right. This coat is pretty warm."

She smirked and shook her head before returning to her magazine. "Can't tell you teenagers nothing, I swear."

"Could you tell Meche I'll catch up with him later?"

"I'll try. He'll probably be sleeping all day."

"How ya doing Mr. Jamison?" Rahmel said as he eased by his snow pile.

"I could be doing a whole lot better if you and your knuckleheaded best friend would help me get this snow off these steps and out the driveway."

Rahmel froze. He just wanted to ease by and start out on his journey. If only Meche hadn't gotten so drunk off the stash he kept in his closet. "Sure," Rahmel said grabbing the shovel.

It took them an hour to get a path cleared from the steps to the street and then another hour for the path in front of the house for pedestrians. His nose felt as if it would fall off, and his fingers were numb even with the gloves. Rahmel was tired, but he didn't say anything. Meche's family treated him like one of its own and always had since they met him all those years ago.

"You know you make me proud sometimes," Mr. Jamison said, taking a break.

Rahmel, stunned by his friend's father and the words that said more than his own father had ever said, stood with the shovel tight in his grip.

"I mean that," he said. "I know things are hard for you sometimes. If you ever need to talk to me about anything, I just want you to know I'm here for you."

Rahmel smiled. Mr. Jamison's offer was unexpected, but he appreciated it just the same. Sometimes he thought Meche took the love of his parents for granted. They were always around, they gave him everything he wanted and he still acted like he cared less. Meche just didn't know how good he had it.

"I think I can handle the rest," Mr. Jamison said, motioning for him to step back. "Why don't you drink a cup of hot chocolate before you start out? Get something hot in you."

After Mr. Jamison said what he'd said, Rahmel didn't want to disappoint him so he nodded before heading back in the house.

"You got some hot chocolate Mama J?"

"Mmmhhmm. Look in the cabinet."

Rahmel took his coat back off and began boiling the milk. His cell rang and he smiled when he saw Asia's sexy face pop on the screen. But he didn't answer it, not with Mrs. Jamison in listening distance. After the boiling started, he made the cocoa, and then Rahmel took his cup and went to the den to call Asia back.

"Good morning sexy," he said when she answered the phone. "I'm surprised you're up already. I thought I kept you up all night."

"I'm surprised, too."

"I guess you must think I'm cute after all."

She giggled. "So did y'all get a lot of snow on the Southside?"

"I don't even know. I'm still in Northwest."

"Oh?"

"I'm by Meche's house."

"Oh for real? How long you goin' be there?"

"I don't know. I was gonna see if they was gonna shovel the streets over here and then be out."

"Oh…if they don't, you should come see me. We can watch some movies or something."

"Or something sounds good."

"Boy, you always so nasty?"

"I didn't even say nothing. Get your mind out the gutter. You're the nasty one."

She sucked her teeth, and said, "Ah ah. It ain't me."

"No for real. I'm not sure. I got something to do at home."

"Oh, okay. It's just that my peoples got stuck out Calvert County last night. I know they won't be here for a while. We could spend some time together."

Surprised at Asia's forwardness and her attempt to help them move things along, he said he'd call her in an hour to let her know, but really he wanted to know if he could borrow some of Meche's clothes since she had already seen what he had on. Meche's parents kept new packets of underclothes and toothbrushes around as if they expected some sort of calamity to occur. Were Meche or his older brother Anwar, who was away at college in Georgia, to ever need them, there was plenty. Rahmel knew Meche still had clothes hanging in his closet with tags on them. His parents were paid, both had high rankings working for the federal government. His mother worked for the General Accounting Office and his father worked for the Department of Transportation.

Rahmel tossed a couch cushion at Meche. "Ay man, wake the fuck up. I need to borrow some clothes."

"Huh?" Meche said. "What for?"

"Asia told me to come over. Her parents stuck out Calvert County."

"You serious?" He said raising his head up. "Oh, shit. Yeah

dawg, go head and tap the hell out that shit."

Rahmel laughed and began thrusting his hips back and forth. "You know I'ma tear that ass up."

An hour later, he walked up the snow-covered steps to her house on Georgia Ave. His footprints were the only ones that had disturbed the soft beauty in Asia's yard. He looked at the address again, 2121. He was at the right one. Before ringing the doorbell, he double-checked that his wavecap was on right and readjusted his fitted baseball cap to make sure it covered his scar.

When Asia opened the door, he smiled. Her white Long John shirt hugged her body like a glove and her breasts were more than a mouth full. He couldn't wait for her to turn around so he could see her butt jiggle in the thin sweat pants. She really did have a dancer's body. Asia had told him about the classes she'd taken at the small studio up the street ever since she was in elementary school.

"Hey you," she said.

"Don't tell me you always look this good in the morning, 'cause you gonna make me fall in love."

"Stop playing Rahmel," she said stepping back, opening the door wider for him to enter. "Take your boots off and leave them right here. Can't be tracking snow all around here."

He did and gave her his coat to hang up. "Where your sisters at?"

"Melissa's over her boyfriend's house and Nicole's in her room sleep."

"Oh. Why your parents all the way out Calvert County for?"

"Dag, you all into that…just come sit down. You want something to drink?"

"You."

"Rahmel…if you goin' keep acting like this, we goin' have problems."

"Why you say that?"

"'Cause I just want to chill. For real, chill."

"All right, all right." He walked over to the couch, where she had BET playing on the TV. She sat beside him, at the opposite end of the couch. "Oh, you gonna sit all the way over there?"

She smiled and turned back towards the TV. "Why don't you take your hat off? I want to see what you look like without it."

Rahmel shook his head and chewed on a toothpick he had in his pocket.

"Why not? You got an egg head like Rich Boy or something?" she asked reaching over, taking a swipe at his hat.

He leaned back but caught her in his arms. She felt soft and warm and smelled like raspberry candy. He stared in her eyes long and deep. "Girl, you don't want to start what you can't finish."

And then Asia took the toothpick out of his mouth and kissed him, twisting her tongue deep inside his mouth. He grew harder by the second. He did what he wanted to do since he met her the night before and palmed his hands on her butt, squeezing and massaging until he lifted her up into his lap. He could feel the heat between her legs penetrating through his sweatpants. She grinded her hips back and forth, in tiny circles, teasing him. Soft moans slipped from her mouth. He thought he was going to bust it felt so good, and yet they weren't even having sex. He raised her shirt and kissed her nipple through her bra, before pushing the cotton over to lick, then suck it.

"Okay, okay stop," she said breathless.

"Why?" he moaned, kissing her breasts.

"Let's stop."

"Come on girl. I didn't walk all the way through this snow just to sit by your sexy ass and do nothing."

Asia stopped grinding and took his cap off and put it on her head.

"Oh, that's what this was all about," he said, relieved he still had his wavecap on underneath. He was still rock hard and Asia's heat seeped through. He slid his hand inside her sweatpants and was thrilled to know she didn't have on any panties.

"Oh, you're a bad girl," Rahmel said smiling.

"I'll take these off, if you take that off," she said running her clear-fingernail polished fingers over his black do-rag.

He looked at her sideways, weighing his options. He knew she would want to know more about the scar once she saw it.

"I know you not goin' to turn this down," she said squeezing her thighs tight, pressing closer to his hard erection.

"Girl, you gonna make a nigga bust."

"Let me take it off," she said in her sweetest voice, her long twists grazing his cheeks. Rahmel thought she was cute and the more he looked at her, he could tell she wasn't a hood rat like her cousin...just a girl trying hard to be bad. She was in the twelfth grade at Roosevelt, a few blocks down the street. One foot out the door, like him only she had plans for what she was going to do next. He thought about going to Lincoln Tech, to get a certificate in electrical engineering, but something told him he needed to get away from D.C. all together.

"Go 'head," Rahmel said. "Take it off."

She smiled, leaned forward and untied it. When she lifted it away, she said, "Your head don't look too bad, it's those ears I'm worried about now."

He laughed. She didn't say anything about his scar, and he was surprised at how relieved he felt.

"So I guess it's my turn now."

He smiled, but said, "Nah, you don't have to. Let's just

take our time."

She frowned, but didn't say anything. She cuddled in his arms, and listened to the soft beat of his heart. He squeezed her tight, before they fell asleep listening to Mario sing, "You should let me love you" on 106 and Park. Rahmel changed his mind about Asia just like that. He didn't want to just smash and be out, like he had planned. He stayed with her until darkness replaced the sunlit room before he finally decided to go home.

It had been a long two days, but he just wanted to spend the last weekend of his spring vacation in his own house. He checked his cell for missed calls. There were three, one from Meche, one from his boy Greg and one from Melinda, the girl he was banging on occasion. He smiled, knowing she wished she could've spent the snowy day with him. But he was tired of her anyway. She wasn't going nowhere with her life. He could tell she was waiting for him to slip up and get her pregnant so she could hit the welfare line.

"Low aspiration having ass," he mumbled. But with Asia, she talked about things like going to law school and studying criminal justice at a college in Virginia. He liked that about her. She wasn't scared to leave the city, and she had dreams even if she wasn't sure about how to go about reaching them.

Rahmel wasn't surprised that his father hadn't called, though he sort of hoped he had. The two lived in parallel worlds. Shifting past one another in the kitchen or the living room—often with not a single word passing between them. Money left on the dining room table, groceries stocked in the refrigerator, but nothing ever said. It was the car accident that created the space. It was his mother and little sister's death, and Rahmel's survival that pushed them apart. Rahmel wondered if his father resented him because his existence was a daily reminder of the wife and daughter he had lost. Sometimes he really wished things could be different, other times, he was just as depressed and too busy getting into petty trouble to see if his father would blink an eye.

Once out of Asia's yard, Rahmel followed the footprints in the snow as he made his way down the block. "Shit, I forgot my fuckin' wavecap," he said as a chill raced down his neck. He looked back at her house, but then he decided he'd use it as an excuse to see Asia again. The thought of her made him smile.

The avenue was shoveled pretty well considering the nine inches of snow. There was hardly anyone outside, and the street was rather quiet for as quiet as Georgia Avenue could be without the usual traffic. Just ahead of him were three guys smoking on the corner of Crittenden, near a lone van parked near the end of the block.

"Is that my nigga Rahmel?" one of the guys asked, as Rahmel got closer. "What the fuck you doing all the way over here?"

"Oh shit, Taariq? Rico?" Rahmel asked a little confused, recognizing two of the guys who used to go to Anacostia High School with him. "Wassup?"

"The fuck you doing all the way Uptown nigga?" Rico asked clasping his hands with Rahmel's. The two of them had stopped going to school in the middle of the eleventh grade. And even when they were there, they were fighting dudes every other day and getting suspended.

"Chillin', seeing some of my peoples up this way."

"You remember Marquan from Stanton Terrace?" Taariq asked, introducing him to the slender guy with shoulder-length dreadlocks.

"Hey, wassup," Rahmel said nodding, not really recognizing him.

"'Sup," Marquan said with what appeared to Rahmel as a slight mug on the guy's face. He noted it, before the guy looked away puffing his cigarette.

"Man, we was at this bangin' ass party last night. The rollers was out, for real," Rico said. "I mean there was some bad ass bitches in that muthafucka."

"No bull…" Taariq said laughing, his round belly shaking. "But, yeah nigga, we got stuck out here. My man Donnell left without us and shit. We were so damn tore up off that Ciroc, man, I don't even remember seeing that nigga dip with one of those broads."

"'Bout to take this joint, right here," Rico said tossing his cigarette to the ground. The cold moist snow instantly sucked the fire out.

"For real?" Rahmel's eyebrows rose up as he turned to the van.

"Look at all these tickets," Taariq said, taking a puff from his cigarette, pointing at the three tickets underneath the windshield wiper. "Since they ain't tow it already, they probably just gonna put a boot on it next. Look like somebody tried to shovel around it already."

"Surprised they didn't tow it in the first place. Dude parked in a snow zone like a dumb ass," Rico said.

"You know the city slow with that shit. It's much easier to write a few parking tickets," Rahmel said, looking over the vehicle. "Maybe something's wrong with it. You sure it works?"

"No, but we gonna see. You down?" Marquan asked, tossing his cigarette to the ground. Rahmel was wise to his game. Before he got involved with it, Marquan only wanted to know just in case Rahmel was the big mouth type.

"It's whatever. I was on my way back to the Southside anyway," Rahmel said. "But we might have problems getting out."

"Nah," Taariq said kicking at the snow around the tires with his Nike boots. Rico started helping him. "We could use your technical skills anyway, college boy."

Rahmel was surprised he'd call him that, since he still hadn't applied for any of the schools. He looked around—a slight stream of cars trudged up and down the slushy street, a man who looked like a crackhead bounced from left to right in front of the corner store, waiting anxiously for someone to come help him with his fix. *Fuck it.* He needed to get home anyway. "Let's do this shit," Rahmel said, pulling his hood over his head.

Rahmel watched Marquan jimmy the lock with the ease of a professional in ten short seconds. Taariq slid open the side door for the other three to climb inside. Once in, Rahmel cracked open the ignition cover and yanked on the red and yellow wires that would start the engine. He tapped the tips together, sparks sizzled and popped the cold air. The car revved twice, but then wouldn't kick over.

"You think it's dead?" Rico asked from the backseat.

"Give me a second. It might just need to warm up since it's been so cold," Rahmel said tapping the wire ends again.

"What the fuck is this wild shit?" Marquan called from the back of the van. "Somebody was a freak in this muthafucka."

"Damn, dude got a bed back there and all huh?" Taariq said looking over his shoulder from the front passenger seat.

"He got a monitor up here with a DVD player and a muthafuckin Play Station. We hit the fuckin' jackpot," Rico said on the edge of the bed next to Marquan.

And then the engine revved again, this time it turned over and Rahmel smiled. Mechanics was the one thing his father taught him that Rahmel could use with pride. Though he was sure stealing a car was nowhere on the same list.

"Aww shit, my nigga," Taariq said smiling. "I knew you knew what to do, wit your smart ass."

"Make a left!" Marquan yelled as Rahmel made a left turn going south on Georgia Avenue. "Let's dip the fuck outta this bitch."

*This bama-ass nigga blowing the shit out of me.* Rahmel smirked at Meche in the rearview mirror. He was getting tired of the stranger. And it was burning him up that he didn't recognize him from around the way.

Taariq began rummaging through the glove compartment, tossing out a lighter, a mini-flashlight, some napkins, an opened box of condoms, some electrical tape and a small tube of lubrication jelly. "Uggh, man," Taariq said flinging the sticky tube to the back, before grabbing the napkins to wipe his fingers. Rico and Marquan cracked up laughing.

Rahmel shook his head and smiled. He paced himself as he drove, careful to obey all the traffic rules as he made a left onto New York Avenue to hit 395 to get them home. Rahmel went under the tunnel that connected Northwest to Southeast. They were only a few blocks away from the Capitol Building, which illuminated the very center of the city especially with the moon's glow bouncing off the pure white structure. Rahmel quietly admired the beauty.

Each quadrant of the nation's capitol, whether it was North-west, Southeast, Northeast or Southwest, was based on the location of that very building. Northwest and Southeast contrasted in so many ways. Most of the federal government business took place in Northwest. Multi-million dollar corporations, most non-profit organizations and the D.C. government operated from Northwest also. Politicians and lobbyists, worked from Northwest. The White House, the FBI's J. Edgar Hoover building and the U.S. Treasury department, along with all the other national government buildings were also in that part of town.

Southeast on the other hand, now on an economic upswing due to gentrification, for decades had been the poorest part of the city. Crime rates skyrocketed along with drug and alcohol abuse only until recently, where condo associations and town home communities sprung up where shoddy projects had long-housed junkies and hopeful residents alike.

But before all the rebuilding, Ward 8 had received all of

the city's leftovers. After the richer districts took the best share for education, hospitals, police departments, sanitation and roads, Ward 8 got what was left. People from Southeast were not expected to thrive. Discount Marts and Check Cashing stores were seen more often than grocery stores or banks. Overpriced liquor stores and Chinese takeout spots were at the end of every corner like traffic lights. Greater Southeast Community Hospital seemed more like a clinic with its less than adequate facilities and equipment. Besides the steep hills, like the ones where Frederick Douglass' historic house or the Anacostia African American history museum sat, the only other thing that was just as abundant in this part of town, were the hallowed out project buildings, cluttering corner after corner. Misery and despair had long replaced hope for the people who headed across the bridge to Southeast after the Martin Luther King riots destroyed Uptown and their prosperous dreams back in the 1960s.

Rahmel noticed that now, even Southeast was being divided up like pie, as people who looked like him were being shuffled even farther out to Maryland's neighboring Prince George's County as the Whites and middle class Blacks snatched up some of the hot new realty. But it was strange watching these people move into the same places where Jamaican neckties had been given to those who stole from drug dealers or snitched to cops. Every time Rahmel walked outside his door he knew that he was Southeast all day. Sometimes he did exactly what people expected. Hung outside on the corner of Minnesota Avenue, all hours of the night. Smoked weed with Meche and the rest of his friends. Stole a car or two, and then sold it to a chop shop in Forestville.

But then there were times when Rahmel showed up for school because he wasn't expected to be there. His teachers were mind-numbing though—either they read directly from textbooks without looking up at the half-sleepy faces staring back at them or they spent the day breaking up fights and trying to get students who didn't want to learn, to pay attention. It was as if they already gave up on them and were just longing for the first and fifteenth, and in most cases, the end of June for summer vacation.

Rahmel didn't care one way or the other, he participated occasionally and for that, his teachers rewarded him with B grades. It was enough to keep his Pops quiet, although it wasn't quite clear if he cared. Rahmel knew those Bs were enough to get him out of D.C. and into a place where he felt he could breathe despite his Dad's solemn gaze and the guilt that Rahmel harbored inside.

"Bingo!" Taariq said back to digging inside the glovebox. "The registration. Raymond Neil Bennett. Residence, 2113 Georgia Avenue. Well Mr. Bennett, we're going to take this piece of shit off your hands. Bet he won't miss this shit at all."

Marquan dug in the pockets behind the front seats and pulled out a map, some papers printed from off the Internet and a manila envelope with an old letter from D.C. Court dated 1997. "Ain't much back here," he mumbled.

"Hold up, let's see what this nigga was watching," Rico said twisting his cap sideways and then pressing play on the DVD player.

Breathless heavy pants and the sticky sound of wet skin slapping on wet skin oozed from the raggedy surround sound speakers. "Yes. Give me that ass."

"What the…" Rico said. "That look like…two dudes, dawg."

"Oh, hell no!" Marquan yelled. "Man, turn that shit the fuck off!"

"Is that a little boy?" Rico asked.

"The fuck y'all niggas looking at?" Taariq asked leaning back to see the screen.

And then at the same time, Marquan and Rico said,

"Uggh," as the man on screen climaxed.

"Youngin' this is some muthafuckin' gay porn. Turn that shit the fuck off!" Marquan barked again.

Rico turned it off, shaking his head. "Man, I swear that boy couldn't be no more than fifteen, sixteen."

"Old freakass muthafucka," Marquan said. "Probably some old nasty ass man who can't get his shit up."

"Shit, he was fucking somebody. Condoms was in the glovebox," Rahmel commented as he sat at the light on Martin Luther King Avenue preparing to make a left onto Good Hope Road.

"I'm about to hurl. This shit is gross as shit," Marquan said staring at the twin mattress. "He probably was raping little kids on this nasty muthafucka."

Taariq shook his head quietly staring out the window. "Sickass. I say let's just set this bitch on fire."

"Shit, I don't give a fuck," Rahmel said.

"Yeah, torch this piece of shit," Marquan ordered.

Caught up in the hype, instead of taking a left, Rahmel maneuvered the van to the right so he could turn into Anacostia Park, the huge area that bordered the Anacostia River. He drove under an overpass about a quarter-mile before recognizing the gate stretched in front of them at that entrance. "Damn."

"Aint that some bull?" Marquan asked. "Shit, pull this mug over and let's burn it right here."

Before Rahmel could respond his cellphone rang. He looked down and smiled when he saw Asia's glowing face. He didn't answer it. Just seeing her face was all the answer he needed. He was tired of rebelling and doing things he knew he shouldn't. Asia reminded him of that, she was refreshing and made him want to be more than average. So Rahmel pulled the van over under the bridge. "Fellas, I'm out," he said shifting the gear into park.

"What?" Marquan asked obviously pissed.

"You out man?" Taariq asked. "All right then. We'll catch up with ya later."

"All right Dawg," Rico said clasping Rahmel's hand.

"You just gonna leave us right here?" Marquan asked pissed. "What kinda punkass shit is that?"

"Dawg, your bama ass don't even muthafuckin' know me! If I was you, I'd just shut the fuck up!" Rahmel fired back.

"Marquan, calm down dude. This ain't even that serious," Taariq intervened.

"Fuck all y'all," Marquan roared climbing over Rico to get out. Rahmel climbed out of the driver's seat, too. He walked in front of the van, squaring his body up, ready for whatever Marquan was planning. Instead of walking toward Rahmel, Marquan walked down the street and around the corner out of Rahmel's eyesight.

"That dude is nothing but a bunch of mouth. I don't know where he been getting all that heart from lately, for real. Shit, even Lil Kenny from Barry Farms whipped that nigga's ass," Rico said shaking his head. "And he in a damn wheelchair."

"Man fuck dude," Rahmel said.

"I feel you. Shit, he only good for that gwop anyway," Rico said switching seats ready to drive.

"No bull," Taariq added. "That nigga a lil' bitch for real. Now he wanna go all hard and shit. He been acting like that for a second now. Nigga done got his folks pregnant and now he wanna start feeling hisself, I guess he a man now and shit."

Rico laughed.

"Man, I don't give a fuck," said Rahmel shaking his head. "Anyway, I'll catch y'all niggas later. Hey, when y'all coming back to school?"

They all burst out laughing at that question.

"Nigga please. You know Anacostia ain't ready for a nigga like me," Taariq said. "Feel me?"

"You never know. Sometimes, I don't like being up in

there, but…I gotta do what I gotta do," Rahmel said.

"Shit, you was good at that shit. Or good at faking it," Taariq said. "Anyway, holla at me."

"All right son," Rico said pulling off and blowing the horn.

Rahmel shook his head at the two. He began dialing Asia's number.

"Hello," she said.

"Hey Sexy."

"You home yet?"

"Not yet."

"Boy, you just don't want to go home do you?" she purred into the phone.

"Nah, not really. I'm almost there though." Rahmel's other phoneline chimed. He looked down to check who was calling. Rahmel smiled as he noticed his home number flashing across the screen. It was his father, and for Rahmel, a sign he did care. Two days had passed without seeing his father, and since he hardly ever called, Rahmel knew his Dad had been worried.

"Asia, let me call you right back. It's my…"

Before another word could escape Rahmel's lips, a loud pop followed by a blistering hot pain sliced through his body. Again. And again. He hit the slushy cold ground, hat falling in the snow. Eyes frozen open while Rahmel's face sunk into the cold wetness. Asia's voice yelling from the cellphone a few inches from his head. Pain. Heat. Tightness of the chest. Rahmel's last breath still lodged in his throat.

"Look who shutting the fuck up now bitch. You didn't think I remembered you, huh?" he said standing over Rahmel's body, sneering.

The moment he saw Rahmel leaving Asia's house, Marquan recognized his face as soon as he saw the deep scar carved in his forehead. Rahmel was one of three guys who carjacked him at gunpoint in Eastover parking lot in August. Even though Rahmel wasn't the one with the gun, he was the one who snatched his keys away and threatened him. Lukewarm piss trickled down Marquan's pants leg that day as he stood frightened for his life, tears slipping from his eyes. The three carjackers had laughed as they let Marquan's crying girlfriend pointlessly wipe the piss off with napkins from their Popeye's bag. The three had even stolen their chicken that day, too. The next day, Marquan bought his first gun, a .357 off a crackhead, and dared someone else to ever disrespect him. The gun had made him feel powerful for months. Never in a million years did he think he'd ever run into them again, but just in case he did, he planned to be prepared.

"Who the lil bitch now?" Marquan spit on Rahmel's face, before turning around and walking away as someone's only child, someone's new lover, someone's best friend and someone with dreams lied breathless beneath the dark underpass.

# LOVE STINKS

*Gena Garrison*
Greer, SC

L ove stinks! It stinks worse than a week old baby diaper. It stinks worse than fifty pounds of rancid garbage lying on the curb. It even stinks worse than that nasty bloated corpse that I kept coming back to and checking on. No love isn't blind it's funky. I know what I'm talking about because I love P.J. At one time I loved this fool more than I even loved myself. I mean he was everything that I'd ever dreamed of and some things I was too stupid to even dream about.

Me and Lesha was sitting out on the steps chillin the first time I saw him walk by. Just so you know, me and Lesha been tight since she moved into our building when I was ten and she was nine. Up until then I didn't have no real friends around here because most of the kids my age were hardheaded boys. All they wanted to do was show me their lil wiggly pee pees and at ten that was the last thing I wanted to see.

At my house on the sixteenth floor of the third building in Fieldcrest projects there was me, momma, my older sister Danielle, and her rugrat Tyra. Danielle's baby daddy Tyrone was there most of the time too but his name wasn't on the lease. I slept on the couch because I got tired of hearing Danielle and Tyrone humping all night. At least in the living room I could drown out their stupid noise, and what they called love.

Momma and Danielle taught me that love not only stinks

but it makes you do stupid shit. Danielle said she loved Tyrone and she didn't even leave him alone when she caught him in Momma's bed. Momma said she loved him too and because of all that love Danielle's got another rugrat and I gots a lil brother. Tyrese and Tyrone Jr. could be twins if they hadn't dropped out of different women only a month apart.

Yeah, love is funky as shit.

So you'd think that after living with the stench of love in my own house I would have known better than to get caught up with P.J. but Outkast is right when they say *roses really smell like boo boo*. Love is like that. It smells sweet at first, but the more you sniff the worse the smell gets.

P.J. strolled by me and Lesha that day like he didn't notice but he was just trying to play it cool. I watched him walk down the block with his pants hanging at just the right spot on his butt. He was Sean John'd right down to his draws. Now me and Lesha was tight, so we didn't usually have no man conflicts. We agreed right after the whole Momma, Danielle, Tyrone thang that if we was both interested in the same dude we'd be upfront about it, and work it out. As soon as P.J. was down the street far enough not to hear me I turned to her and laid it on the line. "Don't even think about it girly. That one is gonna be mine."

"How you gonna just call a nigga like that? He was looking at both of us."

"No, he wasn't. His eyes was all over these big ass titties of mine."

Lesha shut the hell up then cuz she ain't gots nothing on her chest but some overgrown mosquito bites. If we'd been standing up and he'd gotten a look at her apple booty she might have had a chance cuz my booty is wide and flat. But from the front, I was the one who got all the attention and she knew it.

We sat chillin on the steps for about a half hour before P.J.

came back up the street. He was not even looking where he was going cuz his head was down and he was scratching one of those lotto things. I don't know why people keep wasting their money on them damn things. Nobody ever wins the lottery but Mexicans and po white trash. A nigga ain't got a chance at it. But this lotto ticket turned out to be my lucky or unlucky day, depends on how you look at it. P.J. tripped over my foot that somehow ended up in his path and the next thing I knew, he was lying on the steps on top of me. I grinned, he grinned and it was on.

By the end of the week P.J. was on top of me again. We was in his bedroom and he was slamming into me harder than I'd ever been sexed before. It shoulda hurt, he was stroking me so fast and so hard, but it felt so damn good. Two times he had to put his hand over my mouth to keep me from screaming so loud his momma and four sisters would hear. They was in the living room watching TV when me and P.J came in from the movies. We'd held hands and kissed through the whole show and once, he'd even tried to finger me under my skirt. By the time we got back to his house I was on fire. I was polite and said "hi" to all of them, then P.J. pulled me in the back to his room.

I'd been with other boys before, but P.J. was different. He took his time to slowly take off my halter-top and then my mini skirt. Then he stepped back and stared at me standing there in my Victoria Secret lingerie. He let out a long whistle and grinned from ear to ear. P.J. was probably the finest brother living in Fieldcrest apartments. He was tall enough to play basketball but said it bored him. His skin was smooth and supple almost like a baby's and when he held my hand I liked looking at the contrast of colors that meshed together when his hand, which was smooth and cocoa colored, intertwined with my lighter butterscotch.

"You wearing that Babygirl. You look so sexy," he finally said after staring at me for the longest time. "Now take that shit off!"

He didn't have to tell me twice. Within a matter of seconds I was naked and waiting for him on the bed. He turned around and locked his door then he came over and put his face in between my legs. I lay back trying to catch my breath as his tongue moved in and out of me real fast like it was a tiny wet snake.

I don't know when he managed to get his clothes off since he was licking me so good but the next thing I knew he was sliding his thickness up inside me and I was moaning his name over and over.

I think his Momma heard me screaming at least once cuz she gave me a funky look as I was leaving, but I didn't care. I knew that night that I was falling in love with P.J. and wasn't nothing neither she nor nobody else could do to stop it. The stench of love was approaching quickly and it was going to overtake me.

The next day I sat on the stoop sucking on a blow pop the same way I'd sucked P.J. the night before and told Lesha all about it. She stared at me with her big eyes bugging out. "So you two a couple now?" She asked when I finally stopped talking.

"Yeah I mean we ain't said the words, but I know it. Why you ask?"

"I heard that P.J. is a dog."

"Who told you that?" I had to know cuz P.J was the new kid on the block. He'd just moved up to stay with his Momma after his Daddy got shot down in Georgia. When his parents split up, P.J. and his brothers stayed with his Dad and his sisters moved here with their Mom. His brothers were both married and now his Daddy was dead so P.J. didn't have no place else to go. That's why he came to live with his Momma. Nobody knew P.J. around here but his sisters and now me.

Lesha is my girl and I knew she wouldn't just flat out lie but sometimes she carried gossip without checking to see if it had an ounce of truth in it.

"His sister Marlene told me. I was talking to her at the Chinese restaurant last night while you was at the movies."

I remembered seeing all the boxes of leftover Chinese food on the table when me and P.J. came in the night before. My ears perked up. "What she say? I need to know word for word."

"Just that he got two babies and two baby mommas down south."

"Down south? What the hell I care about some country ass bitches down south? P.J. is mine now. Girl I thought you knew something."

Lesha sucked her teeth at me. "I'm just saying. He's new around here and I thought you needed to know cuz you my girl."

"Well P.J. told me all about his kids already so let's just drop it okay." I had never lied to my best friend before in my life. Lesha knew everything about me from the first time I got my period to the first dick I sucked. She knew about the time I'd stole three CDs from the record store, and even about the time I got locked up for writing bad checks. Lesha even knew that my real Daddy was a pimp named Georgia Slim and not that man who was in all the pictures in my house and nobody else knew that but me and Momma.

"So what did he tell you about his kids?"

"None of your damn business!"

Lesha just stared at me as I stood up and walked back up the steps and went inside the building. I knew she was wondering what the hell was wrong with me but how could I tell her if I didn't even know myself.

About three months later P.J. finally did tell me about his

kids but it wasn't the way I wanted to hear it. "What the hell you mean you pregnant?" he screamed.

"I took one of those home tests and the stick turned blue." I didn't wanna look at him because I hated it when he screamed at me. We were at his house and his Mom and sisters had gone out. We'd made love in the kitchen, on the living room couch, and in the bedroom. I thought after getting all that good stuff he wouldn't be so mad when I told him. He was furious. His dark brown face was changing colors and I was scared he was actually gonna turn red.

"You sure its mine? It can't be mine!" He was walking around naked swinging his arms mad as hell but I couldn't help noticing how good his dick looked swinging too as he walked and yelled. Those words should have made me mad but they didn't. P.J. was only human. Every brother asked that question, it was only natural.

"P.J. I'm your girl. You know I wouldn't do it with nobody else," I said.

"Look Babygirl, I ain't neva told you but I already got two kids I can't afford to feed. Why you think I work so hard and still live with my Momma. If I don't send $600 dollars a month down south, they will come up here and lock my ass up. Do you want me to go to jail?"

The thought of PJ in jail and not with me scared me shitless. There was no way I was gonna let that happen. He was my man now, forget them bamas. "No. I don't want that P.J. I want you right here with me."

"Then you know what you gots to do girl."

I knew but I didn't want to do it. This baby was a part of me and P.J. and even though I don't really like kids I wanted to love this one.

"That cost money P.J. I don't know if I have enough saved up." I was lying I had almost ten grand in my savings account. I was saving to move out of that apartment and get my own place. I wanted a place for me and P.J. and now my baby.

"Are you asking me for money?" P.J. asked getting angry again.

"Can't you at least pay half?" I said hoping he'd say no. If we couldn't afford it, then we couldn't do it.

"I just told you where all my money goes, and now you are asking me for more? I thought you were different Babygirl. I thought that you were all about me and all about us. You are just like all those other bitches. You love a nigga for his money and nothing else." P.J. walked over to his dresser and pulled out a wad of cash. He peeled off three one hundred dollar bills and threw them at me while I was still lying on his bed. "That should cover it. Get dressed, and get the fuck out!"

I was about to open my mouth to protest when I heard the locks on the front door turning and realized his Mom and sisters were home. Instead I picked up my clothes, got dressed and left without taking the money. The next morning, I stopped by the bank and withdrew some money, then I went downtown to the clinic and did what I knew I had to do. I lay on my back and counted the tiles on the ceiling while the doctor used something that looked like a vacuum cleaner to suck my baby out of me. When I was done I listened to the nurse, who looked like she'd never had any and desperately needed to get some, give me instructions. Then she asked me how I was getting home. She looked at me with pity when I told her I was taking the bus. "It's a shame when the boy won't even bring you in," she said while scribbling on a piece of paper.

*"Fuck you,"* I muttered under my breath as I took the papers and walked out.

A few days later I called P.J. and told him that it was done. He told me to come over, that he had the apartment all to himself. I should have smelled the stench as soon as I walked in but I'd lived with the smell so long I didn't recognize it. The sweet smell of love was starting to sour like baby's milk.

I ended up back at that same clinic two more times before I finally realized I couldn't do it no more. I love P.J. but every time he put life inside me, he forced me downtown to have it sucked out. The last time I couldn't bear to go by myself and P.J. said he had to work that day. I'd finally told Lesha and she held my hand on the bus all the way there and stayed with me through the night while I rocked and cried. I didn't realize it at the time, but a small part of me went down those tubes with my baby each time. Lesha held onto me tightly as I cried and tried to breathe. The smell was growing stronger, and the stink of love was beginning to choke me.

Standing in the bathroom staring at that little blue stick for the fourth time in two years I knew there was nothing P.J could say this time that would make me go through it again. He'd never said the words but I knew P.J loved me. He was just scared. Those bitches in Georgia were always calling asking for _this_ for the kids, or needing _that_ for the kids. The Christmas before, I'd given P.J. five hundred bucks to buy toys and send down to them cuz they Mommas had spent the child support on nails and fake hair. Those two biddies drained him. But I wasn't like that and as soon as our baby got here, I knew he'd see it my way.

I was gonna wait until I was at least seven months to tell him but one night lying in bed he realized that the tummy bulge was not just extra pizza. P.J. was on top of me grinding deep and slow the way I love it when he suddenly jumped off of me. "What the hell was that?" he said staring at me.

I'd been so lost in the feeling I didn't realize the baby had just kicked him. "What are you talking about?"

"Don't play dumb with me girl. Are you pregnant? I been with pregnant women before, I know what I just felt."

"Come back to bed baby. Your Moms will be home soon,"

I said ignoring him. I pulled him back down on top of me and let him stroke it good and deep and slow some more. He was moaning and whispering in my ear when I answered him. "Oh yes baby, you gonna be a Daddy again," I said while rolling my hips up to meet his thrust.

All of a sudden P.J. started to slam into me hard, really hard. It wasn't the hard that I liked, it was rough and violent.

"P.J. stop that hurts!" I screamed but he wouldn't. He just kept pounding into me harder and harder until finally he couldn't take it anymore. He came and collapsed on top of me. He lay there for a long time catching his breath.

"I'll go with you to the clinic this time," he finally said then rolled off of me.

My thighs were sore and my cootchie burned from what he'd just done to me. I didn't answer him I was in too much pain. I tried to get up, but it hurt too much. I pulled my knees up and lay my face on them. "P.J. you hurt me. Why did you do that?" I whimpered.

"It's too late, ain't it? Too late for the clinic?"

I nodded my head but I didn't look at him. I couldn't believe that he'd just tried to fuck our baby out of me. He was trying to hurt me. He was trying to hurt the baby. The stench of love had never been stronger in the room than at the moment. It swirled around like a thick fog circling us both, daring us to move. After a long while, I managed to pull myself off the bed and go home.

After that, I wouldn't mess with P.J. no more. I lied and told him the doctor said I couldn't. He didn't like it, but I didn't care. I told him I'd suck him as much as he wanted but my stuff was off limits until after the baby was born. He didn't like the idea of the baby either but again I didn't care. I'd already decided that the next time a doctor pulled something out of me I was going to take it home whether P.J. liked it or not.

I told Momma right after that and she just looked at me with a sad look before calling me a whore and slamming the door to her room. So with what was left of my savings, I decided to go ahead and move out into my own place. I found a one-bedroom apartment a few blocks away from Fieldcrest. It had a window that overlooked a breath taking view of the alley and a dumpster. The water was brown when you first turned it on, but if you let it run it would turn yellow, and then finally clear enough to wash in. The stove had two eyes that worked and one burner in the oven. It didn't really matter. I'd lost my job in the mailroom at Prince Construction since I was sick so much from being pregnant and I'd taken one at McDonalds. I could eat anything that was left at the end of the night so I never had to cook.

The apartment came partially furnished, if you could call a broken down couch, a table with two mismatched chairs, and a mattress on the floor propped up on cement blocks, furnished. It wasn't much, but it was mine. P.J. came by at least two or three times a week to get his dick sucked like only I could do it. Then he would grumble about the baby, and leave. Sometimes it bothered me, but then my baby would kick and I'd smile, and then nothing P.J. did, mattered anymore.

I'd watched both my mother and my sister have babies and laughed at the obvious pain they'd felt. But when I woke up in the middle of the night with fire running through my belly, I suddenly realized that this wasn't no joke. I tried to call P.J. but then I remembered I had not paid my cell phone bill and it was off. So I managed to put on some shoes and a jacket and leave my building. I didn't know any of my neighbors so there was no use in asking for help from crazy ass strangers.

I was headed back to Fieldcrest and just hoped I could make it the three blocks without passing out or giving birth on the street. It was at least eight weeks too soon, but the pain I felt was real and I had to get help. I knew it wasn't the smartest or the safest thing to do, but it was the only choice I had. Besides I grew up on those streets and walked them late at night, lots of time. There was nothing out here that could hurt me.

I really believed that until I finally reached my building and stepped inside the lobby. What I saw not only hurt me, it tore me into tiny little pieces that scattered all over the floor.

About five years earlier some people from some big offices downtown had decided to come to the hood and spruce it up for all the little poor niggas to live. They'd cleaned up some of the graffiti on the walls, and put chairs in the lobby. Nobody ever sat in them because they were the hard uncomfortable kind with foam rubber cushions covered in ugly green plastic with hard wooden arms. Me and P.J. used to joke that those chairs were too hard for sitting—the most good they'd ever been was for leaning over and fucking. In my mind I remembered the time P.J. and me had come home late from the club and his Mom had locked him out. We'd been drinking and smoking weed and both of us wanted to do it so bad, it hurt. I was wearing a really short skirt and P.J. had bent me over one of those hard chairs and hit it from behind. That late at night, no one else would be coming or going from the building but even if they did, we didn't care. I was moaning and screaming cuz it felt so good inside me.

Suddenly I realized it wasn't me who was moaning. It wasn't me he was stroking. It was the middle of the night and with the worst pain of my life rushing through my belly, I stood speechless as I watched P.J. stroking in and out of someone else who was bent over the same chair. She must have loved it as much as I did because the echo of her moans filled the whole lobby. She was moaning so loud, it's a wonder either of them heard me when I spoke.

"P.J. what the hell are you doing?"

He stopped and turned around, and so did that apple bottomed bitch. That's when the realest pain a woman could ever feel rushed through me like a roaring freight train. It wasn't a labor pain. It was the pain of betrayal. Lesha's big eyes stared at me as P.J. pulled out of her and tried to pull up his pants.

I started running but the smell kept following me. It was chasing me and screaming my name. The stench of love got closer and closer and I couldn't breathe anymore. It was inside my mouth and made my nostrils burn. I stopped briefly as I felt the bile building up in my throat and I vomited the stench of love out on the street. Then I began to run again.

I finally got to my apartment and slammed the door shut with all my might. Then I turned all the locks hoping to lock the smell of love outside.

I tumbled onto my bed into a ball of pain still gasping for air then I felt a trickle of blood run down my leg. I'd forgotten my baby. I'd forgotten I was in labor. I ran to my tiny bathroom as the blood went from trickles to splatters. I sat or fell—I don't know which one, but I found myself in a sitting position on the floor as blood ran from my body. The pain took over my reality as I looked in between my legs and saw a tiny foot slide out.

My baby never took a breath. She slid out of me onto the nasty porcelain floor already dead. When the pain in between my legs finally stopped, I grabbed a pair of scissors and cut the cord that had connected her life to mine, then I scooped her bloody body up off the floor and wrapped her in a tiny blanket that Danielle had given me when I moved out. I took her to my bedroom and climbed into bed.

The blood on the both of us, and the bed had dried and was hard, but I was still on my bed rocking and singing her lullabies when the sun came up the next morning, and when it went down the next evening. I loved my baby, as she lay in my arms and began to stink. Finally when it was pitch black, I dragged my aching body off of my bed and put her lifeless body inside a hefty bag. I took her and that week's trash out to the dumpster and tossed them both inside.

Several hours or maybe it was days later, I'm not really sure, the sound of knocking woke me up out of a deep sleep. I didn't remember coming back inside, I didn't remember falling asleep. I finally found my way to the front door and opened it. The stench of love engulfed the apartment as I looked at PJ standing there.

This trifling ass nigga had the nerve to grin at me. I heard the words "I'm sorry" fall out of his mouth and I wondered how long he'd known I was a fool. With the stench of love as my guide I stepped aside and invited him in.

I thought it would hurt more, when I screwed P.J. less than 2 days after giving birth to a dead baby but by then I was numb. I didn't feel any pleasure or pain. All I could feel was disgust. I'd told him our baby was dead, and outside in the dumpster and he'd let a smile spread across his trifling face without realizing it. Then he pulled me to bed. The nasty ass bastard didn't even notice the sheets were still stained with blood before he was on top of me poking and grunting. I lay under him and hoped that he came really fast and really hard because it would be the last nut of his life.

As he slept I tried to talk myself out of killing P.J. rationalizing that I wasn't no killer. But as I sat and thought about it, I realized that I was. I had killed before. I killed because of the stench called love. Besides that, P.J thought that killing was the right thing, it was the only thing to do he'd told me once. Because of him I'd killed four babies. Killing another person I loved would be easy.

I went under the cushion of my living room couch and found the gun that my Uncle Cleophus gave me to hide when the police were after him. He'd been in lock up four years and I thought of the gun as mine.

I held it in my hands and fingered the cold steel as I walked back to the bedroom. P.J. had rolled his sorry ass over and was snoring lying on his side with his back to me. It was a perfect target for the four bullets I slowly emptied into it. Then just to make sure I put the chamber next to the back of his head, pulled the trigger, and watched his brain splatter onto my pillow.

A few hours later his cell phone buzzed. I shoved his body over and read the message. *Where are you?* It said.

I typed in my address and pressed send. Then I patiently waited for Lesha to show up. I didn't have but one bullet left so I opened the door and without a word, I placed the cold steel to her temple and pulled the trigger before she even realized where she was. I drug her body inside, closed my door, and went back to bed.

I sat in my apartment surrounded by the stench of love for three days. That's when my neighbors finally realized that the noise they'd heard two days before had not been a car backfiring and the smell of my perpetual love for P.J. and Lesha began to find its way under the doorway and float up the hall.

When the police arrived, I went quietly after telling them where to find my baby so she'd get a proper burial.

By then I knew she'd begun to stink like the shitty diapers she never got to wear. She stank like the garbage that was piled on top of her. She stank even worse than P.J.'s rotting corpse sitting beside me. My baby stank because of love.

My cellmate just stared at me as I finally stopped talking. I supposed she never thought she'd hear so much just by asking me if I'd ever been in love. Maybe I should have kept my answer short and sweet. "Yeah I've been in love, and love stinks."

74     

# BOOGiE DOWN iNFERNO

*michael a. gonzales*
Bronx, NY

"i keep smelling smoke.
I can't tell whether it's real or in my imagination."
"in the south bronx of america"
photo book by Mel Rosenthal
(Curbstone Press 2000)

an abandoned car was parked in front of the hydrant. fire-truck sirens screamed in the night as raging flames kissed the midnight sky. staring at your former south bronx tenament over on 178th and vyse avenue, neighborhood crack zombies were entranced by the vivid yellow and crimison cinders raining down from the rooftop. "oh shit," screamed a young black boy cruising the trash strewn street on a stolen five-speed bike.

this block is filled with ghosts, you thought, still buzzed from the cocaine you had been hitting since noon. feeling as though it were on the verge of exploding, your heart was beating a million miles a minute.

"another bronx building burning," said a weary voiced stranger standing behind you.

looking all offical and shit, you were dressed in the same police academy uniform you wore at graduation that same afternoon. assigned to work at the 48th precinct, your brain was buzzed from the the eight ball of devil's dandruff you scored from some hunt's point homie.

"fish scale," he had assured you, as though it made a difference. all those youngbloods swore they were scarface. fuck the friendly skies, 'cause you was higher than eddie palmieri hanging at casa amadeo record shop bragging about being the baddest piano player in the barrio. sweat rolled down your face like you had stuck it in a oven or something.

besides yourself, no one watching that building burn knew that there was a dead woman on the top floor lying next to a pissy mattress, her messy-haired head cracked like the plaster on an old bedroom ceiling.

chick's name was lisa hernadez, and once upon a time baby girl had been a great beauty with a big booty and supple breasts. still, that was years before the broad had become a full blown crack ho, wandering the streets of the boogie down looking to make her loot by any means necessary no matter how low down.

back in the day, when both of y'all had lived in that red bricked apartment building (her fam lived on the fifth floor, while you were one flight down) you had lusted after sweet lisa since you was a teenager who stared at the ceiling while pulling your pecker.

eyes closed, your nasty daydreams were like private porn movies continually running on a loop in your mind. in that home-made triple-xxx flick in your head, you rubbed lisa's perky nipples through sheer tube-tops, sucked the dirty toes that had been walking the block in red jellies and licked her hairy snatch as she screamed your name.

of course, in the real world, she barely knew that you were alive, so you thought of tonight as payback for all those times she had mocked you, laughed in your face and made snide remarks behind your back. "whose laughing now, bitch" you thought to yourself, trying not to laugh aloud.

*****

welcome to spic heaven: clearly you remembered the days of growing-up on that broke down block of vacant lots, drunken domino players and one storefront church. despite the sweet salsa songs your mother used to hum in the mornings, you never saw any pretty flowers blooming through the cracked sidewalks. unless, of course, they had mutated into dog shit, broken bottles, trash heaps and empty heroin bags.

back when you were a small school boy with chubby cheeks and sorrowful eyes, your mother was your entire world. every friday evening, after leaving her gig at the martin luther king health center, she stopped-off at the cluttered botanica tu mundo up the street. gently parting the colorful floral curtains in front of your living-room window, you patiently waited for her to sluggishly stroll down the block.

you looked at the shattered souls gathered on the stoop across the street, boisterous boys congregated around a chalk drawn skellzie board; a few feet away from jose's luncheonette, a couple of strong armed teens dressed in two-tone sweaters and tight black pants, played congas while a wino ex-boxer drunkily danced wildly and sang out of tune.

minutes later you spotted your mommi slowly walking pass dented garbage cans, carrying a heavy shopping bag. it usually took her ten minutes to tiredly scale the dirty marble stairs to your fourth-floor apartment.

after achingly removing her white nurse shoes, she poured herself a healthy taste of dark rum and flopped on the plastic covered couch. after taking a few gulps, she shared splendid stories about her homeland of puerto rico. with peppermint scented breath, her remembrances of the island were filled with dusty roads and white sand beaches, mystic sunsets and flying cockroaches.

from those tales you conjured images of wide-hipped aunts you had never seen and divine music you had never heard.

"tell me about poppi," you begged after she had downed a few glasses of the potent rum.

"oh, he was such a handsome man with his grey eyes and curly hair," she swooned. a fisherman, he had drowned seven weeks before you were born. while you secretly hated him for dying, you never tired of your mother's verbal snap-shots of their short life together: "it was olokun," she wept, refering the deity of the sea in santeria. with frail fingers she crushed your small head into her full bosom and wept. "olokrun took your poppi away from us."

in the corner of the white walled living-room, below a cheaply framed picture of j.f.k., mommi had constructed an altar. there was a small color photograph of your father lying atop the red and white satin cloth that covered the altar; there was that plaster statue of st. jude, lit white candles, fresh flowers, an apple, an upside down glass of water supported on a white dish and a jar full of coins. with your father's spirit and the santeria gods as her constant companions, it was not uncommon for mom dukes to awaken after midnight to pray that he was at peace.

washing-up in lukewarm water the following morning, you glanced into the sparkling bathroom mirror, slowly searching for a resemblance with the man in the picture. when you were about eight, you noticed that the two of you shared the same haunted grey eyes. at least that explained why your mother never looked into your peepers when she spoke to you. hell, she just couldn't stand seeing your father's eyes in you.

because of your poppi's drowning, your mother feared losing you to "d'evil streets" outside your windows. with those beatbox boys blasting grandmaster flash tapes and nasty domincan girls shaking their bubble butts, to your moms, those barrio blocks were wilder than the waves that had swept away her husband.

once a month she performed a despojos ceremony, gently beating you with whatever herbs the botanica oracle suggested would frighten away evil spirits. she even placed a string of multicolored prayer beads around your neck to protect you from the demons that lurked in the shadows.

as you got older, she slipped deeper into a netherworld of religion and rum. speaking in tongues, she hung crucifixes throughout the apartment and sprinkled the corners with aqua floria. over the plastic slip covered couch hung a picture of jesus that for some reason scared you. affixed to the cross, blood dripped from his hands and feet.

one night when you were nine, your father approached you in a dream: visions of his sun blackened body lying on the white sands of a beach. there were piecering holes where his eyes should have been. with webbed feet and gills like a fish, he stood-up and approached. his hands were cold and slimmy when he touched your fat face.

that rainy morning, you woke-up screaming.

outside of your hollowed home, you were a paradox: gang member and alter-boy, cheeba smoker and teacher's pet, wild in the streets and smart in the class-room. you hung tough with a clique of kids who called themselves el barrio angels.

an everchanging crew that had been around since the days of the young lords, they had originally planned to be an off-shoot of the radical group. but, by the time you got down with them in the summer of '77, the notorious season of the infamous blackout that bought new york to its knees, the el barrio angels dappled in petty crimes that included selling weed, boosting clothes and robbing number taking bodegas.

by '79 ya'll had become infamous in the hood. it was your best friend fast eddie calderon who had put you down with the crew. money grip had got his nickname because he could out-run any mick cop in the precinct.

skinny ass calderon, with his greasy hair and raggedy jeans, had been your homeboy since the two of you were no bigger than fightin' cocks. after his parents had died in a car crash, he lived with his older sister in the projects. at first glance he didn't appear to be the brightest star in the sky, but the boy was no dummy.

"if you look stupid, then people don't expect much from ya," he declared. "that way you can get away with more shit with less consequences." although he was only two years older than you, calderon schooled your punk ass in the ways of the street. "we be like brothers from different mothers," he fondly said.

the meeting spot for the el barrio angels was a decaying tenement a few blocks from the cross bronx expressway. a once stunning structure had been condemned years ago. the once exquisite marble floors, with their faded art deco designs, were chipped and soiled, and the broken windows looked like the eyes of a dead man.

the angels had decided to transform the apartment on the third floor of a crumbling building into a clubhouse. somehow the gang's leader had managed to install lights, an old pool-table, a stained cloth couch and a few tattered chairs. a beat-up eight-track played a constant stream of barretto and bataan. in the dimly lit room there was also an old safe with a broken door where the angels stored bags of weed and stolen loot.

whenever y'all went out, the wild stray german sheperd ya'll named blood was kept inside the room. the canine's constant barking kept the junkies far away. "blood would rip out their throats and eat 'em hop heads like hamburger," calderon laughed petting the dog. "them junkie motherfuckers know better than to fuck around over here."

indeed, the only thing that disgusted you about the building were all those noddin' junkies shooting up, pissing, shitting, fucking and dying in the halls. a trio of nappy haired colored dudes dressed in old vietnam jackets and oily jeans sold five dollar packs of p-funk from a first floor apartment, and throughout the rest of the building.

one dreary twilight in the summer of '79 you and calderon was just chillin' in the club house puffing budda bless. like the villan twins you wanted to be, both of y'all were dressed in your regular el barrio angels uniform of backwards black baseball caps, black pro-keds, white tube socks and black polyester pants.

outside the window, as the sun slowly changed colors from white glare to muted orange, the racket of a rowdy block party ricocheted off of the rickity structures. you just knew that kool herc was in the house.

later that night, there was a surprise raid by corrupt cops on the gang's chill-out spot. the boogaloo music had been so loud that none of the crew had heard those hard heeled police footsteps as they crept up the stairs. guns drawn and popping shit, the blue boys barged into the room.

scared to death when those pigs threatened to stomp anyone who squealed, you knew it was time to jet. in your eyes five-o were just a bunch of pussies with power and guns, flexing their muscles against a roomful of teenagers.

one chalky faced cop swung open the rusty safe door, and began stuffing all the loot and drugs into his pockets. with coffee and cigarette stained teeth, the pig laughed.

there was mayhem in the room as you and fast eddie scattered out of the window and scurried up a rusty fire-escape in beat-up pro-keds. once you reached the roof-top, both of you attempted to leap to the neighboring building.

fuckin' eddie didn't make it though, falling to his death in the darkness.

though terrified, somehow you made it back to your apartment without a scratch. it was then, lying on the bed still

boogie down inferno

and scared shirtless, but wiping away the sweat and tears, that you decided that you wanted to be a cop instead of a criminal.

it was not about knowing right from wrong, but about who had the supremacy in that police state. you've noticed how the fuzz swaggered through the hood with a sense of self-importance; you saw how they never paid for their food in restaurants; you heard stories from the other el barrio angels how the pigs are always ripping-off the local drug dealers, stealing the stash and keeping their cash.

"that's gonna be my hustle," you mumbled, wiping tears away with a tissue. in the next room your mommi slept, unaware of your revelation. "i'm going to be a cop."

ten years later the decade has changed, but the barrio is still the same. or maybe worse. still, on that weary winter morning that you graduated from the police academy, your mother was so proud.

after taking her home to her new spot in riverdale, you hooked-up with a few other friends from the academy for what was supposed to be an innocent celebration in the old hood. in the city's liberal attempt to recruit former homeboy's to police their own, thinking they will be able to relate better to the beamed-up crackheads and wild cowboy drug dealers, this was going to be your beat.

crack had worked a dark mojo on that hood. shit, niggas flipped for that rock cocaine. after it first hit the streets in the early '80s, the bronx barrios had become a surreal circus of ruthless addition and scary monsters who crawled in the night.

you looked at the new jack street dealers with their snarling pitbulls and exquisite foreign cars, and their wealth excited you. hell, you knew that soon you would be sharing in the spoils of the losing war on drugs.

that night, along with three of your fellow graduates, you boogied over to carlito's pub, an old school bar that had been in the hood since you were a kid. the jukebox blared old salsa as though hip-hop had never been created. after hooking-up with your drug dealing homie in the bathroom, you began sniffing the pure coke and downing shots of barcardi as though tomorrow would never come.

"drinks for my friends," you screamed as your mind slowly unraveled like a spool of thread. next thing you realize you are alone in the streets, wandering down the block in search of a piece of pussy gone astray.

the trick was to find one of those rock smoking hoes who knew how to blow like miles davis. it was then that you saw lisa, her skin smoother than black ice as ice. like other lost ladies, she had become as ruined as the neighborhood itself.

"rock star, bitch," you mumbled. "i wonder who broke you down. used to be too good for a nigga…now look at ya."

dressed in dirty jeans, worn nike's and a ratty sweater, you gave her two twenty-dollar bills to buy a few vials of rock before she took you to the apartment building where you used to live when you was a kid.

the block was swarming with illegal business. you walked into the dark building, and heard mumbling voices coming from beneath the steps. most of the creepy apartments appeared to be crack spots, but you were not nervous.

the fifth-floor apartment used to belong to her mother, who moved back to p.r. the year before. you can remember coming to a birthday party here when lisa turned ten, and the apartment was immaculate as the virgin mary. but that was so long ago. now the flat was a wreck, the sticky floors littered with old beer bottles and used condom packages. there are chink take-out boxes and chicken wing bones; there are dirty clothes all over the floor and a jacked-up mattress in the middle of the living-room. there is an unholy stench that burns your nose hairs. there are dirty sheets covering the windows.

after lighting a few candles, lisa invited you over to the stained mattress. you still had coke left, so while she smoked those stinky rocks, you took a few sniffs. lisa chattered non-stop, and what little you caught of her conversation had to do with the baby her mother stole from her. another innocent child born a junkie, but now she was gone.

you didn't give a shit about this mess she was yapping, you just wanted your dick sucked so you could break out. blaring rap songs (eric b. & rakim, big daddy kane) crashed through the closed window like an urban rhythm soundtrack.

touching her bony leg, she told you to wait until she smoked another rock. she is jumpy and nervous, but after sucking that glass dick lisa would be just fine, at least for five minutes.

you lay down, imagining yourself swimming in the ocean. you could feel lisa unfastening your belt and pants. gently she began licking your balls, sucking and gently gibbling with skill. with your eyes closed, in your mind you saw your father emerging from the sea. except, unlike those dreams from your youth, he doesn't look to be at peace. his eyes look angry and confused.

"be a man," your dead daddy said. "be a fucking man."

minutes passed and soon your vision was shattered by loud cackling laughter. despairingly you opened your eyes and saw that it was lisa laughing through fucked-up teeth.

"i been sucking your dick for twenty minutes and you still ain't hard, poppi," she says. "you been sniffing that shit all night long, now your little dickie won't cooperate."

you felt like a drowning man trying to catch your breath. with these simple words, blood rushed to your head. you could feel the anger building in your chest like a wall as her laughter echoed through that room of horrors as though it were coming through a set of hi-fi speakers.

"you're going to regret that you raggedy bitch," you

screamed, and before you could help yourself you punched lisa in the face. on impact, her mouth shattered as teeth and blood rained to the floor.

for a moment she was dazed, but without warning she leapt on your back and began pulling your hair as her fingernails scratched the back of your neck. "fuckyoufuckyoufuckyou..." she cried and screamed and lost her mind. regaining your balance, you flipped the crazy broad off your back. she looked like a broken doll sprawled on the floor, her skull cracked. you noticed your pants and underwear are still around your ankles.

although lisa had not moved since you flipped her a minute ago, her laughter was still loud in that evil room.

she was unconscious on the floor, but still you were afraid. suppose she filed a police report at the same precinct where you were to report to work in the morning.

it would be your rookie word against a crack-head, but who needed the grief. more than likely she would get one of the housing project posse-boys who populated the block to pop your ass on the sneak tip.

pulling up your pants, you buckled your belt and stared into lisa's damaged face. shit, she had bought it on herself, you reasoned. who told the bitch it was cool to laugh at the police.

slipping your dirty hand into your pocket, you felt a pack of newports. you lit one, sucking on the filter like it was a pacifier. lost in thought for a moment, you decided to set the entire pack of matches aflame, tossing the lit matches into a pile of yellow newspaper next to the stained mattress.

flames scaled the cheap plastered walls lined with rotting wood, you could feel the heat on your body and sweat on your brow. as the fire began to spread you could smell lisa's burning flesh. feeling no remorse as you dashed out of the door and down the five flights.

the next day, when you reported to the precient for your first tour working the four to midnight shift, you would hear the story of some crazy crack head who burned down a building doing stupid crack head shit. your fellow boys in blue would make crude crack jokes and you will laugh, showing them you are down with the program. fuck that serpico shit, you was down.

exiting the burning building, the sidewalk was alive with the jumping jive of spectators who now had something to do with their time instead of sitting on the stoop or shooting dice. cornerboys gathered screamed, "meda meda" as though the world was coming to an end. but for you, it had only just begun.

angrily you glanced up at the building. it reminded you of that flick the towering inferno. in your stoned mind, the fire looked like a crimson animal trying to escape from the confines of its bronx zoo cage.

watching that sizzling disaster of your own creation, exhilaration surged through your body like electricity. as the blaze grew even more intense, your little dickie finally got hard.

# SiTTiN ON A GOLD MiNE

### *Da'Neen Hale*
### Cleveland, OH

Yonni sat back on her burnt orange leather sofa in her luxurious apartment. She eyed her surroundings in disbelief. Her life had taken a drastic twist for the better in just the last two months. *Unbelievable what a change of man can do for a girl's quality of life*, she thought as she reached for her White Russian sitting on the end table beside her. She leaned back on the sofa and took a sip from her glass while soaking in the scenery before her.

Her apartment was gorgeous, located in Willoughby Hills, one of the many suburbs in Cleveland. The sunken living room was the selling point as far as she was concerned. When she entered the apartment to take a look before deciding to fill out the application it was the first thing that caught her eye. She also loved about the walk-in closets, the two bathrooms, and the Central Air. The walls were your standard apartment white and the carpet was the standard beige, but there was nothing *standard* about the huge chandelier that hung from the dining room ceiling. The dining room then gave way to four steps that descended into the living room. There was a huge bay window overlooking the pool and Jacuzzi on the apartment complex grounds. The two bedrooms located back up the stairs and to the left, both had walk-in closets and with all the clothes Yonni had, she would probably need both. On the left of the apartment was the kitchen. The island was beautiful with a marble-top finish that was the same on the counters. The microwave hung over the stove which was provided by the apartment complex along with the refrigerator. The kitchen was gorgeous, but Yonni knew she would hardly ever use it. She wasn't the greatest cook and had no aspiration to be one either. Hard to believe this apartment was now fully furnished with Italian leather furniture, a 32 gallon aquarium filled with exotic fish, and a 62' television.

She giggled to herself as she thought about all the people who told her, "Yonni, you know you wrong for what you doin'. Karma is a bitch!"

Yonni placed her drink back on the end table then stood up and stretched her 5'6 frame and smiled. *Haters! That's why they still stuck down in East Cleveland cashing them welfare checks.*

Yonni headed to her bedroom. When she opened the door the July sun kissed her caramel face. She squinted as the sun shined brightly in her eyes. It was high noon and if she didn't close the drapes soon, her room would feel like a sauna. She made her way over to the window and did just that. As she proceeded back to the door she caught her reflection in the mirror on her Victorian-style dresser. She stood there for a moment and studied the reflection staring back at her. She stepped in closer to the mirror to get a better look. She shook her head wildly and watched her sandy brown tresses cascade around her caramel colored heart shaped face and down her back. Her gray eyes pierced her own soul giving way to a sexy sultry look she seemed to have all the time. She stepped away from the mirror this time to get a better look at her small waist and flat stomach that she loved to show off by wearing baby t's. She turned her back to the mirror to get a glimpse of her behind that was labeled a money maker by the likes of Ludacris and Pharell. She shook it from side to side then smacked herself on the ass. *Let me find out Nelly lookin' for a real Apple Bottom model.* Yonni turned back around to face the woman staring at her in the mirror. Her face turned solemn as her eyes danced over her body, then suddenly a smile appeared again. At age 25 her C cup breasts still sat at attention and she could still give any 18-year-old Vixen a run for her money.

Shit, Legend liked it and that was all that mattered. Goose bumps began to form on the back of her arm as she thought about Legend and his magic touch. It was his touch that had started their whole rendezvous. It was the night the Cleveland Cavaliers spanked on the Detroit Pistons and became the Eastern Conference champs. Jaron and Legend had been watching the game in the living room gettin' twisted. By the time the game was over Jaron had passed out in his recliner and Legend was asleep on the sofa and that is where Yonni left them. She turned off the TV and picked up their empty beer bottles and tossed them in the trash. She jumped in the shower then headed down the hall to her bedroom. She turned the light off and slid under the cool covers with her black King James T-shirt on.

Just as she began to drift off to sleep she felt a hand gently stroke her cheek. Without opening her eyes she said, "Stop Jaron, I'm trying to get some sleep." She felt the presence lean closer to her body and she heard him whisper in her ear, "This ain't Jaron Yonni." Yonni's eyes flew open in shock as she turned over on her back and held the covers tightly to her chest. It was Legend standing in her bedroom with Jaron obviously still asleep in the living room.

"What are you doing Legend? Are you crazy?" She whispered, to keep from waking Jaron.

Calmly, Legend bent down on the side of the bed nearest Yonni and explained, "Look Yonni, I'm tired of playing these games. I'm feelin' you and I know you feelin' me. The heat between us in undeniable. All this eye fuckin' we doin' to each other is crazy ma. I wanna get witchu'. Feel me?"

Yonni knew Legend was telling the truth. She wanted to fuck him the first time Jaron introduced them. Their eyes lingered on each other's bodies and the hand shake lasted a little longer than it should have. Up until this point, all it had been was a little innocent flirting here and there. She wanted him, no need to lie about that but the situation was all fucked up.

"Look, you drunk, Legend. Take your ass back out there on the couch and sleep that shit off and we'll act like this never happened," Yonni said trying to play coy as she turned her back on him, praying he wouldn't leave. Truthfully, Yonni wanted this nigga bad. He was papered up and then some. On the real, fuck Jaron! He lost all his juice when he went in the joint and the nigga wasn't even lookin' to get back on. But still if Jaron woke up and caught them it was gonna be a wrap for all parties involved.

Yonni took a moment to mull over the situation, or rather the opportunity and anybody that knew Yonni knew she was the ultimate opportunist. Shit, obviously Legend didn't care about Jaron so why should she? They were the ones who had been friends forever, let them niggas figure it out. Suddenly a wicked grin spread across Yonni's face. *Fuck it! If it's pussy Legend wants, then it's pussy Legend will get.*

"You and I both know you don't want me to go ma," he said seductively as he began to peel the covers away from her body. A shiver ran through Yonni's body as Legend began to stroke her bare legs with those soft sensual hands of his. The heat emanating from her skin told of her willingness to participate in this dance. With each touch she became more and more aroused, giving completely in to her desire for him.

He lifted her black King James T-shirt up just above her waist and found that she wore no panties underneath. His hands rubbed her voluptuous ass as he leaned over and began to plant gentle kisses all over it. Yonni moaned at the pleasure his lips gifted her with. Legend gently placed his hand over Yonni's mouth while sticking his finger inside to give her something to suck on in hopes this would keep her quiet. Legend wanted Yonni but he didn't want to be caught by his boy. He was well aware that this was total disrespect and if they were caught somebody was gonna die. Right now Legend wanted Yonni. He would figure the rest out later.

He began planting a trail of hot kisses down the back of her thighs until he reached the back of her knees. Legend gently turned Yonni over on her back and spread her legs with his head while planting more kisses on the insides of her thighs. Yonni's breathing became labored with excitement and anticipation. By now her clit was throbbing and begging for attention and her pussy was dripping like a faucet as Legend finally made his way to her prize.

He slowly slid his finger from her mouth then opened up her gold mine with his thumb and pointer finger, and blew on her Highness just to tease her a little bit more. Yonni grew impatient and grabbed the back of Legends head and invited him to feast. Each stroke of his tongue on her clit brought her closer and closer to paradise.

He ate her pussy and just when Yonni thought she could take no more she exploded on his tongue calling his name forgetting all about Jaron in the next room. Spent, Yonni lay in bed trying desperately to catch her breath. Meanwhile, Legend exited the bedroom as quietly as he'd entered. It would be the beginning of countless rendezvous they'd have right up under Jaron's nose.

Slowly coming back to reality, Yonni smiled at her reflection in the mirror while shaking her head. *That was fucked up, but that was the hardest a bitch ever came in her life. Oh well. Shit, it is what it is,* she thought as she shrugged her shoulders. And with that Yonni strutted out of her bedroom in her black Enyce short shorts and hot pink baby T-shirt.

As Yonni sat down on the couch and clicked on the TV, Judge Mathis popped on the screen. Yonni folded her legs Indian style as she watched him call somebody's Mamma a crack head. That was one of the things she loved about him. Judge Mathis called it like he saw it. Just as she began to get into the program her telephone rang. Yonni stretched over to the coffee table where the cordless telephone lie. She clicked her talk button.

"Hello."

"Hey Yonni, what's up girl?"

It was her once, good friend Kyra on the other end of the phone. The girls had been friends since junior high but once Yonni decided she wanted something more for her life than just a bunch of kids and welfare checks, it seemed she and Kyra grew more and more apart. Yonni would have thought that Kyra would have been happy for her when she moved out of East Cleveland. No more roaches scattering when she turned on the lights at night, and no more crack heads bangin' on her door looking for Tommy the neighborhood drug dealer, who actually lived across the hall from her. And what about the fact that she could hear Ms. Betty getting her ass kicked every day through the paper thin, paint chipped walls by her alcoholic husband. None of that mattered to Kyra though.

All she could say is "Yonni, that's fucked up what you doin'." Though Yonni was hurt that her girl couldn't be happy for her, she still had a soft spot for Kyra because of the things they'd been through since teenage girls.

"Nothing just sittin' hear watchin' Judge Mathis' crazy ass," Yonni said as she used the remote to turn the volume down.

"Well girl, I was callin' you to tell you I seen Jaron down on 1st off of Hayden last night hangin' out on the block with Boonchie and Richard."

Yonni sucked her teeth and rolled her eyes at Kyra's comment. *Here we go again.* She took a deep breath and slowly sighed and said, "So what Kyra. You know I don't fuck with Jaron no more so why you tellin' me?" Yonni asked as she traipsed across the living room floor to adjust the AC.

"Well girl, I thought you should know that while me and Tammy was standin' around shootin' the shit I could over hear him talkin' about how you fuckin' his boy Legend now and basically he treatin' you like a hoe because he got a baby mamma that he already takin' care of and shit." Yonni made her way back over to the couch and plopped down grabbing her drink with her free hand and taking a sip.

"Did you hear what I just said Yonni? That nigga puttin' bad papers out on you all in the street and shit. But I told you this shit would happen," Kyra sighed.

Yonni turned her drink up and placed the empty glass back down on the table and responded, "Let me tell you something Kyra. First of all there ain't a woman walkin' this earth that ain't at one time been a hoe."

"Uh, bitch, I don't know what you been smokin' on, but I ain't never been a hoe," Kyra said while laughing on the phone.

"You don't think so Kyra?" Yonni asked seriously to her delusional friend.

"I know so," Kyra replied challenging whatever it was Yonni was getting ready to say.

"Okay, try this on for size. When you and Raymond was kickin' it, did you fuck him?"

"Yeah, cause that was my man," Kyra said defensively preparing herself for the verbal battle that was sure to ensue.

"Then you was hoin' for Raymond," she said.

"I think not," Kyra said getting offended.

Yonni rolled her eyes and shook her head as she looked up at the ceiling like she was pleading for God to strike some common sense into her girl. She mimicked her girl's voice and said, "Remember this Kyra, Oooh Yonni, let me call you back Raymond just got paid girl, I'm bout to fuck his brains out. Oooh Yonni, Raymond just came off his grind and I want that new Prada bag I saw at Saks. Girl, I'm bout to suck the skin of his dick! Remember that shit Kyra? Huh? Because the last I heard, ass in exchange for cash makes you a hoe!" Yonni said as she raised her voice a little.

She could feel her temperature steadily rising like the heat in Arizona on a hot August day. Kyra's jaw dropped at the way Yonni had described some of the conversations she'd had with her about Raymond.

"Look Kyra, women been fuckin' men for money, houses, cars, furs, and stability since the beginning of time. Some spit out babies to get that child support check, some get married and lock in the fortune while others latch onto a man and fuck for a buck for as long as it lasts. No matter which way you look at it, we have all fucked our men for one thing or another. Most of they asses couldn't please a woman with their dicks if you sat down and read they asses an instruction manual on how to do it. But because that nigga bringin' in that cash, we fake orgasms, call them Daddy, and tell them how good they sorry ass dick game is because all we want is that cash to do something that really makes us hot and that's shop for expensive shit we otherwise could not afford."

Yonni sat back on the sofa and crossed her legs awaiting a response from Kyra. The phone line was deathly silent when all of a sudden Kyra busted out laughing like Kat Williams had just told the funniest joke she'd ever heard.

"Girl, I always knew yo ass was crazy. That's some off the hook shit you just said. True, but off the hook. Yonni don't go around repeatin' that shit because you could really fuck with a bitch's self esteem," Kyra joked.

Yonni laughed with Kyra for a moment. And for that moment it felt like old times, like they were still thick as thieves cutting classes at Shaw High. But time and different views on life had drifted them apart.

"Look girl, that's fucked up that Jaron is out there talkin' shit about me, but on the real, Jaron just fucked up cause I left his no money havin' ass alone. Is it bad that I'm fuckin' his friend? Well that depends on who you ask. He knew he shouldn't have been bringing Legend over to the house with him and inviting him to spend the night when they had been out drinking. Furthermore, what person on this earth doesn't know you never tell anybody about what your girl or your man does in the bedroom? I don't care if it's your Momma; there are just some things that are not up for discussion. Those are things that Jaron did. Now I'm not saying that I couldn't have chosen to do something different but come on, Legend is fine and a get money nigga. Every bitch in Cleveland is tryin' to fuck this nigga. I got bills and expensive taste just like the next hoe. So when Legend came knockin' I opened up the candy shop. It just so happened that he was my man's best friend. As far as his baby mamma, that ain't got shit to do with me. As long as she stays on her side of Cleveland, I will stay on mine."

Kyra thought about what Yonni said and she couldn't deny that Jaron had done some stupid shit. But that still didn't make it right that her girl was screwin' his best friend. Yonni had driven a wedge between Jaron and Legend who had once been inseparable. They had slung them thangs together for years and when Jaron got knocked a couple years back, he refused to snitch on Legend and did his time like a stand up nigga. They'd been best friends twenty of their twenty-nine years and after all of what they had done and been through together, it turned out a bitch had come between them. It was just a matter of time before some shit was gonna go down between them and everybody on the East side of Cleveland knew it except for Yonni. The beef had been brewin' for the past couple of months. As a matter of fact, ever since Legend had moved Yonni out of EC. When Jaron found that out, everybody just knew he was gonna go ballistic. But he didn't and anyone who knew Jaron, knew he was just a ticking time bomb waiting to explode.

"Hey Yonni, but for real, just watch your back. That's all I'm saying. Niggas is out here crazy these days. I know we are not as tight as we used to be, but I still love you and I don't want to see anything happen to you," Kyra said sincerely.

"Thanks Kyra, but I will be okay. Trust. But look how is that rent thing going? Did you get the money to pay it?"

"Yeah, I got it. Big Mamma gave it to me," Kyra said somewhat embarrassed by the question. Yonni laid down on the couch still holding the phone to her ear.

"Look Kyra, you are a beautiful girl. All that long jet black wavy hair and pretty yellow skin could land you a big time baller. Shit your body is just as tight as mine. You need to find you a sponsor and then you won't have to worry about shit like the rent. Shoot, Legend got a friend that I know would be all over you."

Kyra's interest was peeked. Shit Raymond had been lost his good job he had at Lincoln Electric and the "twos" and "fews" he was bringing in wasn't enough to buy toilet paper with. Yeah the dick was good but who wanted to fuck when the bills weren't getting paid?

"You serious?" Kyra asked like a bashful school girl.

"Hell yeah I'm serious! And the nigga spend money like it's water. You may as well be gettin' that. I ain't never seen him locked up with just one bitch so I know you can scoop him up."

Kyra's brow began to furrow as she thought about who Yonni could be alluding to. Shit, Legend had many niggas that hung around him all the time, but it was one in particular that popped into her mind. Sells. Now Sells was fine and all, standing 6'2 he had the build of a basketball player. He wore his hair in a Caesar and had absolutely no facial hair. People often thought he was about 20-years-old, when in fact he was thirty-one. When he looked at you through those hazel eyes you felt like he could read your every thought. He stayed geared up in Prada, Rocawear, and Sean John. The only thing unattractive about Sells was that word on the street was he had at least six bodies under his belt.

Against Kyra's better judgment she asked Yonni who she had in mind and sure enough Yonni said Sells.

"Get the fuck outta here Yonni! Sells is way out of my league," Kyra said trying to mask the fact that she was scared shitless to fuck with him.

Yonni raised up on the sofa not believing what her best friend had just let slide out of her mouth.

"Are you serious with that shit you just said Kyra? Girl, you are beautiful. Niggas always tryin' to get at you. Look, you only young once. You better use it before you loose it," Yonni said. She got quiet on the phone as she thought back on something her mother used to say to her whenever she messed up. "Kyra, my mother used to go off on me whenever I fucked up in school and brought home bad grades. She used to say, 'Yonni, pretty don't pay the rent. As cute as you may be, folks ain't gonna hire you just because you cute. You are going to need more than just good looks in this life young lady.' Well, I am here to tell you that is a straight lie because I am cute and it is payin' my rent, therefore, I don't need a job. You feel me? Besides you better wake up Kyra and realize that you are sitting on a Gold Mine."

Kyra thought for a moment and almost decided that she would pass until her door bell rang. The door was open and she could see the man from the Electric Company standing on her front porch. *Raymond must not have paid the fuckin' bill.*

"Okay, Yonni set it up and call me back," Kyra said as she scrambled to end the conversation. She needed to get to the door before they shut her shit off.

"I'll do that," Yonni promised then pressed the end button on the phone.

Yonni lay back on the couch with a huge grin covering her face. It was about time Kyra woke up and smelled the coffee. *Shit, she better take a hint from Trina, The Baddest Bitch and try and live the Glamourest Life and act like she know. Maybe I'll buy her ass the cd's so she can take some notes and learn how to come up in this bitch,* Yonni thought as she giggled to herself and prepared to call Legend to make the love connection.

# CARE-LESS

## Dwayne Byfield
Queens/Long Island, NY

I step out my doorway and stretch my arms, all the while sporting a Kool-Aid smile shining bright across my face. It was a beautiful day, but the sun is long gone by now. It's a quarter past nine and time for work. The car of the month pulls up directly in front of my mom's crib and parks. My house may seem like a one family place, but three live here. Moms and I stay on the main floor while the top has a Mexican couple, and the bottom huddles a Puerto Rican family. We never have arguments or shit like that, but every now and again they tend to get a little loud with that salsa, and merengue shit.

The car is an all black Honda Accord with stock tints and wheels. A respectable business car is what we call it. No flash, no gaudiness, no rims; no attention.

This was my last week of work before heading off to school and the very thought of it sent a chill prickling down my spine. By this time next week I'll be setting up my dorm room in South Florida State University. New York was great to me but South Florida, that's paradise. Sun, girls, and oh yeah did I mention the warm sun.

I hop down my porch and step over the large piece of concrete that has protruded about five inches into the air over the past five years. With me saving for school and moms breaking her ass to skate us by, we just never found the time to fix it. You would think that the landlord would take care of it, but I guess things like that don't matter when your big toe doesn't even inch over the poverty line. There were a few things that needed fixing since my pops left, but fuck him, I'll soon take care of everything. I approach the driver's side, and can hear Beanie Sigel's "Dear Self" barely bumping through the rolled up windows. Trev always lowered the volume when he came by the house. He made certain not to annoy my mom with what she called "our poor choice in music." Trev and I have been friends for, well shit we been friends since we could fight. Seeing that's how we met in the second grade and on the account that our mothers have been friends for just as long, respect was always paid to each other's home.

I open the door and slide into the driver's seat as comfortably as if it were my own car. We were both the same height and both drove with the seat all the way back. I like to think our driving this way is to optimize leg room, but we aren't that fucking tall to begin with.

"What's good daddy?"

"What's good?" I reply while giving him a pound. He'd just finished rolling a Dutch as he scraped the leftover guts and scraps of weed off his magazine and out the window. We've both been driving since we were sixteen, but Trev lost his license the same year he got it. We had just turned eighteen and passed our road test together. Unfortunately Trev decided he wanted to go drink and drive. One day he got caught and was charged with a DUI. The judge knew us well and had a thing out for T so he came down hard. He saw Trev's black ass jumping out of his daughter's window in the beginning of freshman year. I would chalk it up to Trev being black and his daughter being as white as the driven snow, but we used to play in his backyard as kids before he became an actual judge and we also went to school with her till freshman year. I could wager any amount of paper on the fact that Trev was fucking the shit out the Judge's daughter, and he could hear her moans and screams as he made his way up the long spiral staircase in his shiny white home. No one knew why the hell he came home early that day, but he did and that was the last we saw of Tiffany Hancock and the first time we met Judge Hancock. Judge Hancock was completely different from Mr. Hancock. Mr. Hancock was a benevolent man but Judge Hancock was a mothafucka. He snatched Trev's license for two years and warned him that if he was caught driving he'd be taking the bus and calling cabs forever. And everyone knows the bus ain't no way to travel on Long Island. Thank God Hancock lived on the other side of town or else Trev would have been Elvis for sure. Dead weight with no way to move or shake, and if you ain't movin' and shakin', you ain't makin no money. This wasn't an option for either of us, so we did our best to play it smart.

I pull off and turn down Palm Avenue headed towards the highway. For the past two years, this has been my job. I know back streets, front streets, main roads, and highways in almost every damn neighborhood from Route 110 to Guy R. Brewer Blvd. Trev butters his bread with what he makes on the streets, and we don't have to be from your hood to sell there. We just simply do it on the low. You never know we're even there. Our clients are usually recommended through a friend, cousin, or just some random pick-up at a club. This has been my nine-to-five in order to pay my way through community college while saving for a University. It isn't the only way, but it is definitely my best. There is no fucking way I'ma wash fucking floors or dishes, and I damn sure ain't gonna fit you for some damn sneakers dressed like a zebra. Nah, that's not gonna happen. I've made far too much money doin' this shit every night. I already made enough money to pay for community college and banked thirty G's to get me down to Florida. Yeah, business has been good and with Trev about to get his license back, an easy exit is right in place for me.

My plans to get money on campus are similar, except no drugs. My uncle owns a few liquor stores so whole sale is in the bag. Only thing left is the clientele, and I doubt I'll have any trouble finding students who want a liter of liquor at ten to fifteen dollars a bottle. I can be very personable when it comes to money, shit why not, that's what a business man does. He may not like you, but any good business man can and will make a deal go through. I turn to take the L as Trev passes while still inhaling a thick grey cloud threw his nostrils.

"So what you selling tonight?" I ask.

He reaches under the dashboard and snaps it off while staring into my face saying "Dreams Jerry, sweet dreams." He fully exposes the bottom lid of the passenger side dashboard, and adds, "Beautiful, white clouded dreams."

Two sandwich Ziploc bags are laying flat in its crevice, one filled with individual packets of powdered white and the other with off-white caps of different sizes. I'm terrible at even knowing which size to give according to price, but Trev can feel a rock and tell the price in a heartbeat. He's been cutting and weighing for quite some time now, and with me going to college and all the people we know from high school both black and white, there's plenty of places to get rid of it all. I see it as a snowball affect, our friends have friends, who in turn have more friends. A vicious cycle, but a cycle nonetheless and cycles can generate some serious paper flow. When the rocks get rolling, it's pretty hard to stop the forward process and 2007 has had plenty of people rollin' and even more blowin'. The 80's started something that will take far more than thirty measly years to go away. Growing up on the Island doesn't mean growing up privileged in some cases. Such was the case for Trev and me. If you don't hustle for it, you don't get it. Whether it's blow pops in sixth grade, cds in middle school, or weed in high school. Something has to be sold, because we got Champagne wishes with our mom's beer money.

I hit the Southern State parkway going west, the direction of the money. "Where we headed anyways?" I barely get the words out before choking on the smoke I inhaled.

Trev begins to rub his stomach. "We gotta go a couple places, but I gotta eat first. You hungry?"

"I can definitely eat," I said. "I only had a sandwich before I left."

"Aiight, lets go to the seafood spot in Freeport. Yeah, I want some crab cakes and lobster...oooohh hell yeah lobsta," he said, smiling while continuing to rub away.

"Lobster, ain't in season fool," I said while taking another hit.

"Shit, it is when you got money. At fifty bucks a plate, you best believe they got lobster."

"Aiight, I guess you'll be having the steak tonight," I said while turning the radio up just as Jay-Z says, "Speech!" The trumpets echo out and into my ears. We ain't movin' shit from Columbia but we sure feel like dope boys of the year. I mean we've been eating at restaurants packed with upper middle class people for the past year and a half, all because that's what we saw outside of our beautiful, shitty neighborhood. It was just last year that we bumped into good old Judge Hancock at Frankie and Johnnie's on the Upper West side. We were reassured then, that we had good taste 'cause his ass is getting fat and it ain't from quarter waters and twenty-five cent bags of chips. While other mothafuckas our age are still sucking down McDonalds French fries, we're ordering our appetizers and sipping on French wine after slipping the waiter $200 cash to over look our age.

We've earned big, we've spent big, and soon we'll live big.

Not from this drug shit neither, nah this is play money. Trev does most of the spending because he knows the situation and the goal. Drug money is like monopoly money, it's not really yours and it ain't real. Real is corporate America. That's real, a seat on the Board of Directors. That's real. And I'm our meal ticket there.

This little drug hustle is our bread and butter for the time being. See the misconception is that we're all dumb drug dealers; wrong again America. Yes, there are plenty of dumb ones running around, but I'm not in the same category. I happen to have two pieces of paper. My high school diploma and my Associate's degree in business marketing, the Bachelor's degree is next. Shit, I might get my master's after that. It's about the long hall. That's what runners my age don't get, but evolution is on its way and I'm gonna lead the pack. A small few have done it, but they're like Jordan, before their time. I'm next and Trev's gonna be right there when it happens.

Trev grabs three rocks from his plate and reaches under re-snapping the lid. He turns to his side view mirror and then to me.

"We gotta make a quick stop first, and then we eat."

"Where?" I ask.

"Roosevelt, you already know what block," Trev said.

The good old Velt, slums and suburbs mixed together the old fashion Long Island way. They have a shitty public school district, similar to ours. A friend of ours moved there about two years ago and hit us with a few fiends shortly after. The blunt finishes and the clip gets tossed right around the time we hit the exit. There was no traffic, which is a blessing considering that a twenty-minute ride could turn into an hour, if there was any. I pull into the Mobile gas station and into our usual dark spot by the vacuum cleaner and air machine. The music gets turned down and the lights go off. Trev looks out his window, then back to me. "Dollar twenty five, damn. Remember when those air machines cost fifty cents to use?"

I lean forward to look at the rusty edged machine and its hefty price tag for usage. "Yeah, I remember we used to fill our bike tires up after we patched them."

"Shit Jerry, things are changing my dude. We gotta hurry up and do something. I swear sometimes I feel like a motherless child just blowin' in the wind out here."

"I feel you. At least you know I'm drifting with you fam," I said.

He turned and looked me square in the eyes and said, "Yeah, but not for long. You got bigger fish to fry and don't forget where you came from. Or else I'ma have to make a random trip to whip the sense back into you the way I did back in second grade."

"T, you know damn well you ain't whip my ass! I had you until I tripped over my cheap ass Batman sneaker laces."

"Hey, a win is a win," he said. "Next time, lace up before you go to war."

We share a well needed laugh before noticing the all white Lexus SUV pull up and flash its lights. I then pull out and take the back streets making as many turns as possible before stopping on a dark corner of Maryland Ave. We are actually in Freeport now. You can tell by the size of the yards. Houses are a lot further away from each other in Freeport. Trev reaches for his black Glock 9mm under his seat and slides it beneath his right knee. It's not for our blond-mopped hair customer who just hopped out heading towards our car. No, it's a precaution for some brave hearted stick up kid looking for a quick come up and more so for when we're in certain parts of Queens. Young souls are a lot braver the further west you go from Long Island. It doesn't happen much, and never to us thus far, but nonetheless it happens, and you never see it coming. So the best you can do is to follow the rules and there are no rules.

The back seat door opens and in jumps our favorite customer Nancy. Nancy is a nurse with two kids, a dog and a dentist for a husband. She lives in an upper middle class section close by in Freeport and sends her kids forty minutes away to private school on the North Shore. Nancy is cool and always down for a good time, and oh yeah she loves her white, probably just as much as she does her kids. Hard or soft doesn't matter to her, it all comes down to how she's feeling and what she has going on for the night. She hates her husband more than anything in the world, but stays with him for the sake of the children. We found this out after she sucked us both off for two grams of white once. She needed to stay awake during the night shift but forgot to stop and get cash, so instead of running to find an ATM she just swallowed us both and kept it movin'.

"Hey boys, how are ya!" Nancy called out.

Trev turns around and answers with a smile. "Good baby, busy as usual you know. I see you're extra bubbly tonight."

"Yeah Peanut, I feel great. My husband went away for the week to visit his mother and the kids are sleeping over a friend's house."

I smirk while checking my mirrors for anything moving.

"So I guess its party time for Nancy?" I replied.

"You know it Jelly, I got my boyfriend coming over and we're gonna fuck all night long" she said laughing that wheezy Marlboro-pack-a-day laugh, and clapping her hands at the same time as if someone just told a seriously funny ass joke. The shit really tickled her to be free of her responsibilities. Why get married I say, if you're not happy? Why waste your time and someone else's? Trev smiles and reaches back clearing her face of her straggly blond hair.

"Why don't we have our own party tonight?" he said, she glanced at me, then into Trev's eyes. "You bring the stuff and I'll supply the rest."

Trev's mood quickly changes as he turns back around, "Hell nah, this shit cost money, baby!"

"Well so do I Peanut. Coke, crack, or money that is," she continued her very unattractive laugh. She's a cute white lady, but somewhere something went wrong in her life and she wasn't gonna bother to fix it. I ain't no Dr. Phil, but even I can see that she's fucked and heading for disaster, but who am I to stop good money from flowin' in? If she ain't buying from us, then she buying from someone else, and that's not good for business.

She leaned forward close enough that I can taste the nicotine on her breath as she speaks. "Hey, when you guys gonna tell me your real names anyways? I mean you know mine and you know I ain't no cop soooo…"

"So what?" I ask.

"I don't wanna keep calling you guys Peanut Butter and Jelly. That's just rude. Your mothers gave you real names right?"

"Sit back Nancy!" I quickly exclaim while scoping my rearview mirror as a patrol car cruises by on the main road behind us. I tap Trev twice, the sign to keep it movin' while answering her nosy ass.

"Yeah we got names, but that'll be breaking the rules and we don't break the rules around here baby. So from now and forever more, we're known as Peanut Butter and Jelly."

"Ok, ok I got it," she said while pulling out her money. She hands it forward and quickly leans back while biting her nails.

"I'm a little short, I only got one forty."

Trev turns and gives her a look as if he wants to slap her silly ass. "One forty, I should cut off ten dollars worth off one of these rocks then, huh?"

"I'm sorry Peanut, I mean you know how it is…the family, bills, the kids and…" Nancy said.

"No bitch I don't know what it is. I ain't got no damn kids, no wife, and no mothafucking house. But I do have this dope and you gonna owe me ten fucking dollars!"

"Here." He tossed the rocks in her lap.

"Thanks boys, you know I love you guys. I'll make it up to you next time, I promise."

"Promise my ass. Take yo ass on before I change my mind. A hundred and forty fucking dollars."

Trev is always cool until you fuck with his money, then all hell breaks loose. With him, it's money, his mom and me, and all three are of equal importance to him. You fuck with any of the three and the reaction is the same. Nancy hops out the car and quickly gets in hers. She pulls off and we make a U-turn and head to the restaurant.

I turn the music up and skip the tracks to Styles and Swizz Beats in preparation to "blow my mind." I pull up to a stop light and turn to him "Yo, roll up and relax man. You gettin' hot over a couple dollars, ain't worth it."

"Fuck that, she knew what she was doing. Don't try to get over on *us*, we get over on *you* bitch."

"Roll up please" I repeat.

"Yeah, yeah," Trev said while exhaling and reaching into the glove compartment.

I pull into the restaurant parking lot and we continue to finish smoking before heading inside. Upon entering, our usual waiter Matt takes notice and rushes over. The place is packed as usual, but Matt sensing an extra $200 dollars gets us seated right away. We're always gracious tippers even if we don't drink, and Matt is the head waiter if there is such a term. Basically, he has juice in the place and we never wait. All eyes are on us and as we take our seats, an elderly couple smile and continue with their meal. We aren't dapper, but we were still fresh to death. Prada sneakers, Seven jeans, and Sean John dress shirts. Not your typical hustler gear, but then again we have never viewed ourselves as typical in any facet of the word.

"Something to drink gentlemen?" Matt asks and smiles while hovering over us like a mosquito ready to suck the money from our pockets.

"Anything French and red is straight," I said.

"Will do sir."

Trev stops him as he begins to leave, "Ya'll got lobster on the menu tonight?"

"Yes, always sir. New England's finest"

"Thank you Matt," Trev said with a polite demeanor as if it's his natural nature. He looks down at his menu with a grin slit across his face.

"What? Say it. I know you wanna say something so go ahead."

"Nah, nah I'm good. I...AM...GOOD brotha."

"Yeah, what the fuck ever Negro. You was right and I was wrong. There. You happy?" I said laughing while he pretended to search the menu.

"You said it not me," he said.

Dinner was good and so was the night. We made runs from Uniondale to Hempstead and down through Huntington. Queens was hot, way too hot. We didn't get a call from that area all night. So we did some reconnaissance. Upon scouting the area we usually roam, we found night crawlers scattered about. Our area was an untouched market, but it seemed as if that has come to an end. Three square blocks had a dude working the corner with back up not far behind in the shadows. Our customers now had a local supplier, but it was only a matter of time before they came crawling back. Night crawlers were usually scraped up by cops after a month or so, or they were slaves to the supply and often ran out. We're different, we are friends with our supplier and we never run out plus we are forgiving to our strayed customers, only an extra ten percent is added the first month a fiend comes back. Springfield no longer has wins for us, but we can still snake in and out of Guy Brew. This isn't our hood any damn way, so actin' up is out of the question. Two against ten never made much sense before, so it ain't making dollars now.

After our last drop in Wyandanch, we head home. It's now almost six in the morning and sleep is calling my name. Trev could go another day and will probably do so once I'm gone and he gets his license back. I step out of the car and give my body a well needed stretch. Trev slides into the driver's seat and slips me my cut of the profit. It's a very good night and we did well over four G's. My cut is about thirty percent. I can feel the size of my knot while placing it in my pocket. The window rolls down and he looks up.

"One more week J, one more and we take the next step boy. You got the biggest responsibility of all. You gotta make it through school."

"I know. I'm ready. It ain't nothing."

"I hope so 'cause I need you. Shit, we need you. You ain't gotta worry about moms when you gone I'll look out for her. She stuck just like mine. We all we got and I'm tired of this drug shit. You gotta hold it down and show me the way once you get there."

"I got you T, you already know."

We exchange pounds.

"I'll see you later tonight," Trev said while turning up the music a little.

"Yessirr," I said before making my way to my porch.

I was stopped in my tracks as I lifted my right foot to climb the four steps to my doorway. My heart paused for a split second and adrenaline starts to pump through my veins as the loud aggressive sounds of sirens filled the early morning air. I run back to my rusty old fence and peer down the block in the direction Trev just headed. Three cars surrounded his, one blue and white and two unmarked DT's. I quickly dash to my backyard and stash the money in a coffee can in my dog's makeshift house. I run back to the front, this time busting through my fence and speed walking toward the scene. I'm not sure what made me think I could do anything, but it was Trev and he was basically my brother so rational thought had no place for debate. I get about thirty yards away when an all black Crown Victoria pulls up next to me. It crept up so slowly that I was startled before stopping. The dark tinted passenger window rolls down. Judge Hancock sticks his head out the window with a conniving grin on his face. His white floppy hair was frizzed and his eyes were gleaming.

"Turn around son, this has nothing to do with you, but it could. So do yourself a favor and turn around," he said.

I stood there for what seemed like an eternity staring into his dark vengeful eyes. I then turned back to see Trev being handcuffed on the hood of his car. He looks up and shakes his head "no" once, before placing his head face down on the hood.

"Turn around son. This is your last chance Jerry. You're a smart boy, so do the smart thing," Judge Hancock's voice echoed through my head as my heart raced like a Derby.

I wanted to spit in his shriveled, pale, disgusting face. But I knew what that would lead to. I somehow gathered myself and turned without saying a word. The race in my chest was over and I lost, all that was left was hurting. Trev would be going away for awhile and I knew it, but I also knew Judge could have taken me with him.

"Hey Jerry," Judge Hancock called.

I turned to see his smirk sharply turn into a smile.

"Good luck at South Florida next week, and tell your mother I said hello. She should be proud. Oh, and by the way, you should go have another bite to eat at Frankie and Johnnie's before you leave, they don't have that kind of steak house in Florida."

His laughter echoed louder than his voice did as the window rolled back up and the car pulled off. The sun slowly came up and I realize that it's a new day, and time for a new plan.

# FRIENDS WITH BENEFITS

## *Nicole Bradley*
Gary, IN

Three months is a long time to be putting up with somebody's bullshit. I can't take this shit anymore," Aris Smith said to no one in particular.

"I know. Who you telling, Bitch?" she answered herself. "This nigger going to make me do something to him. Watch."

Aris Smith was at her wits' end. Her man's cheating was driving her crazy. Well she already was that, mental illness ran in her family on her father's side. It had been a hot minute since she saw the man she called Daddy. Last she had heard, he had been institutionalized somewhere in Chicago where he was trying to climb the walls.

But when she was happy, Aris did a great job of controlling it—like taking her medication. Having a good for nothing man was nothing new to Aris. She had dozens upon dozens of them before. A steady stream of men had entered her life and promptly marched out. She couldn't remember a time since she was twelve-years-old that she didn't have a man. Not a boyfriend, a man. The first time she had sex, it was with her Uncle Ray, who exposed her to a lifetime of misery.

Still Sean was different. Aris was in love with him. He was the first guy to show Aris he cared about her. With him, it wasn't just about sex. He actually took the time to ask her what she felt and what she thought. Most guys she encountered just wanted to get that nut off and then they were gone. Sean was the only guy stupid enough to make a hooker a housewife. He was a sucker for love and he never had it this good.

Aris was a hoe in every sense of the word, but she was a fine one. She was the type of woman who you would have to look at twice. Many a guy had been smacked by his woman for turning their heads to get a second look at her. She was five foot four inches, with a fully endowed chest, thin in the waist, baby making hips, and creamy thighs. Her eyes were the color of coffee with a hint of cream, and her smile was picture perfect. Aris's sandy brown shoulder length hair was the perfect match next to her almond skin.

Sexually, Aris did anything imaginable. Everything a man wanted a woman to do from oral to anal, at the drop of a dime, she assumed the position. To say that Aris liked sex was an understatement. She loved it. Aris had a white liver, an insatiable yearning for sex. She fucked her man Sean, any and everywhere. Aris rocked his world each and every time. She was a young porn star in the making, the type of freak that would put 'Super head' to shame.

"Where is this nigger at?" She cursed. She had it good now.

Probably the best she ever had it and still she didn't know how long she was going to be able to do this. As Aris lay in the bed looking at the ceiling, her mind recalled the many lonely nights she had spent in that same bed looking at the very spot she was now looking at on the ceiling. How many nights had she clutched the pillow to her chest wondering about Sean's where-abouts? Wondering if he was coming home at all? Or had someone left him stankin' in Delaney or Dorie Miller Projects? Just last week somebody had shot up his 300 as he drove down 5th Block.

It ain't no joke in the streets of Gary, Indiana. Back during the times of slavery, the abolitionist, David Walker had once told slaves, "Kill or be killed." And that was the same motto

Sean and the people he rolled with believed in. Living the gang lifestyle, anything was liable to happen at anytime in G.I. which is why Aris kept herself strapped at all times.

Aris knew one thing, if Sean was with another chick, then she wished he were dead. She had a jealous streak inside her that was downright evil. *You would think Sean would get enough of trying to be sneaky. Just last Friday when he came in late from the club, and after he got in the bed and started snoring, I went through his pockets and found a condom. I went into the kitchen and grabbed a butcher knife. And then I came back in the room, sat on his chest, held the blade of the knife to his Adam's apple. When he woke up, I asked him what he was doing with the condom.*

"Uh, Baby. What are you talking about? That ain't mine. I…I don't know how it got there," he had barely whispered.

All Aris could do was laugh. She had that brother shook. He was so scared he couldn't even swallow. He tried to talk but a mouth full of saliva made it difficult. Aris had cackled like a witch and removed the blade from his throat before placing it at the corner of his right eye. "If I so much as think you're looking at another woman, I'll poke your eyeballs out. Understand?" Aris threatened.

Choking on his own saliva, he nodded yes and was glad when she got up and walked out of the room with the knife.

Aris grew tired of lying in the bed, so she got up and paced the floor. Finding herself in front of the bar in the family room, she poured herself an eight ounce glass of Hennessy and swallowed down two of her pills. She needed something to take the edge off. Back and forth she walked, until she got tired of that. Somehow she ended up in the living room, which was closer to the front door and exactly where she wanted to be anyway. Aris didn't want to accidentally fall asleep and allow Sean the opportunity to creep into the house undetected. She wasn't about to let him off that easy, not tonight. Not the way she was feeling.

At this very moment, Aris regretted moving in with this motherfucker. She should have stayed right where she was, at her Aunt Trina's house. Her life would have been a whole lot simpler. But then again, this was all her fault. She couldn't even blame Sean. *'A man gonna be a man,'* her Aunt Trina once told her.

Aunt Trina was Aris' favorite aunt. She was Aris' deceased mother's youngest sister. Aris and Trina were so close in age, only five years separated them. They grew up like sisters raised in her grandma's house. They slept and peed in the same bed, and even shared the same clothes.

*'Girl, you so stupid.' Aunt Trina said. 'You making it too easy on that fool. Don't move in with Sean. Make him earn that coochie and he'll respect you more.'*

*'What?'* Aris said dumbfounded. *'What you talking about?'*

*Aunt Trina replied, 'Sean won't buy the milk, if he already got the cow. Why should he?'*

*'Trina, I wish you stop wit all these old woman sayings. Dang, you sound like Grandma. If I knew you was going to hate on me, like this I never would have told you. I thought we was better than that?'*

*Shaking her head, Trina sighed and said 'You ain't right. Ain't nobody hatin' on you. I'm tryin' to look out for you. But you all in love and got your head up yo' ass, you can't see nor hear shit. We family I only want what's best for you. You trippin' if you can't see that.'*

Her Aunt's words echoed in her head like demons. Aris heard every *'I told you so,'* that her Aunt used to say. Those imaginary words began to eat at her spirit to the point of it further depressing her. *Damn, when is the Hennessy and those pills going to kick in? I can't deal with reality right now.*

Aris continued to pace the living room floor like a mad dog chasing its tail. She glanced down at a photo of her and Sean during happier times. In her mind, they were the picturesque couple. They belonged together. She couldn't see herself with anyone else. There was only one problem, Sean couldn't keep his dick in his pants.

Anxious to relive these happier times, Aris picked up the picture and pressed it to her chest. Sean was a *'Boo'* when he was good. When he was bad, she hated his guts. Aris closed her eyes and reminisced on the good times. It was funny how they met. Aris used to actually fuck with Sean's best friend and fellow Gangsta Disciple, B-Luv. They were first introduced to each before she performed a threesome with him and Sean.

*"Come on Aris. You got to do this,"* B-Luv had coaxed her. *He wanted Aris to let Sean and him run a train on her.*

*"I ain't got to do nothing,"* Aris reminded him.

*"I know. I mean. I'm just saying, the pay-off in the end is gonna be real good."*

*"Byron, I don't know. I don't feel good about this. What if he don't even go for it? I mean what if the plan falls apart and then what?" Aris whined.*

*"It ain't going to fall apart. This dude wants to be me. Everything I got, he wants and look at you, who could deny you? It's gonna work. You'll see and in the end, we'll be sitting pretty. He's been around checking you out. Don't worry," he said kissing her deeply before they set their plan in motion.*

After B-Luv dumped her, Sean decided to put Aris on his team. Even though she was a bust-down, the sex was too good to just let her go like that. Before he knew it, one thing led to another, then they moved in together. Early in the game, Sean made a rule, which was to never mix business with pleasure and to definitely not bring business to his house. That was one of the 10 Crack Commandments he didn't deviate from, until now.

"You did what?" B-Luv asked in his best Lil Jon voice. "Dude, are you crazy? You gave her a key to your place and told her she could move in? Man, you got to be crazy. That chick is crazy, dude. 'Member when I told you I had to pay all that money to the Radisson when we had that party out there after that concert. It was because of her crazy ass. She got up there and went off man. She was throwing lamps out the window…"

"We can't be talking about the same person. Aris is cool as hell, and she—well you know? She got that fire," Sean said and licked his lips.

"Man, you can get some from anywhere. That's going to be your downfall, man. You run a strip club. I know you can't be hurting for some…" B-Luv said trying to figure out where Sean's head was.

"You don't get it. I can go up to The Moon right now and those chicks would be throwing it at me, but I don't want it. I just want Aris," Sean told B-Luv.

"A'ight man, I'm just saying," B-Luv said.

"I know and I heard you. I love this girl. I'm going to make her my wife. That's on the G," the two men did their handshake, patted each other on the back and went their separate ways.

The day that Aris moved into the four hundred fifty thousand dollar home on Lakeshore Drive overlooking Lake Michigan had been pure bliss for both her and Sean. Sean had given her a grand tour and told her to make herself at home.

"Look here, I want to tell you a few things," Sean said very seriously and they settled onto the sofa in the movie room. Aris nodded her head and listened closely. Sean reached into his pocket and handed her three different credit cards. "The red one is for household expenses, grocery, decorating, whatever we might need around the house. The blue one is for you-whatever you might need. Clothes, electronics, so on and so forth. The yellow one is for bills. You don't answer the house phone unless you check the caller ID and it's me. If I ever call you from that number, then it's trouble and you'll know what to do. We'll go over that later. This is my personal cell phone. I only have you and family programmed into it. This is my business phone, which I do most of my talking on. I have people calling me about the club and my business. Ya dig?" Sean told her.

"I got you. So what am I supposed to do all day since you don't want me at the club anymore?" Aris asked innocently.

Sean couldn't help but laugh. This would have been any other woman's dream, but Aris seemed disappointed.

"Baby, we've been through this before. My woman is not going to be on stage shaking it and popping it for the world to see. Here's what you do, get some rest. Keep the house clean, have dinner waiting for me, go shopping. You know what? You said that you always wished that you could have gone to college. Why don't you go up to IUN and see about getting enrolled in the Fall? I saw your transcripts from high school you had a 3.7 GPA. You should have no problem getting in school. Let me know how much it is and I'll make sure that you have the money on your card. Tomorrow we'll order you some checks to go with your account. Let Daddy, take care of you."

Aris was happy but she rolled her eyes and said, "I know you don't think I'm going to call you Daddy?"

"All the girls at the club call me Daddy," Sean said smiling and staring at her with his emerald green eyes. They illuminated his butter-complexion. Aris wondered what she had done to deserve a man like him. It hurt her to know that this was all a façade and would be ending soon. Her loyalties were with B-Luv.

Aris had never gotten over being molested by her Uncle Ray when she was little. Two years ago, she had committed the perfect murder or so she thought. There were no witnesses, no suspects, but what's done in the dark always comes to light. B-Luv saw the whole thing and reminded her daily that at a moment's notice he could end her freedom. He captured the whole thing on video and she had no clue where it was, so her life was in his hands.

"I'll call you Sean," she said and walked to the kitchen to see what she might cook.

Now Aris looked at the dining room table which had been set for two. The food was tucked away in the refrigerator now. It was three o'clock in the morning and she was still wired. She had self-medicated two hours ago and still didn't feel any change. Aris wrapped herself in the custom-made blanket that she had purchased in Cancun last month when she and Sean had gone on a trip for the weekend. Then she flicked through the channels and caught the end of Cooley High. She cried when "It's So Hard To Say Goodbye" was sung. Then she heard the key in the lock turn and the door open. Sean tip-toed in and gently closed the door. When he hit the light switch, Aris said, "Where the hell have you been?"

"No where," Sean said trying to hurry to the bedroom.

"You've been somewhere," Aris said getting in his face and catching a whiff of the Jack Daniels he had been drinking.

"I had to go see about the club. Then I went to pick up something and made some drops in Delaney, Dorie Miller, East Chicago. Then me and B-Luv went out to the Chi to kick it at this studio and lay down some tracks," Sean said running his schedule down to Aris.

"Sean, you must think I'm crazy," Aris shouted.

He wanted to say, "Nah, I know you crazy," but instead he fanned her away. He was startled to see what his boy B-Luv was talking about. Maybe this hadn't been such a good idea— moving her in. *I don't need this ignorant type mess up in my house. I should just kick her out.*

"Who you think you fanning at?" she asked grabbing his

shirt and turning the two hundred pound man toward her. Her strength shocked her. It was no way in the world that she imagined that her one hundred twenty pound-frame would be able to spin Sean around.

Annoyed by the fact that she had spun him around, he said, "Go on Aris. I'm not in the mood for this tonight."

"It's morning now. Not night. You didn't come home last night. And is that lipstick I see on your collar? Hell naw. By the way who is Monie?" Aris fumed.

"What?" Sean pretended not to know what Aris was saying.

"Who-is-Mo-nie?" Aris said very slowly.

"I don't know. You tell me?" Sean said walking away.

Aris picked up his personal cell phone from the desk and scrolled through it and brought up a picture of a woman in a bikini and showed it to him, "Her! Who is that?"

Faced with the evidence, there was no way for him to deny knowing her so he said, "Oh, her. Girl, you crazy. That's just somebody trying to get on at the club. She ain't got nothing on you Lil Momma," Sean said and slipped Aris's camisole straps off her shoulder and bent down to lick her nipples. Then he sucked on her nipples.

He took her over to the couch and laid her down and pulled her lace thong down with his teeth.

"Open your legs," he commanded her. She did. She could smell cheap perfume on him. Aris moaned as his tongue explored her. When he flipped her on her over and licked the length of her back to her crack, her toes curled. When he kissed and sucked on her cheeks, she screamed and got up. She liked being in control. Hastily, she removed his clothes and told him to follow her into the bedroom. She gave him the ride of his life on the waterbed and kissed him deeply. He moaned loudly and she kept riding him. He gasped for breath and she laughed.

"I can't take it anymore," he stammered, "You keep this

up and you're going to kill me."

"Exactly," she mumbled. When she was satisfied that she had given him the ride of his life and zapped his energy, she got out of the saddle. Still on her knees, she reached into the headboard and withdrew the small handgun. He was snoring now. She kissed the gun and eased out of the bed and aimed the gun at his head. Then her head. She wanted to end this mess right here, right now but she couldn't. Aris didn't have the heart to pull the trigger. She loved Sean and despite the fact that she felt like he was playing her, she couldn't kill him. She wanted to end her own sad, miserable, pathetic life, but she couldn't bring herself to do that either. After killing, Uncle Ray she vowed she would never take another life.

Her cell phone vibrated on the nightstand. She picked it up and ran to the bathroom. Her heart pounded as she hit the button to accept the call.

"What's up?" B-Luv asked. "I guess he's sleep?"

"Yeah," she sighed and rolled her eyes.

"Did you do that?" B-Luv asked.

"Yeah. Why you keep asking me the same thing over and over? I told you earlier that I transferred the funds to your account. How many times I gotta tell you that?" Aris asked.

"Now, what about the safe and the stash? You got that?" B-Luv asked.

"No, I can't touch that until I'm ready to make a move. If I touch it now, he's going to know that I messed with it and…" Aris stuttered. She didn't feel comfortable taking Sean for everything he had.

"Look, you need to get it now. He's talking about putting you out anyways. He said that he's tired of you. What's up with you? You had it easy. Never mind that. Get your stuff together and I'll be over there in fifteen. The gig is over," B-Luv demanded.

"What? You think I'm just going to get up and leave in the

middle of the night. I got too much stuff…" Aris began to cry.

"Get your stuff together. I'll be over there in an hour," he said and hung up.

Aris took a quick shower and then dressed quickly. Most of her things were already in the trunk. Whatever she left behind, she just left behind. She hopped into her Lexus and called B-Luv, "Meet me at the spot," she said.

"Why did you leave? I told you that I was coming by," B-Luv told her.

"Just meet me at the spot if you want Sean's stuff," Aris said.

"I'm on my way," he said smiling and hanging up. *She transferred all of dude's money to my account and now she's getting ready to hand over all of his dope to me, too. I'm set. I don't need her. Sean is going to know that she stole from him and will end up killing her. It'll never get traced back to me. Sean'll handle it and I'll be long gone,* B-Luv thought.

When Aris pulled into the parking lot of what used to be her elementary school, a sense of nostalgia fell over her. It was in this lot that her life had begun and ended. One day she had sat on the rails waiting for her mom to come pick her up from school, but she never did. Instead, her grandmother did. Aris would not let her grandmother pull out of the lot until she told her why her mom hadn't come to pick her up. Finally, her grandmother told her that her mother had died earlier that day. It was strange how one moment could change your life.

"'Bout time," B-Luv said as he got out of the car and walked to his trunk. Aris followed with two suitcases. "So, this is it?" B-Luv asked as he tried to stuff the bags in his trunk.

"Yeah, this is it," Sean said before shooting him three times in the back. He signaled to a car across the street to come clean up the mess. Then he hopped into the car with Aris and they drove off. Sean smiled at her and said, "You're my girl for life. You don't have to worry about me messing around. What you've done for me? I don't have words."

# THE LAST PLACE ON EARTH

## *Russell Little*
### Philadelphia, PA

Hello, everyone my name is Jonathan Taylor. I'm a twenty-year-old Anglo-Saxon male. I'm from rural Pennsylvania, a tiny town called Hershey. You know, like the chocolate bar? I graduated at the top of my class in high school. I'm a journalism major at Temple University. And as you may have guessed by now, I am a writer. Well an aspiring one, anyway. It won't be official until I graduate and land my first job. At the moment, I spend my most of my free time as an intern at the Philadelphia Daily News. It's only *thee* biggest newspaper in the city.

Writing is my passion. For me, it's a true labor of love. I came to the city of brotherly love not only to go to college, but to cut my teeth in the journalism field. To me, there's nothing like plying your craft. Taking the knowledge that you've studied and learned in class and applying it to real life stories and real individuals. You know, writing about the people, cultures, places and events of modern day Philadelphia? And let me tell you, there is plenty of subject matter to write about. This year alone the city of Philadelphia had the dubious distinction of being the murder capital of the world. Yep, you read right: "THE MURDER CAPTIAL OF THE WORLD."

The idea for this story was something I totally came up with. I had been pestering one of the senior editors at the paper for a chance to do a big story. I was tired of writing the want ads, car classifieds and things of that nature. I felt my talent was being wasted.

One day another writer fell ill and suddenly I was the front runner. The senior editor called me into his office, and said he wanted me to write a story. Me, Jonathan Taylor. He wanted something that really represented the city and its people. He told me he wanted a tough-as-nails story with no gimmicks and for it to be gut-wrenching. But above all else, he wanted the truth.

This was the moment I had been waiting for all my life, and there was no way I was going to let this opportunity pass me by.

"Can you handle this kid?" he asked.

"Of course, sir. I'll try my best," I said.

"Don't try, do it! Go out there and bring me back the best freaking story possible. Boy, you write your ass off!"

\*\*\*\*\*

My search for a subject for my story had taken me from the comforts of the newspaper building, to the heart of the ghetto, North Philadelphia. The last place on earth any white person in their right mind would want to be, unless they were buying drugs. My adrenaline was pumping so fast, I had no time to fear for my own safety. I had a deadline to meet. And nothing short of death was going to stop me. I stumbled across the person who would be the topic of my story accidentally.

Carla "Candy" Simpson had been standing in the cold for the past six hours, looking. Her coat was open, exposing her dirty and ripped black dress. She's what most people in this area refer to as a crack whore. Her legs were ashy, hair knotty and her front teeth were missing. The old shoes she wore, were pointing toward the sky. Her skin was calloused and her hands were bruised from providing maintenance to her crack pipe.

The scar under Candy's eye reminds her of the rape and how unsafe the mean streets are, although she boasts about how she survived the sexual assault from one of her customers. Drugs have ravished her body, making her look older than she actually is.

Many people may have seen Candy "hugging the block" as they call it around here. She is more faithful than any drug dealer I've ever seen or heard of. She has a wealth of knowledge that I'm eager to tap into. Candy knows who's selling what and where. She brings in customers that are undercover smokers and freaks, people are likely not to suspect. She knows who has the good drugs and whose dope is funny. She keeps track of who has weighty bags and knows if a worker has been skimping on the bags. But don't take her for granted, she is very influential.

Although there may be a half dozen or so of people, in a two block radius, who function like Candy, don't be fooled— she is one of a kind. And knowing this woman could possible save someone's life, which is something I'm counting on. Candy can definitely get one a "*ghetto pass*."

Oh you know her. Candy faithfully brings that money, running back and forth. When she is having a bad day, someone still tosses her a bag to get her started up and focused. Even now a couple of people in the neighborhood hold her in great esteem. She doesn't care how, but she gets what she wants.

I've watched her for hours on end. Sitting on that stoop next to the corner with her legs spread open, enticing strange men to exchange sex for drugs. She finds no takers. Even though I am personally repulsed at the idea of touching her, I am reminded that she has single-handedly opened and set up shop on the corner of North Philly for business. She has clientele. And I even witnessed a bidding war for her services.

Candy stands or sits in front of the Korean-owned warehouse under the swinging billboard waiting for her next visitor. She patrols the streets on duty, looking for a patron to solicit her services. Candy walks from one end of the corner to the other end of the street smiling at the passersby, trying to attract some attention. When her hectic schedule slows to a snail's pace, I approach her.

"Excuse me, Miss?"

She ignores me. It's as if she doesn't even see me although I almost upon her.

"Hey, you? I'm talking to you," I say.

"Who you the po-lease? If you is, you ain't git that shit from me. I ain't sell you shit?" Candy insists.

"No, no. I'm not a cop," I assure her.

"Then who the hell are you Cracker? And what you want with me? Huh?"

"I'm a reporter. My name is Jonathan Taylor. And I'm looking for some information for a story I'm doing."

"Wait a minute, what kind of information? You one of them God damn crime stoppers? If you is git the fuck away from me, cause I ain't no snitch!"

"No, no, Ma'am. What did you say your name was?"

"I ain't said shit."

I could feel the chance of a lifetime about to pass me by. I had to do something fast.

"Look, I'll give you some money," I told her. "All I have is a hundred bucks to my name. But here take it, it's yours."

Candy stared at the money as if it were marked. It was as if I was pulling some type of trick on here. Just knew I thought she would turn me down flat, she snatched the money out of my hand.

"Now what you say your name is? You work for the newspaper, ain't that what you said?"

"Yes Ma'am. My name is Jonathan Taylor and I work for

the Philadelphia Daily News."

Before she uttered another word, Candy looked me over suspiciously.

"Lemme see yo ID," she said.

I complied with her order, handing over my newspaper credentials. Once they met her strange security requirements, Candy kindly handed them back.

"Hey, white boy, I still don't believe you. If you want to talk to me, I gotta search you first. To make sure you not wearing no wires or nuttin'. Ya boys could be hiding on the rooftops or around the corner for all I know."

"But I told you I'm not a cop. I showed you my ID."

"Motherfucker, I don't believe you!" Candy snapped.

I felt like a fool as I stood at the bus stop getting frisked by a drug addict. But at this point, I didn't have much of a choice.

"Hey, white boy," she said, "You gotta big dick? You gonna have to let old Candy here give you a blow job before you go. I ain't never been with no white man before."

As Candy released the hold she had on my genitals, I could only hope she was playing. I would do a lot of things to get a story, but having sex with Candy is where I draw the line.

"I'm just kiddin' white boy!" she laughed as if she could read my mind.

A wave of relief washed over me. Without saying a word, Candy started to walk off and I followed right behind her. My all access pass to the hood had suddenly begun. I had Candy as my tour guide, this should be great.

*****

Somerset Street crosses Broad Street and curves into Glenside Street, which sits over the train tracks. By night the streetlights are dim, and an abandoned car sits parked where

Candy climbs in and out of to stay warm. For close to an half an hour, we don't exchange a word. It's almost as if I'm not there. I'm more content to observe Candy in her element rather than constantly interrupt her with clumsy questions. There'll be time for that later.

The corner of Broad and Somerset is going through a transformation. The new strip mall down the street has the sneaker store, Path Mart, a Laundromat and Family Dollar. The final stages of gentrification are going on in this neighborhood. The Septa is pouring million of dollars into the semi-abandoned Train station that has an unused parking lot as big as two football fields. However, walk one block up and see the drug dealers standing in front of the bodega still selling their wares. The old abandoned row homes are used when Candy does her business. There used to be several abandon homes, but they have been demolished and turned into empty lots.

It's quite evident Candy's hard knock lifestyle has caught up with her. She walks with a noticeable limp, an injury she suffered some years ago when she was shot. The shooting incident, Candy claims, was a case of mistaken identity. I find that statement hard to believe since Candy is truly one of a kind. She has more scars and old war wounds than I could possibly count.

"Candy, who shot you?" I ask.

"Some lil nigger trying to make a rep for himself. It was over some 'he say, she say, I stole his package' rumor. He got me mixed up wit another bitch who really did it."

"Did taking revenge ever cross your mind?"

"You damn right!" she said. "But you know what? I didn't have to do a thing to that boy. Somebody else did. He got killed two weeks after he shot me. Right here on this very block. So you see, God don't like ugly."

I didn't respond while Candy continued to brag about the

young man's demise. Somehow I get the impression that out here in this concrete jungle, there wasn't a premium placed on human life.

"Wait right here. I'll be right back," Candy insists.

From a distance I observe her approach a group of African-American youths. Although the exchange happens in a blink of an eye, I can tell Candy has scored some narcotics. The transaction has caused Candy happiness. She floats over back to me.

"Let's go. Got something else I wanna show you."

Now I'm having a hard time keeping up with Candy. She's in a rush. She leads me to what appears to be an abandoned building, then she pushes aside a large piece of plywood that's clearly marked, "KEEP OUT". In a blatant disregard of the law, we enter.

Once inside Candy uses her lighter to illuminate the way. Never in my life did I fear for my life, more than at that moment. I expected some assailant to spring from the shadows to rob and kill me any minute. I said a quick prayer as I expected to meet my maker. Much to my surprise, nothing happened.

"This is where I live."

A quick thought ran through my mind, *This isn't living. It's not even existing.* I couldn't help but notice that Candy shares her quarters with a multitude of stray cats. A siren of meows begins to serenade us. Suddenly, I begin to feel a few furry feline rub up against my legs. I clutch Candy's arm even tighter. She feels my fear.

"Don't worry about them. They don't mean you no harm."

Carefully, Candy continues to navigate this dark maze of trash and cats. We climb the stairs together. She enters what I assume is her makeshift bedroom. She shuts the door behind us to prevent the small army of cats from entering. Candy immediately walks over to the windowsill and grabs a small candle. The light it emits is slightly better than the lighter. But now I can see that the room is furnished with a urine-stained mattress and a bucket. I assume for Candy that these are the bare necessities she needs to entertain her guests.

"Have a seat."

I observe Candy as she conducts a quick search of her person. It's a search that produces some sort of crackpipe and then Candy retrieves the drugs she purchased. Now she is in business.

"Don't mind me. Just need a quick pick me up!"

"Sure, go right ahead."

I watched Candy as she packed her crackpipe with the drug, place it inside her mouth and ignite the drug. Over the cat's meowing, I can hear the crackling of the drug as the heat disintegrates it. I smell the nasty stench of crack cocaine as Candy inhales deeply.

Suddenly, she exhales a cloud of smoke. As I watch the smoke disappear, I can't help but ask myself has Candy's life gone up in smoke with it.

"Candy?" I suddenly call out, only to find my subject is unresponsive. I know now that my subject is in the clutches of one of the most addictive drugs known to man.

Candy holds up one finger as if to say, hold on for one minute. I respect her request. I wait until she gets herself together. Clearly the crack cocaine has suddenly made her paranoid. She walks to the door and makes sure it's locked, countless times. She enters a state of paranoia that takes her close to twenty minutes to recover from. Once her high wears off, I proceed once again with my line of questioning.

"Candy, why do you use drugs?" I ask.

"Why?" she repeats. "I really don't know. I guess it makes me feel good. And when something makes you feel good, you gonna keep doin' it over and over again…until it kills them. What they call that? The pleasure principle."

"If you know that much, then why do you continue to do

it?"

"Good question," she admits.

For the moment, Candy is dumbfounded by the question. Perhaps if she knew the answer she wouldn't be in her current predicament. Surely, her drug abuse has contributed to her free fall in life. Not wishing to cause any unnecessary burden on Candy, I move on to another question.

"Have you ever sold your body for a fix?"

Even before Candy responds, I already know the answer. Of course, she has performed sexual favors.

"Yeah. And any bitch out there that tells you they haven't is a goddamn liar." She states, exposing her rotten teeth.

Candy recalls all the moves for getting over on her johns, especially the ones that smokes with her. She would pinch out of the bag and stick the rocks under her fingernails, burn the drug fast so it could melt in her pipe, charge ten dollars for a five-dollar bag, and (this is her favorite) remove the screens loaded with the potent drugs.

"Are you scared somebody will attack you for swindling them out of their dope? What about AIDS?" I ask.

"I ain't scared of a Mother Fucking thing! NOTHING THAT'S MEANT FOR ME IS GONNA GET ME. AND NOTHING THAT AIN'T MEANT FOR ME IS GONNA HIT ME…and, what about AIDS? We all gotta die from something!" Candy yells as she exposes the rusty old razor cradled in her pocket. My guess is somehow I've offended her. As I attempt to continue my interview she looks me up and down as if she is trying to intimidate me. I inform her that I'm just looking for a story and that's it. I quickly change the subject.

"Do you have any kids?" I ask.

Silence, I could see that her strong and tough demeanor wanted to melt away. She remains silent and never quick to answer.

"How many kids do you have?" I ask.

"Seven, I have seven kids," she says, still remaining proud.

"Do you see them?" I ask.

"Sometimes," she says.

I am amazed she has seven children and I immediately believe all of them are motherless and somewhere in the system. I'm overcome by an urge to condemn her. She ought to be ashamed of herself. I am horrified! I begin to speak and I could tell by her body language, she was bracing for the long speech about how she can change her life and how she can be a better mother.

"I just want to tell you, that you don't have to live like this. There is a much better way and I am willing to help you. Can you see that the drugs and the lifestyle are slowly killing you? I'll help you get into a drug treatment program, so you can get a job and possibly reunite you with your children," I quickly say, hoping my plea didn't fall on deaf ears.

"Really? You would do that for me?" Candy says, with a glimmer of hope in her eyes.

"Yes really," I tell her. "I have a professor at school who is really well connected. Let me talk to him, I'm sure he can help. He's a very compassionate person."

"Oh yeah?" Candy says. "Well, what makes me so special, that he would help me? My life is over only God can help me baby."

"Don't talk like that. There's always hope," I say looking to spark something inside of her. But nothing happens. Her face is blank and has grown annoyed at my attempts to plead for her life.

What Candy does next deeply disappoints me. She pulls out another crack cocaine rock and takes another hit of her pipe.

"Fuck that shit," Candy says before she inhales deeply.

My head falls forward, stunned by her ignorance. I want to somehow save her, but I recognize that Candy does not care about her life, which is the essence of a true addict. How can one save someone else, who doesn't want to be saved? I believe Candy's latest act of getting high was a feeble attempt to rid herself of me. She was uncomfortable with being around me, and now she wanted to end our arrangement.

"Let's git the fuck outta here!" she suddenly says. "I'm ready ta go."

I follow her back through this pitch black house of horrors, holding on to her as we head outside. No sooner than we reach the outside world, Candy hits the ground running. She's walking fast, looking around nervously, surveying the area. Immediately, she recognizes a familiar silhouette, but fails to move away. Candy stops in her tracks, holding her ground. She removes a long rusty screw driver she had in her coat pocket, and immediately, her adversary gets the point.

"That bitch better stay from round here," Candy mumbles. "She know she ain't got no bizness 'round here. Carry yo ass on up da block."

By the time I turn around Candy is walking away with her Paramour. A police car drives slowly down Somerset Street and recognizes the petite woman. She avoids making eye contact with the car or the officer who is driving. The officer appears tired of warning her and arrests her. Suddenly, the police siren wails and the lights flash. The squad car screeches off to another more pressing matter.

I am convinced had it not been for that call, the police officers would have accosted us. After all we were a strange looking couple, a clean cut white boy and a black drug addict in the heart of the ghetto. However, this time God was with us. Surely, I would have been the primary target of the police officers. As a result, I would have bore the brunt of any line of questions.

# The Last Place on Earth

It didn't dawn on me until later, had the cops searched Candy they would have surely found drug paraphernalia and possibly drugs in her possession. We could have both been charged with a crime. My life, not to mention, my story, would have been ruined.

"Look Mighty Whitey, this is where we part company," Candy suddenly announced. "You slowin' me up. I can't get my hustle on. So I gotta go."

"Okay, Candy thanks," I tell her. "Thanks for allowing me into your world. Thanks for allowing me to tag along."

"No problem, White boy. No problem," she says, knowing she doesn't mean a word.

Suddenly, Candy did something totally unexpected. She reached out and embraced me, lovingly. Just like my own mother had done so many times during the course of my life. This simple act of humanity spoke volumes to my soul. And I was touched.

I swore I saw a tear in her eye as she turned and walked away.

"I'll see you later Candy. I promise. One day I'll be back." Now it was my turn to lie. My turn to give her some lip service.

"White boy stay away from here. If you ain't from here, don't come here. There is nothing to see. Just write your story white boy…tell the truth…chase your dreams…live yo life…"

Intently, I watched Candy as she disappeared into what appeared to be a nearby crack house. By this time, the first signs of the sun's rays were beginning to penetrate the sky. This, coupled with Candy's absence, was my cue to leave. I turned my back and walked in the opposite direction making my way out of the last place on earth I'd want to be.

The time I spent with Candy was intriguing to say the least. It certainly was an enriching personal experience. The things I saw that day opened up my mind to how the other

136      *Hood₂Hood*

half lives. The images I witnessed, both good and bad, will never leave me.

I felt a moral responsibility to do what Candy asked, to tell the truth. I felt a moral responsibility to give the voiceless a voice. Suddenly I heard the unmistakable crackle of gunfire in the distance. I said a silent prayer for Candy. I hoped like hell she wasn't the intended victim. But my gut instinct told me Candy would be all right. In the last place on earth, Candy could surely hold her own.

# DiE BY THE SWORD

*Rhonica Wesley*
Shreveport, LA

Right where the run down buildings came together on East Nineteenth Street and Vine was the heart of the ghetto, but also the place Isaiah called home. Queensboro or QB as it was called, wasn't much to look at to some. It was just a muddle of decaying buildings and crack houses long over due to be torn down. On the other side of the long winding railroad tracks was where the Addison Park projects started, and civilization ended. For most of the inhabitants of the ghetto when greed and power took over, rationalization was out of the question. Grown men with starving families would stop at nothing to put food on the table. Their motto was "By any means Necessary." They were aware of the consequences, and even though they went to jail sporadically, these hustlers, drug dealers and con men had already taught their elder sons how to take care of the family while they were incarcerated. That was how it went down in the projects, young men were turned into soldiers, to defeat poverty and adversity.

The hood was a breeding ground for hustlers, whores, and drug addicts. The other half of the residents kept to themselves and gave a deaf ear to illegal activity they knew went on.

The lollipop stick rested on Isaiah's lower lip as he raced through the downtown streets with his backpack slightly draped over one shoulder, and his Walkman clamped onto the waist of his sagging Mecca brand jeans. For every pedestrian that walked pass, he would nod his head, acknowledging their presence.

Isaiah was six foot four, and his long legs stretched as he walked turning every step into a rhythm. The southern heat soon forced him to eliminate his sweat shirt, leaving him dressed in his white T-shirt and baggy jeans. Isaiah inspected his boots for dust or scratches, and when he saw they were still as good as new, he moved along the sidewalk again headed towards his destination. Just like the other young men in the hood, Isaiah was not born with a silver spoon in his mouth. His father had been robbed and killed when he was just a toddler, ordaining him the man of the house. His manly ways did not sit right with his mother, and she eventually put him out on the streets to fend for himself at the age of sixteen. That was when Isaiah met his father figure who went by the name of G.T.

G.T. was the leader of one of the worst drug operations in Louisiana hands down. He was a murderer, a felon, and even the police were afraid to approach him. He had offered Isaiah a part in his operation, and that was when Isaiah began to rob and kill with no remorse. Isaiah always said it was "Every man for himself." He didn't care about what happened to those around him, he was sick of looking out for everyone else. He was a hustler and a con man, G.T. didn't have a conscience and he was pretty sure he didn't have a heart.

Isaiah dumped his backpack behind a trash bend, and looked around to make sure he was alone in the alley before he attempted to change clothes. It was hard to rob stores on foot, but Isaiah had been known for his speed and agility. Isaiah changed in a hurry, his ski mask atop his head, not yet ready to conceal his identity. Isaiah stood at the corner of the Chinese restaurant and spotted his partner heading his way.

During the morning hours, there were no people in the run down Chinese restaurant. The Chinese used their restaurant to cover up a counterfeit operation they had run for many years. Isaiah planned to steal real and counterfeit cash, and whatever else he could find of value. He made sure his forty five millimeter was loaded and ready to go, before he met up with his partner at the entrance door. He quickly pulled his ski mask down over his head and signaled to his partner that it was time to take action. With guns drawn, they rushed into the restaurant and demanded everyone down on the carpeted floor. The people did as he asked, but one lady would not stop screaming.

"Be quiet bitch..." Isaiah's partner said trying to calm the woman down. She would not listen and continued to beg and plead for her life. She stood up on her knees and grabbed Isaiah's pants leg.

"Please do not kill me," she pleaded.

Isaiah gave the woman one look through his mask and pumped four bullets into her skull. She lay on the floor in a mass of blood, and Isaiah turned his attention to a small Chinese girl kneeling near the entrance. He instantly grabbed the frantic girl by the throat and threatened her.

"Where is the money?" he yelled.

She mumbled in Chinese, and Isaiah became aggravated with her.

"Speak English bitch! Where is the money?" he yelled again.

"Please sir, she does not speak English. Do not harm her, I will show you," an elderly Chinese lady said.

"Well, hurry up bitch! You wasting time," he cursed.

Isaiah grabbed the older woman and shoved her to the floor as she struggled to get to the back. Isaiah knew he only had four more minutes to get out, or it was his ass.

Isaiah's partner held his gun on the four other remaining

people as Isaiah followed the elderly woman. The woman took him to a dusty old room, filled with crates and spider webs. She opened a small vault and crouched in front of it, as she was scared to move.

"This is all the money we have…" she trembled.

Isaiah back handed the woman with the butt of his gun. "You lying bitch! Where's the counterfeit money?" he growled.

"Wait, wait…please I know nothing about counterfeit I swear…"

Isaiah shot the woman in the chest, and hurried to fill his bag with money. He didn't have time to argue about the counterfeit money, he had to move before the cops were alerted. He rushed to the front of the restaurant, and ordered the other four people to lie down. He and his partner proceeded to execute them all, and hurriedly rushed out the restaurant, leaving the six dead corpses.

Isaiah did not want to draw attention to himself, so he removed the mask, unaware of the pedestrians around him. Isaiah parted with his partner before heading back to the dumpster. He switched clothes again, and stuffed the money in his backpack. He threw the other set of clothes inside the dumpster, and walked back up the street towards the Addison Park projects.

*****

Isaiah arrived home only to find his six month pregnant girlfriend, Nacelle sitting on the stairs, her head in her hands. Isaiah didn't know what to think, but he still wondered what was going on.

"They put us out," she sobbed.

"What?" Isaiah was dumbfounded.

"They evicted us. They evicted us because your ass didn't

pay the fucking rent this month. I'm sick of this shit Isaiah.
I'm going home to live with my mama. I can't take this shit
anymore. Where you been…hunh? You were out robbing and
stealing. I swear to God that I hate your guts!"

She was cut off by Isaiah's back hand slap across her
face.

"If you hate me, then why you still standing here? How
I know that kid mine anyways? We all know you a hoe!" he
yelled.

Nacelle started to swing at him, but was unsuccessful
at landing a blow. Isaiah tried to grab her but she fell to the
ground.

"I fucking hate you…you stupid no good nigga!" She
screamed and cried at the same time.

"I hate you too bitch!" Isaiah screamed and traveled up
the stairs. He tried his key in the door but it didn't work. He
started to violently demolish the door with the bottom of his
Lugz.

"How they gonna evict me from my own shit? Fuck them!"
he yelled.

He slammed what was left of the door, and entered his
bedroom, where he lounged still in his clothes and shoes.
Nacelle walked in with tears streaming from her eyes. She
found a duffel bag at the foot of the bag, and began to fill it
with clothes and personal items. She looked at Isaiah from
time to time to see if he was watching her. She finally grew
sick of his lack of attention and stood with her hand on her
hip.

"So you don't give a damn whether or not I leave. You raw
Isaiah, and I hope you die a slow painful death," she said.

"Damn if you gonna leave, go on with all that bullshit
Cel," he said looking up into the ceiling.

"You know what, fuck you Isaiah. And don't call me when
your ass face down somewhere, 'cause I ain't bailing you out

this time." She exited the room, and Isaiah waited for the door to slam before he went into the bag of money to count it.

"One-Thousand two hundred and eighty five dollars," he counted.

Robbing that restaurant had been a waste of his time, he could usually clear at least ten thousand in one attempt, this only meant that he had to plan another robbery and soon. Isaiah heard a rapid knock on the front door, and was sure it was Nacelle back again to start an argument. He opened the door, only to be greeted by a half naked light skinned sister with long wavy hair and a set of piercing gray eyes. She grabbed the back of his head and planted a wild kiss on his lips. Once she came up for air, Isaiah began to speak.

"Where the fuck you been Jazz? I told your ass I needed to borrow your muthafuckin car this morning," he scolded.

"I'm sorry baby. I been working. Damn bank has me stretched out."

Jazz sat down on the couch and started to remove her shoes. She was a stripper by night and a bank teller in the day. She and Isaiah had been messing around for years and if it wasn't for the fact that Nacelle was claming to be pregnant by him, he would be with Jazz no strings attached. She sashayed over, and grabbed Isaiah by the hand. Leading him to the sectional sofa, she sat him down and began to unzip his designer jeans. Every once in a while, she would glance into his eyes, but the stare that she got back was blank. Soon she buried her face in his lap and pleasured him with her lips and tongue. Once she was done, Isaiah saw her out the door and flopped down in his bed for a long nap. He had no feelings for Jazz whatsoever. He just kept her around because she did things that Cel wouldn't do.

Isaiah turned over, but to his surprise, the front door was being knocked off the hinges. He tried to reach for the gun underneath his pillow, but he was staring down the barrel of a rifle.

*****

"I told you man, I don't know shit about no robbery at Cheng's. I was at home fucking my baby's mama's brains out." Isaiah smirked.

"Do you think this is a game Mr. Davis?" the cop said to him growing impatient.

"You ain't got shit on me, so can I go now," Isaiah said calmly.

The cop extended his hand towards the door, and Isaiah got up to walk out.

"I'd suggest you get a lawyer Mr. Davis. I plan to take you down, if it's the last thing I do," the cop said.

Isaiah went to the pay phone to call Nacelle. He had to get out of there. He was so nervous he could barely dial the number.

"Lemme speak to Cel," he ordered over the phone.

He waited for a moment, and his girlfriend picked up the phone.

"Cel, come pick me up from the police station. Fuck all that, just come get me." He slammed the phone down and went outside in the one o'clock heat to wait for her arrival.

Just like always Cel was there. She drove up in her ten-year-old Maxima, looking like she was mad at the world. Isaiah got in the car, and that's when she started to talk.

"I don't know what the fuck you called me for. I should have left your ass there. Your ass is all over the news. Some old ass white broad seen you and that dumb ass nigga Deuce coming out of that restaurant earlier today. Nigga you as good as gone this time," she said.

Isaiah wasn't listening. He just knew he had to find that old lady and shut her up.

Even though they had not mentioned the old woman's name on the news Isaiah had friends who worked at the news station. He planned to go to his informants and shut the old lady up for good.

"Her name is Helen Norris. She lives over in Broadmoor. She's some rich old dame. Says she seen you and Deuce running from the restaurant earlier in the evening. I'm sure the cops are casing her house. If I was you man, I'd forget about it," Gerald said.

Gerald and Isaiah had grown up just three buildings down from each other, and had been tight since sixth grade. Gerald was different, because he was not a hustler, or a drug dealer. He was one of the few who had chosen to go to college and better himself.

"Look college boy, I ain't trying to hear all that. I got plans for that old lady…and believe you, me, I'm going to follow through."

Isaiah would inform Deuce of his plans, and once and for all, give the cops nothing to go on.

*****

"This ain't right Isaiah. I don't feel right. Something's wrong," Deuce cringed in the bush, and whined.

"If you gonna be a bitch man, I suggest you head back to QB," Isaiah scolded.

Deuce closed his mouth, and Isaiah put his hood over his head proceeding to cross the street to a massive house with a Pickett fence and a flower garden in the yard.

"I'm going in. Watch my back," Isaiah ordered.

He didn't mind intimidating some old broad. He was sure that she lived alone, and had some valuable items. Isaiah went around the back of the house, and spotted a back door, that looked worn enough for him to enter. He used a knife to open the screen door, and to open the front door. Just as he was about to duck into the house, a light came on in the kitchen and there stood an old man with a gun. The old man released a shot, and the bullet stuck deep into Isaiah's shoulder. When Isaiah ran out of the house, he dropped his knife. And the old man could identify him. Now, Isaiah was really in deep.

*****

"Yo, chill out with that damn needle Wes!" Isaiah whined, as Wes stitched up his shoulder.

Wes had been a doctor in the army, but had been given a dishonorable discharge when he was caught with underage Russian prostitutes.

"Take two of these, and make sure you keep the wound clean," Wes said. He was a chubby white man with a beard, and a mustache that covered his thin pink lips. Even though Wes' operation was illegal, everyone in the hood went to him when they needed a medical favor. From abortions to bullet holes, Wes did it all, and he was deemed "the hood doc."

Isaiah threw his shirt back on and headed out the door. It was now night time and the moon was half full. The sound of crying babies and sirens in the projects was all too familiar to Isaiah. He strode up the street, lighting a cigarette with a single match that he had struck on the curb. A car coming up the street dimmed its light, and Isaiah stopped in his tracks. The car halted as well. Isaiah walked a few inches further, and the car started to move. Isaiah broke out to run. The faster he ran, the closer the car got to him.

Isaiah ran through the alley, and tried to climb the brick wall, but was unsuccessful. There was no way he would let the cops take him. He was a hustler, and he would never spend his life behind bars. Born and raised in Shreveport, Louisiana, Isaiah was nothing near a sucker. He had to escape; he was too smart to get caught up. Isaiah took out his gun and started to spray. The police fired back.

Suddenly, he could remember every person he had ever killed, and all the elderly people he had robbed and beaten. His life flashed before him like a movie. He had no remorse for anything that he had ever done. Twenty-five shots rang out, but only four of them entered his body.

Isaiah Davis was just another young black man who had become a product of the cruel streets of Shreveport. He had made opportunities for himself, where there were none for men with little education or a lack of standards. His unborn son would only hear stories of him, and be told of what a hardened criminal his father was. He would follow in his father's footsteps, breaking his mother's heart. Isaiah's son would also choose to live by the sword and take whatever he wanted; therefore, he, too, would die by the sword.

# CAUGHT UP

## *Angel Mitchell*
Bradenton, FL

The door opened and the music followed Kendra when she walked into the bathroom wearing only a gold thong and gold nine inch heels. Her blonde weave clung to the sweat on her back and her face glistened in the bright light from the bathroom.

"You're after Fonda girl. You ready?" she asked.

I tied the string from the bikini top around my neck and shrugged. "I guess so."

"Well, what is it going to take for you to be sure? You need another drink? You want me to get an 'E' pill from Notti?" She asked. Kendra picked up my MAC lipstick from the counter and applied a coat to her full lips. She pressed them together and smiled. "I know, do a line with me, you'll be ready then."

"You know I don't get down like that Kendra." I looked in the mirror and adjusted my false eyelash. "Just break the money down to me again," I said.

Kendra stood behind me and gently massaged my shoulders with her sweaty hands. She stared at her reflection as she spoke.

"Notti charges all the boys at the door, that's the "house". We each get a part of that off top. What we make on the floor is ours to keep. The harder you work, the more money you get. You feel me Dix?"

"Yeah."

"V.I.P two fifty guaranteed, but it's up to you to go that route. Niggas are gonna press you, but you don't have to do anything you don't want to do. Remember that," she said.

Six months ago, I would have never imagined myself in the predicament I'm in now.

Before Bryce got hemmed up by the Feds I was living on top of the world. Money was the least of my worries. Now, it is my only worry. I went from a four bedroom house on the Southside, to living in a two bedroom apartment in the Gardens projects with my little girl. I'm working part time at the mall, and taking classes during the day. I miss not having to worry about anything. Bryce took care of everything, now he's gone and I'll be fifty-six-years-old by the time he sees the light of day again.

The day Kendra strut her powderhead ass into the store last weekend, she must have recognized the "brokenness" in my eyes. She talked a good game. She sold me on the dancing thing with words alone. She said that Notti, a legit party promoter in the area, was looking for a few more "pretty girls" to dance at some of his private events. She thought I would be perfect. Kendra said the money was easy, fast and good. She promised all I'd have to do is look cute, shake my ass a little, and I would make more in one night than the mall could pay me in a month. I needed the money…bad.

Fonda walked into the bathroom talking loud as usual. "I need a fucking drink! Those niggas are animals!" she said.

I stared at Fonda's slender naked body while she looked in the mirror. To me she was entirely too pretty to be dancing for dollars, she looked like she should be in someone's Hip-Hop magazine. She was tall with beautiful long hair, and perfect skin, but Fonda was far from the woman she appeared. She was right where she wanted to be, doing what she wanted to do. Fonda's money was long, and she surely put in the work for it.

"I have two VIPs lined up already. Rent is due bitches!" Fonda tapped me on the shoulder and I jumped. "Notti said, 'hurry your ass up, Dixyn,'. You're supposed to walk out as soon as I'm done," she said.

"You sure you don't want any of this?" Kendra said, holding up a small mirror with four lines of cocaine resting on it.

"No, I'm good." I said.

I stood up and adjusted the small bikini. I ran my fingers through my hair, and stared in the mirror. Kendra slapped me on the ass and laughed.

"Shake what your mama gave you bitch."

What my mama gave me was good sense and morals, but all of that went out of the window when I started fucking around with Bryce Winters. Bryce wasn't well known, because he had been an outstanding student or athlete in high school or college, or because he had a prosperous legitimate business in the community. Bryce Winters was well known because he moved units. Major units. Before Bryce Winters, Dixyn Green didn't even know what a 'unit' was.

I was lucky enough to be raised by both of my parents on the Southside of Tampa. I'd been an honor roll student all through high school, and was starting college dead set on becoming a Child Physiologist. Before I knew it, I was caught up in Bryce's drug game. I was doing things I'd only watched in the movies. My old life was history. I lived and breathed the street life. My parents wanted no part of it, so when Bryce was taken in I was literally left on my own with my baby girl.

I stepped toward the door, which led to the small room. I looked back at Kendra, and half smiled. I couldn't believe it. I was really going to take my clothes off for money. I took a deep breath and opened the door.

My Neck, My Back was blaring in the background, and fifty or more men surrounded the small platform that was supposed to be the stage. They were shouting and clapping as the music bumped through the speakers. I quickly looked around and didn't see anyone I recognized, so I smiled and walked to 'center stage'.

The dancing was easy. It was the "taking off my clothes" part that had me scared. Notti didn't half step when it came to his private parties. He charged the boys one hundred and fifty dollars a head to get in, with the guarantee of seeing some pretty pussies.

While the bass pumped through my body, I remembered what Kendra told me. "Just pretend you're alone in your bedroom." After shaking my ass all over the floor and grinding on a few dudes it was time to show the goods. I wound my hips to the beat, and loosened the bikini top and dropped it to the floor. I turned around to show the horny men, my average breasts while they dropped their bills around me. I sexily licked my lips and gyrated to the ground. I lay on my back and pretended I was alone in my bedroom as I slid the bikini bottom over my long legs. I rose to my feet and continued my sensual dance. Hands were everywhere, grabbing me, and touching all of my private areas. Notti promised there would be no touching, but with a bunch of rowdy men, and one woman, it was hard to control. I looked at the bills around the floor, and smiled. It didn't matter what I was doing. Fifties and twenties were scattered everywhere. I needed that money. An older gentleman even stuck a one hundred dollar bill between my teeth after I bent over in front of him. The money was too easy, just like Kendra said.

Before I knew it, my turn was over, and Notti was collecting my funds from the floor. I walked into the back room, and Kendra ran to me and gave me a hug.

"You did the damn thing Dix! Girl, you are a natural."

"I was scared as fuck. Where's Notti with my paper?" I asked.

"He'll be here. He's probably just seeing who wants VIP with you."

"Aww hell no, Kendra, I'm not doing no VIP," I said.

Notti walked into the backroom and sat in the chair beside me. Dixyn Green here's your check," he laughed.

I took the stack of money from Notti, and started counting. I was up to six hundred dollars when he interrupted my addition.

"I have a business proposition for you Dix," he said.

"I'm not doing VIP Notti."

"It's better than that. Someone wants to take you on his boat tonight. Just you and him."

"I'm not for sale Notti."

"He just wants to spend time Dix. He's willing to pay for it."

"Who is this guy that is willing to pay for 'time' Notti?"

"He's legit."

"Send Kendra," I said.

"He wants you."

"No Notti. I'm not a whore."

"Okay…it's your loss." Notti stood up to leave, and I grabbed his arm.

"How much is he willing to pay for time?"

Notti leaned down and whispered the amount in my ear. I looked at him like he was crazy.

"I don't have to have sex?"

Notti leaned down and whispered in my ear again.

"Let me meet this dude," I said.

All the girls cleaned up and headed out for the meet and greet portion of the night. Notti always had his girls mix and mingle with the men after the show, to ensure they received their monies worth. It was during that part of the night when most of the contact and VIP negotiation took place. The girls could easily walk out of one of Notti's parties with a couple thousand dollars in their pocket, if they played the game right.

I looked around for Notti. I wanted to meet this mystery man who was willing to pay for some 'time' with me.

"Dix!" Notti yelled from across the room.

I held up my hand to acknowledge him and made my way through the raucous crowd. When I reached the table the mystery man was facing the opposite direction, talking with another party patron. Notti tapped him on the shoulder and when he turned around my heart dropped to the bottom of my feet and I stopped breathing.

"Bryan, this is Dix. Dix this is my boy Bryan."

I extended my shaking hand to the man, and he kissed it. "Nice to meet you shawty," he said.

"Well I'm going to let you two get to know each other. Dix, let me know when…I mean if you leave," Notti said.

"So Ms. Dix, how'd you get this gig? I thought you were holding it down at the mall. At least that is what my brother told me the last time I talked to him."

"Bryan, please…you can't tell Bryce," I pleaded.

"I'm not going to say anything, if you come with me to-night."

"Okay Bryan, I'll go."

"Do you promise to make it worth the money I gave Notti?"

"I promise," I whispered.

"Let's go."

On the way to the dock, Bryan questioned me, like a con-cerned older brother, but the look in his eyes, said something else.

"How long have you been getting down like that Dix?"

"Tonight was my first night."

"I can't tell," he said.

"Well, it was. Kendra put me on. I needed the money. You haven't come around to check on me or your niece since your brother got locked down, and you promised him you would," I said.

"I have had some shit of my own going on. My life has been fucked up since he went down too. You ain't the only one. Do you know how hard it was to recoup all that lost money?"

"Don't know, don't care. I'm still living in the projects."

Being on Bryan's boat brought back memories of the times that me and Bryce had long ago. I closed my eyes and wished I could go back in time and make it right.

"Do you want to change clothes?" Bryan asked. "There is everything you need in the bathroom, towels, and a robe… whatever."

I walked into the bathroom, and washed the night's activity away from my body. I hoped that Bryce's brother didn't actually expect me to have sex with him. What happened between us the night Bryce was taken away was an accident. I was vulnerable, and scared. When I told him it could never happen again, I meant it.

I wrapped the plush white robe around my body and went to sit with Bryan.

"I'm in a position to help you now Dix. I am going to take care of you and that little girl from now on. You don't have to worry about anything anymore. Dancing, taking off your clothes and shit, that's not even you. It ends tonight."

"How can I trust what you say?"

"You just have to trust me."

Bryan and I talked until the early hours of the morning. When I woke up I was on the bed, and Bryan was on the chair with his head resting on the arm. Before I left that afternoon, he handed me a wad of money, folded with a rubber band wrapped around it.

The next day Kendra called to find out if I would be doing the next party.

"They are all asking about you Dix," she said.

"I can't Kendra. It's just not for me," I said.

"Well let me know what's up, if you change your mind."

I wish that I could change my mind and go back to before I'd ever got caught up in this crazy life. I had become accustomed to fast money. There was no turning back for me. I'd do anything to get it now. I didn't know which was worse, taking off my clothes for a bunch of over-sexed brothers with nothing better to do with their money than pay for pussy, or getting ready to board the train with major weight in my luggage.

I knew Bryan wasn't going to let me off that easy. He reminded me when he dropped me off at the train station... nothing in this life is free.

# THE BLOCK

*Kevin Wiggins*
Baltimore, MD

As the sunset, Baltimore Street, also known as "the block", began to pulsate with life. The neon sign flickered in the nightlight advertising the wares of fast food takeout joints, pornography shops and strip clubs like Norma Jeans, The Players Club, The Gentlemen's club and the Pussycat Dolls to name a few. This red light district stretched two city blocks. It's like a modern day Sodom and Gomorrah, where pleasures of the flesh were bought and sold nightly. Drug dealing and prostitution run rampant, and any sexual act under the sun, was committed here. It was for this reason and this reason alone, that men from all walks of life were drawn to this infamous strip like a moth to a flame.

What was once a place of legitimate adult entertainment has been transformed into a block of ill repute. Low lives, businessmen and scantily-clad strippers alike all congregated on the strip and in these clubs to engage in the sex trade, in one form or another. The pimps, tricks, and strippers were all good for the economy of the block. They all fed off each other and they were all dependent on each other. It was just one vicious food chain, one big vicious cycle that each person perpetrated on the other, over and over again. Most of the illegal prostitution transactions took place inside the confines of the strip club. Often times, deals were made at the bar and carried out in the VIP areas, or in other secluded places in the club.

Selling pussy may have been just a side hustle for the strippers who worked the clubs. For the women of the night, on the other side of that door, it was a full-time occupation. These street walkers had to walk the track, pound the pavement, in search of customers. For them it was a never-ending quest, especially with a pimp pressing them for money and watching their every move. Monye Bell was one of the poor misguided souls who had the misfortune of having a pimp.

"Dollar, these heels are killing my feet. Can I get in and take a load off my feet? Huh, Daddy?" she asked.

Momentarily, Dollar looked away from the Baltimore Sun newspaper Sports section that he was reading. He was pissed off by the sudden disturbance. Quickly, a wicked frown spread across his lips and Monye knew she was in for a tongue lashing.

"Bitch!" Dollar barked. "If you don't get the fuck away from this car with that dumb shit…I swear I'll make you regret the day you were born, hoe! I don't give a fuck how bad your feet hurt. Hoe, I don't care if you have to walk on your fucking hands, go git my money!"

Monye regretted even mentioning her problem to him. She knew Dollar didn't have any compassion. He was a cruel, foul mouth, bastard. What else did she expect him to say? Dollar didn't respect anything but the almighty dollar, and a money-making hoe. Money was his God. His hoes were just a tool he used to attain it.

"Sorry Daddy. I'm okay. It won't happen again," Monye said.

"Beat it Bitch!" he mumbled.

Wisely Monye heeded his warning and renewed her search for tricks. Meanwhile, her pimp eyed her evilly until she was out of sight. Then once again, Dollar began to read the newspaper.

Monye felt a tinge of guilt deep inside her soul. It was the submissive act of being a whore and calling some nigger young enough to be her older brother, daddy. Although it may have seemed easy, it wasn't. Monye detested the way the word easily rolled off her tongue. Dollar had forced her to address him in this matter, just like he had done all his hoes, by going upside their heads with his fist, a time or two. Dollar was a new age pimp. He possessed none of the earmarks of pimps from yesteryear. He didn't where outrageous clothing that called attention to himself. He didn't have a fancy car. He didn't have expensive jewelry or fur coats. All he had was the gift of gab.

To his credit, Dollar could definitely pull a hoe. But he couldn't keep one to save his life. His leadership and management skills left a lot to be desired. Dollar couldn't lead a horse to water. That was because he had violent tendencies. Either Dollar had heard or saw it somewhere in a movie that pimps were violent. So he transformed himself into a cold calculating motherfucker. He was a brutal pimp who used intimidation and violence to keep his hoes working and productive. But eventually his act would wear thin, even with the most naïve hoe.

When it came to pimping Dollar was outside of his element. Dollar thought just because he had fucked the majority of the girls in his hood that this qualified him to be a pimp. This whole idea started out as a joke. He talked a hood rat into selling some pussy for him to a couple of his homies. This act turned him into a monster. One chick turned him on to another, which eventually led to Warren renaming himself Dollar and taking his show out the hood to the block.

Just looking at Dollar, one couldn't tell that he was a pimp. He looked like a normal cat from the hood. He stood an even six feet, weighed one hundred and eighty pounds. He was dark skin with short wavy hair and two gold teeth in his mouth. The older pimps on the block had no respect for Dollar, because he didn't respect the game or abide by the rules. They made fun of him behind his back. They couldn't wait to relieve him of his hoes. They loved it when he bought fresh meat to the block, because it would only be a matter of time before his hoes would be theirs.

While Dollar busied himself with the box scores in the Sport's section of the paper, Monye walked up and down the block looking for her first trick of the night. She needed that first bit of action to get her started. She needed some cash in her hand just to get her adrenaline going. Knowing Dollar, she knew she was going to be in for a long night. Although her feet hurt like hell, making Dollar some money would ease her pain.

*****

Monye Belle was an eighteen-year-old runaway from nearby Howard County. She was brown skin, stood 5'6, weighed 150lbs, with long straight black hair. Monye was attractive in every sense of the word. But as attractive as she was, Monye was equally as naïve. She had fled the safety of her parents' home, fueled by visions of fame and fortune.

Since she was a child, Monye had always wanted to be an actor. She didn't care if it was on the silver screen or up on stage in a Broadway play, she wanted to perform. The only problem was her parents weren't supportive of her dreams. At home, she lived in a fish bowl. Monye's every move was being scrutinized. Her parents lived vicariously through her, hopping that she would follow in their footsteps and attend college and enter the corporate world. But Monye had other plans. After graduating from high school, one day Monye went off to her part-time job at Burger King and never came back. She took a bagful of her belonging and hopped on a bus, to Baltimore.

Her destination was close but it was oh so far. Monye was a county girl from suburban America. She had been to Baltimore only a handful of times. The city wasn't a popular destination for her parents. Its high crime rate always made it an unattractive destination for them. They feared Baltimore and all its inhabitants. In order to avoid any potential trouble, they stirred clear of the city. When they wanted to go out for a night out on the town, they usually opted to go to D.C., Annapolis, or the Eastern Shore.

On the radio, Monye had always heard of all the concerts, events and the black stage plays that were being promoted in Baltimore, so she promised herself that she would go there one day, in hopes of auditioning for a stage play. When Monye finally got to Baltimore, she auditioned for a role in some play in the producer's hotel room. Instead of reading for the play, she landed on the casting couch. The producer had his way with Monye a few more times, then he skipped town before he could make good on his bogus promise. Slowly, but surely Monye's money and luck were running out. Down in the dumps, Monye was set to return home to her parents, when she had the misfortune of meeting Dollar at Lexington Market. A chance meeting turned into a nightmare. Monye didn't know that that a five-minute chat could get her into a world of trouble.

On the block Monye's acting skills would serve her well. The stage was set, all she had to do was play her part.

\*\*\*\*\*

*Damn I can't believe its Friday night and it's dead as hell out here* Monye mused.

Nearly an hour had passed, and there wasn't a trick in sight. Dozens of cars passed by, men looked but didn't stop.

Then suddenly a trick appeared.

"What's good Shorty? You working or what?" The man asked.

Normally, under no circumstances would Monye consider going with this guy. For one reason, he was black. From her experience, Black men tended to give hoes a hard way to go. They were hard to please and never satisfied. Even Dollar had warned her to stay away from Black guys. In the time it took to serve one, a hoe could have easily served three or four white men. Since Monye was dead broke she was willing to take a chance on the man. Right now money didn't have a face. She was selling a product and he was a potential buyer.

"Yeah, what's up? What can I do for you?"

"A nigger need a lil head that's all."

"You ain't the police, are you?"

"Do I look like a cop?"

"That's not what I asked you? Now answer the question."

"No, I ain't no fucking cop!" The man barked. "You gettin' in or what? It's hot out here!"

Monye was easily convinced by the man. She quickly hopped inside his car and they merged into traffic.

"How much for some head?"

"Fifty. And you pay up front."

"I ain't got no problem with that. But where we gonna go do this?"

"Since you only gettin' some head, we can do it right here in this car," Monye said. "I gotta spot I can take you to. We'll put these tinted windows to some good use."

The man looked at the young woman in his passenger seat in disbelief. Her confidence overrode her innocent appearance. She looked like an angel but talked like a seasoned whore. Giving the man precise directions, they arrived at an out-of-the-way side block, not far from Baltimore street. Once the money exchanged hands, the fun was set to begin. But for

Monye it wasn't fun at all.

Monye hated the act of sucking dick. She wasn't really big on sex for that matter, either. If someone would have told her that she would be selling her body for money right now, she wouldn't have believed them. Who could have predicted such a fate for a straight-A student from a middle class family? Dollar had duped her into believing that he was saving a portion of the money that she earned from turning tricks to buy a plane ticket to New York City and pay for a few months room and board. Once there she could pursue her real dream of acting. *"Sucking and fucking was only temporary,"* Dollar promised.

Once the money exchanged hands, Monye received a rude awakening. A swirl of blue and red lights suddenly doused the car and backup vice units converged. Monye's head began to spin as the vice squad officers removed her from the car. A female officer conducted a bodily search of her person.

"What's this?"

"It's a knife. I carry it for protection."

"Why? Who or what do you need protection from?"

Monye didn't bother to reply.

The woman police officer tightly slapped the handcuffs on Monye's wrists. "Miss, you're under arrest," the cop suddenly announced.

"But I didn't do anything," she cried. "What are you arresting me for?"

"Prostitution."

Monye went numb as the cop read her rights.

"You have the right to remain silent. Anything that you say or do, can and will be used against you in a court of law…"

By the time the cop was done reading her rights, reality had set in. Monye was crying her eyes out as they placed her in the back of a police car. It wasn't the fear of jail or the shame that she had brought to her family's name that caused tears, but it was thought of what Dollar would do, once he found out.

*****

Dollar posted bail for Monye. There was no way he was going to let her sit. She was no good to him in jail. When she was released from custody, she was given back all her personal items that weren't considered contraband like her purse and pocket knife. Dollar was waiting outside the courthouse to take her home.

"Daddy, I'm sorry. I didn't know that guy was a cop," she told him. "Please gimme another chance I'll make it up to you. I swear."

"Don't worry about it Babe. It happens to the best of them," Dollar said.

Despite what Dollar said Monye knew there was cause for concern. Dollar's cool attitude was not the norm. It hinted that he possibly had something up his sleeve. Now Monye wished she had called her parents to bail her out instead. But she didn't have the guts to do that. The thought was just wishful thinking because she didn't trust Dollar. Still she was glad to be free. In her mind all her troubles were behind her. On the contrary, they were only beginning.

In no time, they arrived at Dollar's non-descript rowhouse located in the slums of east Baltimore. As soon as they crossed the threshold, Dollar flipped the script on Monye, exposing his true intentions. He led his *property* into the bedroom. Dollar wasted no time when he tossed Monye onto the bed. She was caught off guard by his actions, but she still didn't protest.

"Bitch, you been a bad girl," he stated. "Now you got to pay."

Unlike most pimps who didn't fuck their whores, Dollar did. He had a pussy habit that would rival any hardcore junkie's heroin habit. Dollar just loved to fuck. The younger and cuter the hoe, the more frequently he fucked her. Instantly Monye knew she was in trouble. She looked back at Dollar and saw he already had whipped out his large black penis. It stood at attention waiting for some oral satisfaction.

"Come suck this dick bitch!" Dollar ordered. "And it better be good."

Submissively, Monye crawled across the queen-size bed towards Dollar's exposed manhood. As soon as she reached him, Dollar manhandled her, shoving her head toward his groin region. Monye responded by opening her mouth wide and taking his long thick dick down her throat. Dollar forced his dick so far down Monye's throat, she began to gag. Surprisingly, he released his grip and allowed Monye to establish her own pace. Slowly she went back and forth, up and down, sucking Dollar's dick.

"That's it bitch!" hHe coached her. "Suck dis dick hoe!"

For some reason Monye felt funny, disrespected. It was as if the spell that Dollar cast on her was lifting. Monye felt like crying but she didn't. She fought back the tears, relying on her acting skills to carry her through. And they did. Dollar thought she was enjoying the oral sex as much as he was. The act of fellatio had turned Dollar on. Now he was ready for some pussy. He wanted to run up in Monye so bad it was killing him. He had had enough oral sex, now it was time to fuck. "Bring your ass here. I want some pussy," he said.

Quickly, Monye popped Dollar's saliva coated dick out of her mouth. She took off her skirt and slid off her panties before assuming the position. She laid spread eagle on the bed waiting for Dollar to penetrate her. Monye couldn't help but feel dirty. She knew her pussy had an unfavorable scent to it, especially, after being in police custody for two days without being able to take a shower. But if Dollar wanted some pussy, then she was going to give it to him. She would do anything to get his mind off the blunder she made the other night, getting arrested.

Without any foreplay, Dollar shoved his dick deep inside Monye. He went raw. Although Monye didn't like the idea, she didn't say a word.

"Ummm," Dollar moaned. "This pussy good as a mother-fucker." As Dollar let out loud gasps of pleasure, tears escaped Monye's eyes. Dollar's big dick was tearing up her insides.

"Stop Dollar you're hurting me," she whispered.

"Shut the fuck up!" he yelled. "Bitch this my pussy. I do wit it what I want."

Dollar bent Monye into a variety of positions. He was hitting it from every angle imaginable, missionary, cowgirl and doggy style. Dollar pounded away at Monye's vagina, not taking her pleas into account. Finally, Monye's fat ass sat high in the air as she bit on the pillow. Dollar caught glimpses of Monye's asshole. It winked at him as he thrust in and out of her. He saw this as a personal invitation to violate her anus. He spat into her small opening, and combined that with Monye's bodily fluids that soaked his dick. Without warning, Dollar removed his dick from Monye's pussy then he rammed his dick inside her asshole.

"Ahhhhhh!!!" she screamed.

Monye let out shrieks and cries of sheer pain and discomfort. She was a virgin when it came to this. Monye had never engaged in anal sex before. She tried to wiggle off of Dollar's dick, but he wouldn't let her. He chased her up the bed until he was able to insert all of his manhood inside her. The snug fit of her asshole around his dick only excited Dollar. He pumped his dick in and out of her asshole with reckless abandon. Dollar got off on seeing young girls screaming and in pain, and the louder she screamed the more he enjoyed it. Dollar reached around and squeezed her tightly around the neck, he began choking Monye. Just as Monye was about to lose consciousness, Dollar suddenly climaxed and released his grip. Even the foul odor of shit couldn't stop Dollar from violating Monye.

He was a butthole bandit. He loved anal sex more than any other form of sex. And Monye's ass was unexplored territory which made the sex that much better. Dollar was a pervert, fucking virgins gave him some sick sense of pleasure. It was sadistic in a sense. Now Monye had come to experience it firsthand.

"That asshole was good." Dollar remarked. "We need to do that more often."

On the bed Monye laid paralyzed by pain. She heard Dollar but at the same time she didn't. Nothing he said seemed to matter at this time. The pain in her rectum was all she was worried about. As Dollar withdrew his dick from her asshole, shit began to freely ooze out. Soon the stench was overwhelming. Unable to take the smell, even Dollar had to abandon the room.

"Bitch git yo ass up! And clean up this motherfucking shit," he ordered Monye.

Suddenly, Monye sprung to life as she summoned the strength to get up off the bed and go to the bathroom and clean herself off. Inside, Monye used washcloths and toilet tissue, whatever she had at her disposal to freshen up. Still no matter what she did her asshole throbbed with pain. It served as a consistent reminder of the despicable act that had just taken place. Monye busied herself cleaning up.

Meanwhile downstairs, Dollar replenished his body with refreshment as he mentality prepared for the second half of his plan. Out of nowhere, Dollar reappeared. Monye never heard him re-enter the room. As she bent down, putting the finishing touches on her clean up session, Dollar crept up on her and punched her in the rib cage. The force of the blow knocked Monye to the floor, where she withered in pain.

"What I do?" she cried.

"Bitch, don't think I forgot. Your stupidity cost me money. You disobeyed the rules. What I tell you bout datin' black guys huh?" Dollar didn't wait for her reply, he pounced on Monye.

An onslaught of punches and kicks rained down on Monye's body. Everywhere Dollar saw an opening he seized the opportunity to land a heavy blow. With the preciseness of a boxer, Dollar badly beat Monye's body. He was careful to avoid striking her in the face since that might mess up his money. No man in his right mind wanted to turn a trick with a badly beaten prostitute. Monye would be like damaged goods, useable until she healed up.

"Stop Dollar. Please. That's enough," she pleaded.

"Bitch don't tell me when to stop! I orta stomp your brains out yo, fa fuckin' up my money," he swore.

The brutal beating had left Dollar winded. He doubled over in an effort to catch his breath. He threw a few more punches and kicks at Monye, but either they were weak or had no effect on her. She laid motionless on the floor.

Dollar began to worry, he thought he had killed her. "Git up bitch, you ain't hurt!" He gently kicked her until Monye began to stir. A sense of relief washed over him. He was so happy she was alive. Dollar thought he caught a body. But he had merely knocked her unconscious.

Dollar went back downstairs to retrieve a cup of ice cold water. Once he came back upstairs he dumped the water onto Monye's head. This really brought her around to the point that Dollar thought she was functional. He hovered above her waiting for Monye to climb to her knees. What Dollar didn't know was Monye wasn't as hurt as she appeared. She was playing possum.

"Bitch git yo ass up! I need some head hoe." Dollar's zipper made a loud sound in the scantily furnished room. Upon hearing this noise something suddenly snapped in Monye's mind. In one swift motion, Monye removed the pocket knife from her bra and blacked out stabbing Dollar repeatedly in his abdomen.

At first Dollar thought the blows Monye was hitting him with were punches. He had the audacity to laugh at her feeble attempt to put up a fight.

"If that's all you got bitch, then you in trouble?" he said as he let Monye reach her feet.

In Dollar's mind, he was really going to whip her ass now. How dare she hit her Daddy back? Just as Dollar was thinking about all the damage he was going to do, Monye lunged at him with the weapon. Dollar didn't bother to block what he thought was a punch; instead he tried to weave it. Unfortunately for him, he was a tad bit too slow. The knife found its mark, the jugular vein. Monye left it stuck in her victim's neck as she scrambled out of the room.

Dollar's confidence quickly disappeared when he realized he had been stabbed. Fear spread throughout his body, much like the fear he instilled in his hoes. It caused Dollar to panic. He pulled the small knife that protruded from his neck, free. Blood began to gush everywhere as he staggered out the room and collapsed in the hallway. Dollar's body hit the floor, making a loud thud.

Too scared to leave the house, Monye came back upstairs to investigate, once she didn't hear any more commotion. To her delight, she found the man responsible for her own personal hell, on the floor in a pool of blood, dead.

"Yeah, motherfucker. You finally got what you deserved! Suck ya dick, huh? Now look at you!" She mocked him.

Death wasn't good enough punishment for Dollar, at least not in Monye's book. She went downstairs to the kitchen and came back upstairs with a butcher knife, she began to mutilate the body. She pulled down Dollar's draws and with one swift motion, cut off his dick. Then she stuffed it into his mouth, she stood up and admired her work.

*Nigger explain that to your people* Monye thought as she exited the house.

In the blink of an eye an innocent child had become a killer. Monye laughed at the thought when, or if, the police discovered Dollar's corpse with a severed dick. She thought nothing of what she had done. In Monye's mind Dollar had it coming. If he didn't die by her hands, then surely it would be by someone else's. She took great pleasure in the act of murder, Monye knew that another girl would never suffer the same fate she endured, at least not at the hands of Dollar.

Monye didn't have a clue what she was going to do next. All she knew was she had to get the hell out of there. She opened the door and disappeared into the Baltimore landscape and it was as if nothing ever happened. Her destination, unknown.

# UNDER THE " L"

*Eric White*
Bronx, NY

## HANDS OFF, HANDS ON

The nearly empty Bx. Number 41 bus made the left off of Gun Hill Road, stopping in front of the Te-Amo smoke shop where a light crowd waited to board for their chauffeured ride to unknown locations. While up the street a small group of physically fit women in tights and sweats conversed in front of the Lucille Roberts gym about the vigorous Step class they had just completed. It was an unseasonably warm evening and the "Boys in Blue" also known as The New York City Police Department were out in full force, continuing to maintain order in the streets once bullied by murder-minded drug dealers and ruthless Jamaican gangs. On every other street corner, spanning from 211th Street to 241st Street, their police presence was evident and visually blatant on the infamous White Plains Road, previously known as the "Murder Mecca" of the North East Bronx. With the constant pressure of arrest and deportations of unruly foreign felons, the crime rate took a significant dip allowing local businesses to flourish again on the lucrative two-mile strip.

The moment Beauty and Kuntry pulled up, she jumped out of his BMW 7 series, slammed the door and adjusted her skirt, as she walked towards the tinted-glass doors of the lounge. With every step, she could feel the warmth of his jism beginning to stream downwards from between her legs. She despised that fat bastard and everything about him for all the anguish and pain that she was being forced to endure. This was the third time this week she'd had to allow Kuntry to have his perverted sexual way with her. She hated him with a passion and with every punishing down stroke he emitted into her body, her level of resentment for him grew ten fold.

Feeling morally disgusted and physically violated, she reached into her handbag and grabbed a handful of Kleenex to blot her tears and wipe away cum that now clung to her inner thighs that her thong panties could no longer contain.

*Dammit, I keep tellin' this muthfucka to stop nuttin' in me and he jus' refuses to listen. I swear if I ever come up pregnant I'll kill myself and take my child with me.*

"Umm, excuse me lil lady. What's up, you ain't got no words for me tanite? You jus' get out my car, slam my fuckin' door and walk away?" Kuntry said through the open window.

"Are you serious Kuntry?" she said with both hands on her hips. "What should I be sayin' to you? Have a good night? Thanks for the dick? I just don't get it! What more needs to be said? You got what you wanted and still that's not good enough! Well listen, I don't have nuthin' more to say to you. I was always told if you have nothing nice to say, then shut the fuck up. So you figure it out!" she barked as she turned and began walking away.

"Alright Beauty, you got that one. And it's cool. You ain't gotta say a word! But anyway, listen. I got some business ta go handle downtown, but I'll be back shortly. And when I'm done, I'ma swing pass here to pick you up and that smart ass mouth of yours and drop you da fuck home. I'll call Lorraine when I'm on my way, so don't have me out here waitin' on your ass like I see, you like to do, you hear me?" he said with a devilish grin as he drove off.

The way he touched her with his dirty lust sent her mind into a frenzy, making her chocolate brown skin crawl with hives that chewed on her flesh from the inside going out. When he would bathe the inner lips of her love with his tongue, she wished that somehow, someway he would suffocate and die from his animalistic oral greed. Just the thought of him gaining pleasure from her pain sickened her. The grunting and groaning sounds that he'd emit during their one-sided moments of ecstasy was enough to make her silently pray that God would find a reason to call her home, so she'd be eternally released from his hold. But as for now, she was trapped with no help in sight like a butterfly stuck in the web of a giant arachnid, struggling to break free before becoming devoured whole by its hungry occupant.

In Kuntry's twisted mind, he knew he'd be up in that tight pussy later on that night and the night after, for that matter. The thought of her being bent over while he dug out her sweet box from her blind side, made the hairs on the back of his neck stand up and rise to attention. He loved the situation he was in, along with the power and the control, he had over Beauty. And silently, he praised her brother Jha'ton for making that foolish mistake he made that night, allowing him to be in this position. The little attitudes and feistiness that Beauty gave off to him whenever she spoke only enticed him more, adding fuel to his already burning fire for her. But she just didn't know it.

It didn't even bother him in the least when he looked into the rearview mirror and saw her giving him both middle fingers as he pulled off. He knew he was the high man here, and Beauty had to do whatever he wanted, whenever he wanted, or else!

Before she entered the lounge, Beauty stood outside taking a moment to calm her nerves and gather her composure. She couldn't believe that Kuntry, the same man who used to run the number joint with her dad was now disrespecting his name and violating his only daughter. She couldn't fathom how he could do this to her after breaking bread in her home with her family so many times. The secret he held over her head was ruining her once peaceful life and turning it into a living nightmare that she wanted so bad to wake up from. And to make matters worse Damian was starting to ask questions about why he wasn't seeing her that much anymore. She loved him so much and it was killing her inside that she couldn't tell him what was going on. Damian would never understand, and she wasn't willing to lose her man over this. Not now. Not ever. She wished her dad was still here to guide and protect her, but he was gone and Kuntry was taking full advantage of his absence.

"Hey Beauty!" said Lorraine, from behind the bar as she came through the doors.

"Girl, the phone been blowin' up in here for you all nite. Damian been callin' askin' if I'd seen you or if you were comin' in. He sounded like it may be important, so give em' a call as soon as you get settled in okay, sweetie?" Lorraine saw that Beauty was visibly upset and knew right away it had to do with Kuntry.

"Will do Lorraine! I'll call him in a few," Beauty dully replied, as she walked pass, dabbing her eyes with her crumpled tissue.

Lorraine kind of knew what was going on between the two and hated what Kuntry was doing to her. She didn't have all the facts, but she knew whatever the reason Beauty was sleeping with him, it couldn't have been on her own free will. As much as Lorraine wanted to intervene, she wouldn't dare. It was Kuntry's bar and she needed her job to support the two young mouths she had at home. She knew Kuntry was a bastard, and had a very nasty demeanor. It would be nothing for him to put her out on her ass if she opened her mouth without thinking twice about it, kids or not.

Up until the day he died, Beauty's dad worked hard making sure she and her younger brother Jha'ton stayed focused. He was big on education and always preached on how minorities, especially black folks, needed to be educated and have their own businesses in this white man's world. He schooled them as best he could about the streets and the characters that inhibited them. And he never glazed or sugar coated anything. That's what Beauty respected and admired most about her dad. He was real and always kept it funky no matter what.

"Real Eyes, Realize, Where Real Lies" was the motto by which he lived and once explained to her. Beauty understood just what the words meant. He was a good man who hustled hard to provide all the basic necessities for his broken family, and he only wanted the best for his children since he was all they had left. His plan was to make sure they were well prepared for life's nasty challenges and that they didn't end up like him—hustling' all his life or becoming even worse, a dope fiend like their no good mother.

Her mother left when Beauty was about seven. Her mother felt that her younger, drug dealing jump-off was a better look for her financially than being at home raising her own family. So without warning she packed up her shit and moved to Florida to be with him. There were no calls made to her family to check-in or even so much as a card in the mail for their birthdays or holidays. She just removed herself from her husband and children's lives and went on as if they never existed. It was a difficult adjustment not having her around anymore, but they managed and continued on with their father in place, playing both parental roles.

Before their mother left though, she was fighting a head to head battle with her own personal demons. She'd developed a heroin addiction which they knew played a huge role in her disappearance. Three years later, around Beauty's tenth birthday, her mother was found dead at dude's home in Miami, sitting on the toilet with a hypodermic needle still stuck in her arm. Her dad, although stressed about having to raise two kids on his own, never swayed. He did what he had to in order to keep the family tight. He possessed no real form of education but when it came to street knowledge, he was a Rhodes Scholar and a great businessman.

After doing the number running thing for many years, he and Kuntry found a location and opened up a social lounge on White Plains Road in the Bronx which they named "The Labyrinth". The name was chosen as a reminder to all the obstacles that were placed before him and that he'd conquered or had overcome. The lounge did excellent and with the money coming in, Beauty was able to follow one of her dreams and attend John Jay College, where she pursued her degree in Law and Forensic Science.

When the cancer began eating away at Beauty's dad, everything started spiraling downhill quickly. He became very weak and could no longer take care of himself, so she had him moved from Jacobi Medical Center in the Bronx, to St. Luke's Hospital downtown, which was closer to her school. This way she could be with him daily between classes, and now take care of him. Before he passed, he told Beauty where his money was stashed, and transferred the apartment lease so it would be in her name. He also gave her instructions on collecting his portion of the proceeds that the lounge was bringing in. He requested several meetings with Kuntry as well, but of course he never showed.

In Kuntry's mind, he couldn't wait for the nigga to die so he'd be the sole owner of "The Labyrinth". He had his own plans in mind of what it was to become next.

When Beauty asked Kuntry if he was going to see her dad

on any day, he always had something to do or just didn't go. Basically he was saying "Fuck Ya Father" without actually saying the words and she knew it.

Three weeks later, Beauty's father had succumbed to his illness and everything went awry from that point. Her brother dropped out of Evander Childs and started hustling with some greasy, bottom of the barrel losers up in Edenwald Projects. And he rarely came home at night. He began getting into trouble and racking up on minor charges of loitering and disorderly conduct, and Beauty knew it was only a matter of time before those minors would become majors.

Kuntry, too, had changed and became very disrespectful to her. He would frequently make sideways comments out his mouth and many sick references in regards to Beauty's physical attributes. Now every word of out his mouth was about "her fat ass *this* or her big titties *that*", and what he'd do with her if she ever gave him some pussy. She thwarted off all of his sexual advances, but he continued to be very persistent and demanding.

He'd tried to get at Beauty in any way he possibly could, and when all else failed, he stopped giving Beauty her dad's take from the lounge proceeds in hopes that she would give in but she still refused. So to make ends meet, Beauty took on a job as a beautician at her friend's salon, "Hair It Is" on 145th Street in Harlem.

Months had gone by since Beauty buried her dad and her life was beginning to gain a bit of normalcy. She was still managing to get by on the money her father had left behind and the salon was in full swing, so she maintained a steady source of income. Kuntry continued to hold out on the loot from the lounge, but it didn't even matter to her anymore. And unbelievably, he paid for the whole funeral service without her having to say a word. With him footing the bill, she was able to give her dad a fabulous send off for his return back to the essence, complete with a tombstone displaying his motto for all to embrace.

Beauty hadn't seen her brother since the services and decided to let him be his own man and make his own choices. He was too far gone to be helped, but she still prayed for him in hopes that he, too, would find himself and straighten up his out-of-control life. But then it happened.

While working at the salon one afternoon she received a very disturbing phone call, one that would change her life and set the wheels in motion on a crash course with turmoil and despair.

"Hair It Is, this is Beauty speaking. How may I help you?"

"Hey Beauty. What's up? It's Kuntry," he said in his faded southern accent.

"Kuntry?" she asked puzzled. "Yeah, what's up? And why you calling me at my job?"

"Hold on now, before you start gettin' all fly out da mouf'. I know you all busy doin' hair and shit, but we need to talk. Come outside. I'm parked across the street in the B.P. gas station."

"Talk? What me and you need to talk about Kuntry? And how you get my damn job number?" she said, annoyed by his call.

"Neva mind how I got the damn number. What cha you need ta do is stop whateva the fuck you doin' and bring ya ass outside and come see me," he barked back.

"Wait a minute. Who you talkin' to like that Kuntry? I'm at my place of employment and I don't have time for your B.S. today or on any day. Listen, I'm hangin' up and this conversation is ova'. I got work to do," she said through her tightly clenched teeth.

"Alright, you can hang up. But know dis' before you go lil lady. If you don't get out here in the next fifteen minutes, ya lil brutha ass goin' ta jail. The clock startin' right da fuck now," he said, before hanging up on her.

*Fifteen minutes huh? He got alot of damn nerve speakin' to me like that, like I'm his god dam child or sumthin'. I swear, Jha'ton betta not have done no dumb shit out there that's gonna cost him his freedom.*

Beauty hadn't seen Jha'ton since the funeral and just figured he was out there doing him, hustling hard and getting his money right. With Kuntry making threats that placed her brother and jail in the same sentence, she knew it must be something serious. As much as she didn't want any conversation with this man, she knew this meeting was definitely mandatory.

"Nadine! I'll be back. I need to step outside for a few minutes. You want anything from the store while I'm out there"? Beauty asked.

"Nah B. I'm cool but bring Monica back a big Pepsi. You know that bitch be needin' her caffeine fix to keep her ass calm up in hea'," said Nadine, pointing at Monica with her curling iron.

"Alright, will do!" said Beauty, chuckling as she walked out the door.

A few minutes had passed as Kuntry anxiously waited to see if Beauty would actually show. He'd already planned what was going to be said. It was to be a real simple trade off, a favor for a favor. It would be more beneficial to him but she too would gain from the deal..She would get to keep her brother. Her time limit wasn't up, but the anticipation was killing him so he picked up his cell phone off of the passenger seat and began dialing Beauty's number again, but then he spotted her across the street awaiting clearance so that she could cross over.

*Goddam, what a difference a little time can make* Kuntry thought to himself. Beauty had definitely grown into her name. She was always a very pretty girl which was how she adapted that name. Her dad used to call her "Beautiful Lady" damn near from the time she began to take her first steps. For anyone to call her by her government name of Carla was unheard of and they may not have gotten a response had they done it.

Now all grown up, her pretty face was now gorgeous and her previously nice figure had upgraded to thick and solid. Her hair had gotten longer, he could tell by the way it was draped over her shoulders. Her breasts, even from a distance, looked full and firm like they wanted to be set free from the tight fitting button-up shirt she donned. Beauty now looked more like a model than a beautician and a student. Kuntry couldn't take his eyes off of her. It was like he was seeing her for the first time all over again. The closer she got, the more he wanted her and couldn't wait to put his plans into action.

When she got in the car, she kept it very impersonal. She didn't say a word. Her eyes should have told him the whole story of what she was thinking. *Ok, you sorry muthafucka. I'm here, what do you want?*

Before he could get a word in, she felt her cell phone vibrating. She looked down to see if it may have been Nadine calling, possibly needing her or maybe wanting something from the store. But it wasn't, it was Damian once again trying to speak with his woman and once again being ignored.

"Well, hello to you, too, Beauty. Long time no see. Wow, you lookin' just like a younger version of your mother," said Kuntry.

"Yeah, Yeah Kuntry. Thanks but we not here to discuss her or anyone else. What you know about my brother and what did he do?" Beauty demanded.

"Ya know what? You're absolutely right," Kuntry said. He began speaking and informed Beauty in detail, about everything he'd witnessed on a late night three weeks ago. Kuntry was in the midst of getting a blow job in his car from a young Puerto

Rican girl he'd scooped up from a bar party on Boston road. While he was getting rocked behind his tinted windows, a dude was getting rocked in the K.F.C. parking lot across the street. At the time, he didn't know it was Jha'ton and Poundz putting in that work but he knew whoever it was, they were beating and stabbing the bullshit out of guy. Come to find out, the victim was a rival hustler from 219th street who'd tried to put his workers out in Edenwald on Poundz's time without permission. They had followed him from Cafe Lous' down the block and found an opportunity to get him and did. It wasn't until they got in their car and drove past Kuntry that he noticed them. Instead of trying to be inconspicuous after doing something of that nature, they drove past him windows down, music blasting like your average inexperienced thug would do. It wasn't until three days later while reading the New York Post's "NYPD Daily blotter" section, did he realize that the man they assaulted died and the murderers were being sought.

Beauty's phone buzzed again. She ignored Damian's call a second time since she couldn't believe what she was hearing. Kuntry presented her with the news clipping but that didn't prove to her that it was Jha'ton. Was this just another pack of sordid lies put together in an effort to further damage her already torn family? Was there really any validity to these allegations? She was so confused and had no way of immediately verifying if Jha'ton actually did what Kuntry had claimed.

"Ok Kuntry, I heard you out, but what is it that you want from me? I haven't heard from my brother in months and I have my own life to live," she said, trying to sound unconcerned.

"Well now lil lady let me see!" he replied as he clasped his hands rubbing his palms together. "We seem to have a situation here that can become one of two things: win, win or win lose. The outcome is totally in your hands."

"Listen, Kuntry. I'm at work and I don't have time to play

these guessing word games, speak your mind. Once again, what is it that I can do to make this thing go away," she said hesitantly.

"Ok Beauty, I'll make this real simple and cut to the chase. If you want me to forget about what I know, I'm gonna need your assistance. You'll need to start putting in some of that same quality time with me that you be giving to that boyfriend of yours. I want the same thing he be getting and just maybe, if its good enough I'll forget about what I saw the other night. The choice is yours!"

Feeling numb behind the news she'd just received, she exited his car and walked away without saying a word. Beauty knew she had to find Jha'ton to confirm if he'd really committed this heinous act. And if he did do it, how could she avoid Kuntry's request of sexual favors for his silence. Her mind was in a state of confusion but this had to be dealt with, and dealt with soon. Beauty knew how grimy Kuntry could be, and it wouldn't be long before he'd be contacting her again. Beauty's cell phone went off yet a third time. Damian was calling and still, he got no answer from Beauty.

Kuntry sat in his car pleased with how the conversation went. He knew that right now Beauty had no wins here. He'd give her a day or two to figure things out before he started applying the real pressure. The day was already off to a good start in his mind, and he smiled to himself as he started his engine to pull off. As he did, he looked in the direction of the salon and thought to himself of how good that pussy was going to be and how he couldn't wait till she got back to him.

As he made the right out of the gas station heading towards the 145th Street bridge, so did the Maxima that had been following him for the past week.

# THUG PASSION

*"Anonymous"*

**San Francisco**

When Dante left the room I was still on my knees. My face was still wet from the explosion that came from his dick when I finished sucking it. His weed sack and Philly blunts were still on the glass table, not far from the black leather couch he jumped off of when he heard pounding on the door. Dante was scared for reason only. He didn't want anyone to find out about us. The two of us having sex was suppose to be kept on the down low. This was our little secret. *Huh! If his friends, better yet his girl, could see him now.*

Who would have thought a simple little knock at my front door would have scared Dante shitless. While he ran for cover, I wiped off my face. I stepped around the clothes that were spread out over the zebra pattern on the carpet and moved to the peephole. *Damn, it was Joss.* I ran over to the pile of clothes, picked up Dante's Roca Wear boxers, jeans and shirt, things from his wardrobe that I knew she would recognize, if she would so happen to gain entrance to the house. I opened the bedroom door and threw them onto my king sized sleigh bed where Dante was resting across the black and white comforter, butt assed naked waiting for me.

"Who is it?" He asked nervously.

"It's Joss! Now what are you going to do?"

"Fuck you mean what am I going to do?" Dante repeated.

"You better do something! Whatever you do, don't let her ass up in here."

Dante jumped up and grabbed his underwear, as soon as he put one foot inside, his cell phone started singing it's "I'm so Hood" ring tone.

"That's her now," he said.

"Well answer the motherfucker," I said going into the bathroom, to rinse my mouth and wash Dante's kids off of my face. I stared in the mirror while Dante talked to his Barbie doll looking girlfriend, who is also my best friend. As I washed my face I overheard Dante lying to Joss for the hundredth time. I couldn't help but shake my head in disgust. I was wondering when or if ever this nigga was going to be a real man and tell his girl about us. I always felt it ain't what you do, it's how you do it.

Unable to bear another word of their pathetic conversation, I turned my head to the side and stared at my profile. I needed to get to the barber shop to let Kingston, that fine ass Jamaican brother with the King Kong dick taper me up. My little black curls were still tight and shining at the top of my head, but my line wasn't distinct like I liked it. I ran my hands down my back and looked at my hand. Small hands for a small man, but small hands made it easy for me to grip those big assed dicks I loved to put my mouth on. Especially Dante's he likes when I wrap both hands around it, and move them in opposite directions, while I allow him to work my mouth like he worked Joss's pussy. That nigga big dick stretches my mouth to the limit. Still I love every minute of it.

I didn't feel the least bit guilty about leaving my friend Joss standing at my front door. If she was handling her business in bed then her man wouldn't have to stray. Not if Dante was getting all that he needed at home.

"You done?" I asked.

Quickly, Dante put his finger up to his lips to quiet me.

I walked back into the bedroom and kneeled in front of

Dante. I held onto the elastic waistband and held the boxers open, and Dante slid his foot inside. As I pulled the shorts over his knees they trembled. I softly touched his knee cap and kissed it. Dante placed his hand on my cheek and forcefully pushed my head away. He hated all of that kissing and touching. He said kissing made him feel guilty. To him it was more intimate that oral sex. Besides that I think it was the fact that the act was with another man. I knew it was because he didn't want to admit that he was truly attracted to me and possibly falling in love. I have that effect on men. See what bomb ass head will do for you?

"I don't know, I ain't seen that nooka since Wednesday," Dante said. "He's probably getting his hair cut or something, you know how he is. That Miss Thang keeps her shit together... oh, you at his crib? The car is out there? I don't know baby girl, did you call his phone?"

Dante was a trip. You would think that the hardest brother in the hood, by way of Hunters Point, wouldn't carry himself like this. This gun slinging, gang banging, set tripping ass nigga was an undercover punk. Although Dante was fine as the day was long. He had smooth chocolate skin, thick braids and a swagger that was matched by few. Dante Simms was the shit, six foot six inches tall, thick and ripped from all that working out and busting his gun to keep up the "image". Dante could hold his with the best of them. His sagging jeans, oversized t-shirts, Timberland boots that he never laced to the top, and fitted caps made him look the part of the straightest brotha you ever met.

His Lincoln Navigator, sitting on twenty four inch Rozzi chrome rims, was the talk of the town. Everybody around town believed Dante was a big time hustler, copping "ki's" and moving weight but that was the furthest thing from the truth. Dante Simms had secrets and I knew most of them. The nigga was fronting. His grandmother had passed away and left him a couple of dollars in her will. He immediately went 'crazy' and blew it all on a ride and some clothes. So now he was mooching off my home girl Joss. This bitch is fucking stupid, she is so in love with the dick, she can't even see that Dante's using her ass. I must admit I did try to tell her on numerous occasions.

As soon as Dante mentioned my phone I ran to the living room to get grab it off of the table. The ringer was on the highest setting and the ring tone was Beyonce's screaming ass singing "De ja vu. I silenced the phone and returned to the bedroom.

"Yeah, yeah, just call me when you get finished," Dante said.

"She leaving?" I asked. I sat on the edge of the bed and crossed my legs. "Well is she leaving?"

"Yeah man, she's gone."

"Well now can we finish what we started?" I asked greedily.

"Nah, I'm good." Dante said. "I gotta go. How the fuck could you be thinking about some dick at a time like this? Bitch, git your mind right."

"Please Dante. Don't do me like this."

"I said no!" He snapped.

The anger in Dante's voice made me finally realize that this nigga was serious. I didn't want to push my luck and run the risk of him hurting me in here. Physically I was no match for him.

Quickly I changed the subject. I twisted my one hundred and thirty pound body toward the bathroom to spray myself with the new cologne, I picked up from the mall.

"Come here D...smell this."

Dante walked toward me, and I held out my wrist. He inhaled the scent and smiled.

"That's nice Mari," He said.

"You like it daddy?" I asked. I tugged at the elastic on the boxers, and rested my hand inside. I leaned in closer to

Dante's body and placed the side of my face on his neck.

"Do you like it daddy?" I whispered.

Dante didn't bother to reply, he just shoved me away. I flew across the room like a rag doll until I landed harmlessly on the floor. Suddenly I began to cry my eyes out. Dante had hurt my feeling more than anything.

"Man, what the fuck is wrong with you?" Dante asked. "Nigga git yo punk ass up. You ain't even hurt…Oh, my god I swear, all faggots are crazy!!!! Something is definitely wrong! Y'all elevator don't go up to the top floor…."

As I lay there crying my eyes out in front of my lover, I had to admit to myself Dante was one hundred percent correct in his assessment of me. *I am crazy. Crazy in love with his ass.*

*****

When Dante left I immediately called the Barbie. Joss was my best friend. We met when she came into the salon to get her "already too blonde" hair highlighted once again. Her regular stylist was on vacation, so I was given the duty. People wondered why I chose to work in a white hair salon, when so many sisters in the hood needed a good stylist. White girls are where the money is. Even Dante knew that.

When Joss walked into La Salle, I did a double take, and I don't even look at women like that. Joss is gorgeous. She could give any of the top models a run for their money if she wanted to. Joss wasn't your average "white girl". She had a pear shaped figure, and every outfit she wore showed it. She had long blond hair which I layered every two weeks. Her blue-gray eyes changed to hazel depending on what time of the day it was. Joss visited a tanning salon twice a week, which was too often if you asked me, but she insisted it was the 'norm' for them. If it wasn't for that golden hair she might be mistaken for Hispanic, or maybe even a light skinned sister. Perfectly kept makeup and nails were a must. My girl had it going on. What attracted me to Jossilynn Spears was her personality. She was easily one of the most admirable women I knew. Joss went out of her way to help others. Sometimes too far, like when she helped Dante get off on that murder charge. He owed her, but he didn't love her.

"Hey girl, what the hell is up? You have been blowing up my phone all day." I said when Joss answered her phone. "You want to go eat? Hell yes I'm hungry as hell, absolutely famished Jossy." I walked over to the window and stared at the view of the Ocean. "Alright I'm getting ready now; I'll meet you at Chino Basil's. Bye girl."

## Dante

I ain't no fucking fagot. I just like getting my dick sucked, and Mari is good as hell. I close my eyes and just imagine that it is Melyssa Ford down there, maybe even that chic from the Flavor of Love TV show, Deelishis. I think of anybody I can. I keep my muthafuckin eyes closed the whole time, because I don't want to accidentally look down there and see Mari's pretty assed light brown eyes looking up at me while he has my entire dick in his mouth. Naw, fuck that I ain't no faggot. Mari is the only man I have ever been with in my life, and how he talked me into that shit, I'll never know.

Joss was out of town on visiting her family, she hadn't told them about me yet. She couldn't tell them that she was seeing a black man. Omari came over to check on the fucking cat. Joss knows I don't give a fuck about her cat. I hate that fucking cat. But Joss treats that cat like family. P-Hil is her name. The motherfucker is fat as hell, from all that boiled chicken Joss feeds her, she could have gone weeks without eating. Still with Joss gone, Omari was named her official guardian.

I'd just finished a strenuous workout at the gym. I stopped at Joss's house to get the shirt I'd left last weekend. It showed of my physique which made the bitches to go crazy. Once I got there I decided to chill for awhile. I poured Hennessey and coke into one of the glasses with the gold bottom that Joss always used for my drinks. I took off my gym shorts, and slipped off my socks and sports sandals. After I took off my drawers and wife beater, I stepped into the Jacuzzi. I set my drink on the platform and rested my head against the edge the same way that Joss did, when we chilled together after a fuck session.

The Hennessey and coke started to take effect after the fourth glass. I was feeling good. I closed my eyes and let the

*Hood₂Hood*          189

music soothe me. I jerked my head forward when I heard keys jingling inside of the house. I thought it was a burglar or something. This nigga Omari was the furthest thing from my mind. I swear.

"Yo, who the fuck is that?" I yelled. "Joss is that you?"

"It's not Joss mother fucker. It's the one and only Mari!"

I peeked out the door, with a towel wrapped around my ass just to make sure it was him. This dude looked just like a bitch. He was wearing a light pink shirt and some tight little jeans that made his ass look like a woman's. Two gold hoops in each ear as always, and fucking lip gloss.

"What the hell are you doing here Dante?" He said.

Now his ass was standing in the doorway with his hands on his hips. I looked him over. *Are those fucking heels on his boots?* I thought to myself.

"What the fuck you mean what am I doing here, what are you doing here?"

"I came to check on P-Hil, you know, make sure she had something to eat, I know your ass ain't going to feed her Dante," Mari said.

Why do faggots always make people's name's long? Like a song or something. The way Mari says Daaahntaaayy gets on my nerves. Now he's in the kitchen, I'm watching him from the patio. He's moving around all fast and feminine, clackty clacking those heels everywhere. What is wrong with him?

"You want something to eat Dante?"

"Why? Are you going to me cook something?"

"Yeah I wouldn't have asked if I wasn't. You know Barbie has some good shit in here. Why let it go to waste?"

"Bet. If you cooking, I'm eating."

My workout had left me hungrier than a motherfucker. In fact I was so hungry I was willing to over look the fact that a faggot was preparing my meal. And I have to admit Mari can cook his ass off, I'm sure he got that from his mama. Hell, Mari probably got everything from his mama, that pretty assed cocoa butter complexion, those high assed cheekbones, pretty eyes, pretty hair. Mari is pretty; I can see why he is gay. He should have been a woman.

When Mari finished cooking I still hadn't gotten my drunk ass out of that water. I wasn't going to either, the jets pushing water against my tense muscles felt too good.

"Get your wrinkled ass out of the water Dante."

Mari was standing beside the Jacuzzi with one hand holding my plate, pizza boy style and one hand on his hip. He was looking at my dick flapping in the water I could feel it. I covered myself with my hands. Right then and there a warning sign should have popped up in my mind, telling me to proceed with caution. But it didn't.

"Nah man, I think I'll just chill."

"What? You don't want me to see your lil dick Dante? You ain't holding." Omari commented. "Anyway you ain't got shit I ain't either had or seen before."

I replied, "I don't know about all that but you ain't about to get your jollies off on me. You ain't going to reckless eyeball my dick. Now would you please get the fuck out of here and let me get dressed."

I watched as Mari turned around and headed back to the kitchen with the food. Once he was gone I stepped out of the Jacuzzi still covering myself with my hands. I grabbed a towel from the storage cabinet wrapped it around my waist, and went to join Mari, where he'd placed one of Joss's candles in the center of the table. I was more hungry than drunk. So much so that I never realized how scantily clad I was. I just wanted to get my eat on.

I got right to it, cutting my steak into manly portions, and wolfing it down. Meanwhile across from me Mari chewed his food with a woman like etiquette. He chewed small portions of food well and swallowed them. Frequently he used a paper towel to wipe his mouth. The nigga posture was even perfect. He sat with his legs crossed, straight up with his back against the chair. And of course the fork dangled from his broken wrist. Mari was a true faggot indeed.

"What you looking at me like that for Dante? What did I do to you?" Omari suddenly asked.

*'Damn, I hadn't realized that my inspection of this punk was so obvious'.*

"My bad! I was looking at you but I was thinking of something else." I explained. "That ever happened to you? You know you looking in a person's direction and suddenly you get lost in a thought...anyway, say man, have you ever thought about modeling?"

"Boy please, I aint tall enough," Mari said standing up. "You want another drink?"

Mari reached for my glass and I handed it to him. He took my glass over to the bar and filled it to the top with ice and my drink of choice. He sashayed back to the table and crossed his legs when he sat down.

"You don't have to be tall, you could do head shots or something like that. Catalogues and shit. Know what I'm saying?"

"Why you think I'm cute Dante?" Mari laughed.

"Stop playing! I don't get down like that..." I told him. "...Nah man, I was just saying. Just making conversation that's all. Ain't got no plans with a man."

The dinner with Mari was one of the most uncomfortable nights of my life. I watched him hard. He reminded me of Prince, his petite size, and feminine facial features and movements were exactly like the singer's. I placed my hand over my dick whenever he stood beside me or reached across my body to pick up my plate from the table. My dick moved. The shit was getting hard by the second. I couldn't believe it. But it was I swear to God. I turned my head out of shame. I was trying to fight the feeling. I couldn't even look at him now. What the fuck was happening to me? I had to be drunk; the Hennessey was fucking with me. Yeah that was fucking it. It had to be the alcohol because I ain't no faggot.

"You want another drink Dante?" Mari asked.

"Hell, yeah. I'll take another one of these shits." I replied, looking for something to take away the lustful feelings.

I held my glass up and Mari took it from my hand. I looked at his fingernails. They were perfectly manicured just like Joss kept hers, except he didn't have the French tip. Just clear polish.

"You haven't sipped on nothing Mari," I said.

"Are you asking me to have a drink with you Dante?"

"You could. We are in here chilling. You are too hyper man. Sit ya ass down and relax." I said.

Mari cleared the rest of the dishes, and walked back to the patio with two drinks. He sat down and crossed his legs.

"How the fuck do you walk in them boots?"

"It's easy. I've been wearing heels since I was in high school. I'm a small person. Heels make me feel big Dante."

"You don't have to say my name after ever sentence that comes out of your mouth dawg."

Mari took a sip from his glass and smiled. "I like the way Dante sounds coming from my lips," he said.

I put my hand over my dick again. I hoped that Mari didn't see me. The way he said my name, had my dick rock hard this time. My dick was poking through the towel. I picked up my glass, chugged the rest of the alcohol and slid a piece of ice into my mouth and sucked hard. I needed to cool off.

"Want some more?" Mari asked.

I nodded and held up my glass. I watched Mari twist toward the kitchen. His ass was nicer than Joss's. Don't get me wrong Joss has a banging body, but Mari's shit from behind is damn near perfect. How the hell a man's ass could even conform to that shape was beyond me. The shit was unnatural. No wonder Mari was turning out so many brothers. He had a reputation around the District. Men you would never expect to be kissing dicks were letting Mari suck and fuck theirs. Husbands and fathers, preachers and teachers even a few of the neighborhood dope boys were rumored to have succumbed to Mari's charms. Not me. Omari wasn't *that* good. All the liquor in the world couldn't make me go out like that. Nah, I loved pussy too much.

Mari returned to the table and I put my hand over my dick once again and tried to stick it between my thighs. He went in there and took off his shirt. His little ass was sitting in front of me in a black wife beater and those tight assed jeans. He crossed his legs and grabbed his thin gold chain.

"What Dante? You keep looking at me like I did something to you? Let me guess, you staring off in space again? Right? Come on Dante keep it real." Mari asked, running his index finger back and forth underneath his chain.

I ignored his suggestion. I continued to talk about what I want to talk about.

"What did you take your shirt off for?"

"I'm hot! Motherfucker what do you think?" Mari said.

"Hey, watch ya mouth. I ain't going to be too many more of those."

"Well don't be asking me no shit like that. What do you think? I'm trying to do seduce you or something? I already told you, you ain't nobody Dante. You just another nigga to me. I ain't pressed about you."

"Seduce me?" I chugged some more Henn and laughed. "Dawg... ain't no seduction here."

"I said that already Dante."

"Well lemme say it again. Just so you know."

I repositioned my dick under the towel and stood up. "I'm

going to take a quick shower. I'll probably stay here tonight. No sense in driving all the way across town tipsy. I don't need no DWI."

"I'm going to clean the kitchen, and then I'll leave," Mari said.

"Whatever man, knock yourself out. Take your time."

What the hell did I say that for? I just gave this punk a free pass to stay a little longer. When I walked out of the bedroom, this diva brother had cleaned the kitchen *and* made a snack. I walked to the living room and took a seat on the white extended armchair which Joss called a chaise. I was feeling the Henn a little too much, because when Mari took mango slices, strawberries, and grapes from the tray, placed them into a bowl and handed it to me, I accidentally grabbed his hand.

"You are touching me Dante," he said. Mari put his hand on his hip and smiled. "Like you want me or something."

"Nah, my bad! I don't want you. All I want is conversation. Let's talk." I said.

Mari sat at the end of the chaise and crossed his legs. "Talk Dante."

"How do you...you know? You know what I'm saying?"

"No."

"Come on Mari, how do you put your lips around a dick, dawg?"

"What do you mean Dante? The same way you put your lips on nasty pussy lips that bleed once a month and discharge all kind of bacteria. That's how. Easy!"

"So what do you do with *your* shit, while you are doing somebody? Huh?"

"What do you do with your shit when you are doing Joss?" Mari said.

"Alright what about when you are finished, what happens after that? Does one person get theirs and then it's the other man's turn? How do you get satisfied? I don't mean no disrespect but I've always been curious brother."

"What happens when you are finished with Joss?"

"These ain't no rhetorical questions. They require answers. Are you going to answer my questions or what man?"

"You want me to show you instead?" Mari said.

I shifted in the chaise and shifted again. I rubbed my hand over my chest and then sat up.

"You or no other punk in this whole wide world could ever get my dick hard dawg." I lied.

"Your shit has getting hard all night Dante. I'm a man remember? I know."

Mari caught me off guard with that statement. I didn't think he had noticed. Still I played it off anyway.

When Mari's small fingers accidentally grazed my leg I didn't flinch. He did it again, this time it was on purpose. I looked at his feminine ass sitting on the edge with his legs crossed and closed my eyes. For some reason I couldn't wait for him to wrap his thin lips around my dick. The anticipation was killing me.

Closing my eyes was the cue Mari needed. He uncrossed his legs and moved to the bottom of the chaise. When his warm hands touched the bottom of my feet I opened my eyes for one fifth of a second. His hands were soft. Mari massaged my feet like a professional. I opened my eyes and lifted my head to the ceiling when he gently placed my big toe into his mouth. Mari's tongue swirled around the tip and I almost came. I could wait for him to swirl it around the tip of my dick. Mari bobbed up and down on my toe until I couldn't take the shit anymore. I grabbed his chin and stood up.

"Open your mouth," I ordered him.

I pulled down my shorts with Mari's chin still in one hand. I used my legs to push the shorts down my leg and held my dick with my free hand. "Open your mouth bitch nigga."

Mari opened his mouth and I forced my dick into it. I held Mari's chin until he wet me to my satisfaction.

"Hurry up," I whispered as Mari's head bobbed back and forth. "Hurry the fuck up."

I closed my eyes again when Mari wrapped both of his soft hands around me and slowly turned them from left to right in opposite directions while he bobbed back and forth softly sucking my head. My toes curled and my stomach tightened. I wanted to fuck Mari's mouth hard now. I grabbed his head and pushed my dick in and out until I heard him gag. I opened my eyes and slowly pulled out. When Mari wiped his mouth with his hand and stood up I saw his dick print through those tight assed jeans.

The minute I came I felt like a sucker. I wanted to get as far away from Mari as possible. I promised myself that something like this would never happen again. But it did. Over and over again. Still I don't give a fuck what nobody says, I'm not gay. I'm just letting the faggot suck on my dick.

## Joss

When I moved to San Francisco two years ago I was just looking for a change of scenery, a change of pace, something different. I never expected to meet my best friend Mari, or the love of my life, Dante. Mari is definitely different from any of my girlfriends I had in the past and Dante is unquestionably different from any other man I'd previously dated. I never dated a "real" black man before. I'd been approached on several occasions, but the pursuers never appealed to me, but it was something about Dante that had me hooked from the start. Maybe it was his 'thug appeal' as Mari would say.

Coming from Hollywood hills I didn't get a chance to deal with many black men. At boarding school I heard a lot of rumors, the obvious of course was how big a black man's dick is. This was a rumor I was dying to either confirm or dispel. It would take months for me to get my chance. But it did happen.

One night on a camping trip, while the rest of my classmates were asleep I followed a black guy into the woods. Where he was suppose to be letting nature take its course. But behind the tree, in a moonlight night I could see he was jerking off. So of course I offered my assistance. If I wasn't in the closet then Brian definitely was. They say it takes one to know one, I knew Brian was gay the day we first met in the library.

I did Brian and then Brian did me. I must say in Brian's case it wasn't true what they said about Black guys. I was disgusted when I found out he wasn't packing at all which led me to believe that he wasn't one hundred percent black. It wasn't until I met Dante did I realize that the big dick thing wasn't a myth after all.

My father was a big time Hollywood film producer, who shall remain anonymous; he never accepted the fact that I was gay. When I went to Brazil for my sex change operation, he really flipped his wig. We didn't speak for damn near five years. My mother was the go between relaying messages for the two of us. He banished me from the house, but his financial support never stopped. Sometimes I found our arrangement odd. Still I never questioned it. I'm not one to look a gift horse in the mouth.

In my quest to find the right atmosphere suitable to my new lifestyle, I chose to move to San Francisco, for obvious reasons. In gay circles it's known as the place to be. Flamboyant parties and parades all year, San Francisco was definitely the place for me.

I had to make a decision and make it soon. Lately Mari has been pestering me to tell Dante that I used to be a man. I think he's just jealous that I have somebody who loves me and he's just whoring around. Regardless, I must admit he does have a point, but I love Dante and he loves me, so gender, race, economic position shouldn't matter. Love conquers all right? The truth is I'm scared. Not of what Dante might do to me, although that has crossed my mind. I'm really scared I'll lose Dante forever if he finds out. I know one thing I better tell him before Mari opens his big mouth and spills the beans.

The drive from LA to San Francisco wasn't bad at all. Besides thinking about my reconciliation with my father, I pondered my future with Dante. I made up my mind tonight I was going to tell him the truth. I hoped like hell he was ready for it.

When I pulled up to my condo, I immediately spotted Mari's car. I thought it was kind of strange to see his car parked at my house this late at night. I decided not to go in through the front door. Instead I walked around to the patio. I noticed a candle flickering in darkness, soft jazz was playing in the background and the jets from the Jacuzzi were still running.

I walked toward the backdoor and peeked through the

small glass window. I noticed Dante lying naked on my chaise. Unsure of what was going on, I watched in silence until Mari appeared. I couldn't believe what I was seeing. While Dante lay with his head against the back of *my* favorite chair, *my* best friend kissed his chest and massaged his hard dick. When Mari placed his lips on what I thought was *my* dick, I knew that I was supposed to be upset, but something fluttered down below. Watching Dante get a blow job from my flamboyant homosexual friend was actually turning me on. Was Dante one of those "down low" brothers I'd heard about on Oprah? He surely seemed to be enjoying the head action. He was smiling, and running his hands back and forth across Mari's head while he worked his mouth magic. I placed the key into the deadbolt and unlocked it. I smiled as Dante and Mari jumped up and ran for cover.

"You don't have to run. I've been watching for awhile, I saw *everything*," I said.

"Joss Baby girl, it's not what it looks like…" Dante started.

"Jossy, forgive me girl…please, I'm so sorry!" Mari screamed. He fell to his knees and started sobbing uncontrollably.

I ignored Mari's theatrics and looked Dante directly in the eyes.

"Its okay, Dante you have secrets, and I have some too. Would you like to hear mine?"

Dante grabbed his pants from the floor and covered himself. "Yeah Baby girl, tell me whatever you want," he said.

"Why don't you both get dressed and we'll all talk over a drink."

While the men who betrayed me fumbled around nervously trying to get dressed, I walked into my bedroom and pulled out an old photo album. When I walked into the living room, Mari fixed drinks for the three of us and Dante sat on the couch as far away from Mari as he possibly could. I sat next to him and opened the album.

"What do you think about this person?" I asked.

"What you mean? Nothing. Is that your brother or something?"

Mari sat on a stool in the corner swinging his crossed legs back and forth swiftly. He knew what was coming next and I could tell he was nervous for me, but after what I'd witnessed, I was sure that Dante would keep his cool. He didn't want his secret to "accidentally" get to his boys.

I took a deep breath, and ran my finger over the plastic covering the picture.

"This person...used to be me Dante."

"Wha...the fuck you mean Joss?"

"I mean...this man used to be me, Dante." I flipped to another page in the photo album and pointed to a different picture. "See...look closely."

Dante grabbed me by the neck and applied pressure to the sides.

"No Dante!" Mari screamed.

"I should kill you bitch...nigga, whatever the fuck you are!"

"Dante please," I said, as I tried desperately to take air into my lungs.

Dante tightened his grip around my neck as he stood over me with his eyes full of fury.

"I should kill you bitch!" Dante shook me forcefully causing my head to hit the back of the couch. He tightened his grip, and continued to shout obscenities. "I should kill you!"

I was slowly loosing consciousness, I tried to fight the sleepiness creeping in, but with no air to breathe it was a lost cause. I stared into Dante's eyes and he suddenly released his death grip.

"Baby girl, I'm sorry," he whispered. "You should have told me...you should have just told me."

"I didn't know how you were going to react, and I didn't

want to loose you."

While Dante and I stared into each others eyes confirming our love Mari jumped off of the stool and raced to the kitchen.

When he appeared in the doorway he was pointing my nine millimeter glock directly at Dante.

"Aww hell no mother fucker, you are going to make a decision right now. Me or her! Right now Dante! Tell her! Tonight isn't the only night you wanted me! Tell her!"

Dante raised his hands in the air and slowly walked toward Mari. "Give me the gun dawg."

"You better tell her, before I do! You think I'm the only man your man has been creeping with Jossy? No, this big nigga is an undercover faggot, and has been for a long…long time! Tell her!" Mari walked toward Dante waving the gun back and forth.

"Okay…" Dante sighed heavily. "Yeah, I'm confused, I want you…and I want her. There I said it nigga, you happy now?" Dante stretched out his arm and Mari slowly set the gun in his hand.

I breathed a huge sigh of relief when Dante turned to me and smiled.

"Baby girl, secrets can kill you. Some you have to take to the grave. You feel me?"

Afraid of what Dante was thinking, I nodded hesitantly. Dante pointed the glock to his temple. "I ain't no fucking faggot," he said.

# FAST GIRLS

*Josie N. Bradley*
Charlotte, NC

## PROLOGUE

When I first started packing my bags to leave Brooklyn, I almost couldn't believe it. Brooklyn was my everything. My heart. And Trina was like a sister to me. Never in a million years would I have thought that things would have gone down the way they did.

We made a pact to never let niggas get to us. We were in it for the money and the game. I, myself, didn't even see it coming, especially with my girl. But then looking back, there was a lot of shit I didn't see coming. My moms wanting to move to the ATL, her linking up with Vincent, and then the ultimate, that shit that happened with Trina and Raheem.

Michael and me...well, that was a story in and of it self. I guess I need to start from the beginning, right? Cuz now that Trina is gone and not here to tell her side, shit is all fucked up in the game. But that's how it is when you a true Trick Mami. It's all about game anyway.

Let me start back from the beginning. Way back in the day…

# CHAPTER ONE
# BACK IN DA DAY
*1989-1990*

The first day of school and I gotta look fly. I go to one of the freshest schools in Brooklyn, Boys and Girls High school. I had to call Trina to see what she was wearing. There was no way I was gonna look wack for school. She picked up the phone on the third ring.

"Girl do you know what time it is?"

"I have a clock hoe. Tell me what to wear!"

"I thought we were wearing our red and white outfits with our Jordans?" Trina said still sleep.

I laughed as I remembered. "Oh yeah I forgot."

"Bitch, I will talk to you when it's time to jet. I needs my damn sleep."

Before I could respond, I hear a dial tone in my ear.

That was Trina's style, so I didn't trip. The only reason I called her so early in the first place was because I couldn't sleep. I felt nervous and scared at the same time. I couldn't play it cool like Trina all the time. I mean, she never let anything get to her. One time last year, we almost got busted by the truant officers who patrol downtown Brooklyn by Albee Square Mall. We were just hanging out by the food court, all cool and shit. I spotted five-o out the corner of my eyes so my first thought is to jet. But Trina plays it cool and pulls me in the direction of Orange Julius. She walks up to the dude at the counter and asks for applications. He looks at us and shrugs, and then he gives us two forms. I am sweating bullets now. I just know we are busted.

Five-o is advancing towards us. Two big ass black cops, looking mean as shit. The counter guy gives us the forms as Trina whips out her pen to fill it out. The cop stares us down and I look away and reach into my Fendi bag for a pen to fill my application out. They pass us with a wearing glare and Trina gives them the finger as they walk away. My heart is beating like an African drum and Trina hasn't lost her cool yet. We walk out the mall to catch the A train to 42nd Street to meet some dudes from Park Heights High who we know from around the way. Trina looks at me all smiles, and then she hugs me reassuringly like everything is cool. I'm still shitting bricks. Shook like hell.

"Stick with me kid. I'll make ya famous," Trina said laughing.

I just smile back breathing a sigh of relief. Everything is cool now. Trina has taken care of everything like always. That's my girl.

See Trina is my homegirl. My best friend. We tight like a small-sized girdle on a three hundred pound fat broad. She grew up with me in Herkimer projects and I knew her ever since I was six. She is like the sister I never had, cuz it was always just me and my moms. Trina, on the other hand, had a house full of niggas. She got her moms, pops four brothers, one sister, grandma, uncle and a cat. My moms always worked. She just started working at UPS, so now she always gone at night and sometimes for the day shift. I hardly see her, which is cool. I stay over at Trina's crib all the time.

Trina taught me about my period, how to fill my bra, wear shit that makes my ass look less flat and how to wear makeup so I could look eighteen to get into spots like The Sound Factory uptown. She was a pro at getting over. But today was gonna be the real test. High School was a different world from Junior High. No more kiddy niggas. We would be hanging with the major playas.

Glancing at the clock that was at the edge of my bed, I tried to decide what to do next. I didn't have to meet Trina until a quarter to eight, so I needed to kill time. The clock said

6:45. Might as well get ready. I head to the shower so I could get dressed. Today was gonna be The Day.

But The Day turned out to be a very fucked up day starting from the beginning. First, me and Trina walked into the High looking fly as shit. Both wearing our velour short sets and red and white Jordan's. Shit was sweet. We couldn't rock our jewels like we wanted 'cuz the principal got a rep for confiscating gold. He was on the news showing a box of people's beepers, four finger rings, and jumbo doorknocker earrings. Like some Brooklyn version of Joe Clark on *Lean on Me*. So we stashed our jewels in our Coach bags. Shit, I heard once he takes it, you never get it back. I worked too hard to get my shit to have that fat bastard taking it. I was not having it.

Trina and I had plans to go to homeroom and jet afterwards anyway. No way was we gonna stay all day. We were looking too damn good to waste it on the High. Plus we heard about a back-to-school party going down on Ralph Avenue. I was amped. My first back to school jams. Trina met me at the back of the High by the track. We had to play it smooth pass security so we could hop the train at Utica Avenue. I met Trina at the row of townhouses that were the projects everybody in the hood called Smurf Village. Trina was outta breath as she ran up to me.

"Yo Queen. I just saw Rondu up the block," she said as she caught her breath.

I rolled my eyes and sucked my teeth in disgust.

"So fuck that nigga. What he want?"

"He wanna know if you gonna come to his spot."

"The weed spot on the boulevard?'

"Yeah, but don't go Queen. You know he just wanna fuck."

I laughed at the thought. "He a four stroke creep he got a

big dick and don't know what to do with it"

Trina burst out laughing.

"Girl, don't make me laugh, cuz then I'm gonna have to pee."

"That's my word. If it wasn't for the fact that he got that good ass African black and that Thai, I wouldn't even fuck with him."

"That's all right. We gonna find us some ballin' niggas, for real."

"We need to 'cuz I am tired of these cheap ass Bed-Stuy niggas"

We walked to the station so we could party. Trina passed me a token so we could ride. We walked to the lower platform to the A train going towards the Far Rockaway side. There were a whole lot of kids getting on the train. Trina stopped me mid-stride and pointed to our bags. I nodded and reached into my bag and started to put on my link and my earrings. I left my rings at home in a rush, but that was aiight, I still had my gold bangles that this Panamanian cat named Primo gave me. We switched pass these three cats standing on the corner near the poles. They looked like they were seniors at the High. I recognized one of them as Dante. I had seen them on Marcus Garvey boulevard once with this cat named Alphonso. Dante tugged on my bag to get my attention.

"Yo, don't I know you?"

I just looked at him and smiled. Trina looked back at me and eyeballed Dante.

"Don't I know you?" She asked.

"Me? How I know you, shorty?"

"Oh, so now you got fucking loss of memory?" Trina snapped "I met you at the Sweat box on St. Marks and Bedford with ya boy Knowledge. I was with my girl Candice."

Dante squinted trying to remember. "Ok. Ok. You was with that chick Peaches, too, right?"

Trina nodded.

"You that chick with that bomb ass pussy," Dante said holding his dick, nodding at the memory.

Trina smiled at the compliment. "And you know this."

Dante's friend eyes her up and down as Dante whispers in his ear and laughs. Trina don't give a fuck. They act like I'm not there, so I stand against the pole as Trina flirts with Dante *and* his friend. I am used to this shit. Trina is always pullin' niggas. She is called "light and lively" on the Ave. She is redbone with long straight hair, Cuban and Black with Cherokee Indian mix. Big ass titties and a fat firm ass. Only fifteen, but can easily pass for eighteen. Me on the other hand, I am a nice butter-cream brown with shoulder-length hair, nice sized 36 Cs, ample hips and thighs and I have a little ass. I did aiight most of the time gettin' Trina's leftovers. Most niggas preferred the redbone chicks first, for some reason.

Dante looks at me and Trina, and winks at his boy. "So what y'all about to get into?"

Trina looks at me. "Why?"

"Cuz, I was thinking maybe we could swing by my boy's crib in Far Rock."

"Y'all must be crazy thinking we gonna roll with y'all all the way out to Rah Rah like that," Trina said.

"Damn shorty. Cool out. We gonna make the trip worth y'all while," his boy said.

"First off, we don't even know your fuckin' name," I said.

"I'm sorry," his boy said. "My name is Rob. What's your name shorty?"

I can tell I am not gonna like this cat already, and there is no way I am gonna go all the way out to Far Rockaway with these lame ass niggas.

Trina looks at me trying to tell where I am coming from.

"So what's the deal shorty?" Rob asked.

I'm looking at Trina not sure what to say next.

"Lemme check with my girl," she said, then pulls me to the side, all smiles so I know that something is up. But I don't say shit. "Yo, Queen. I know we can cop money off these sorry ass niggas, for real."

I look them over.

Dante is short, brown skin. He has on some Karl Kani jeans, some fresh Jordan's, a Polo shirt and some jewels, looking fresh with a faded haircut and a beeper hanging off the side. I can tell he got some ends. His nails look clean. He doesn't look like a bum nigga. His friend on the other hand, looks like he drooling. Rob kept staring obviously at Trina's ass as we were talking like she was a fresh piece of meat in a dog pound. Hell naw.

I shook my head.

"Naw, T fuck that."

"C'mon Mami. All we gotta do is get these niggas high and then give them some ass, get the cash and split. We might even get the jewels Queen."

I didn't trust Queens niggas, especially Far Rock. "You know how I feel about Queens, T."

Trina sucked her teeth and sighed. She turned abound and faced Dante.

"Well, sorry but me and my girl are gonna have to catch up to you later. Lemme get ya number, maybe I can get witcha sometime this week."

Dante seemed pissed but he gave Trina his number anyway, and his boy shook his head eyeing Trina's ass like he just knew he was gonna score. We walked further down the platform to catch the A train away from those bums. I was happy as fuck.

"Herb ass niggas," Trina said walking away laughing.

"Where you hook up with Dante?"

"I met him at the Sweat Box that time you didn't want to

go with me and Peaches. She hooked up with me and his boy Knowledge and then we went to her crib on Kingston Ave."

I nodded remembering.

"I turned that nigga out. He got a scar on his side and I licked that shit, right? He nutted all over his self lovin' it with his freaky ass."

We laughed.

"All you gotta do, is remember to keep a nigga hooked, you gotta turn his ass out. Don't give it up to these crab ass niggas with no dough, and make sure you got game about your shit. Word up," she said.

I was taking it all in as Trina schooled me about the game. She knew her shit. The train pulled into the station and we got on. It was off to the party on Ralph Avenue.

When we got to the party, I saw mad niggas going up into the spot. It was in a basement of a brownstone at the corner of Ralph Avenue and Decatur Streets. They had mad cuties out, up there. And I spotted a few that I recognized from the High. Trina looked at me and licked her lips. I know who I am getting with already. I was trying to take it all in as we entered the spot.

It was real smoky down in the middle as niggas was passing around fat ass blunts of weed. I wanted to grab one, but it smelled funny.

"Yo, Queen. We gonna split up aiight? Meet ya later?"

"Bet."

We would hook up later and compare how many numbers we got. It was custom. Trina dipped to the left; I dipped right, trying to find a spot to chill. I parlayed over in the corner by the DJ when I spotted a chocolate dip chillin' in the cut, smoking a Black and Mild, and babysitting a Heineken. I gave him the eye from head to toe, letting him know that I was feelin' him and he stepped to me after a short pause.

"Yo, shorty what's your name?" he asked.

"Queen."

"I'm Dre."

I nodded, barely able to hear him over the music. He was a cutie looking even better up close with his chocolate brown skin and deep dimples. He had a baby face that was spotted with the beginning of facial hair underneath his chin.

"You live up this way?" he asked.

I shook my head. "Nah, I'm from Nostrand Ave."

"Word? You know Gift?" he asked.

Gift was a nigga from the Decepticons posse around the way. He also rolled with the niggas off Gates Avenue, Shakim and Divine.

"Yeah. He used to fuck with my friend Trina," was all I said trying to play cool.

"Gift is my cousin."

I wasn't impressed. I chilled and nodded my head in time with the beat, getting bored with the conversation already. He must have caught on because he stopped running off at the mouth for a minute. I guess he was trying to think of something to say when all of a sudden, somebody screamed in the middle of the dance floor, and everybody went on pause.

"Oh shit five-o!"

Everybody started scrambling like roaches and I took off too. In the back of my mind, I'm wondering were Trina is. No time to think as I run in the direction of Ralph Avenue towards Fulton Street. I could go to Kingsboro. I knew Cookie and True would be home chillin' as usual. I could hook up with Trina later, if she didn't beat me there first.

The cops were speeding down Ralph. I stopped dead in my tracks and slowed my roll dipping into the corner store for a hot minute. I heard Trina calling my name as she was speed walked up the street.

"Queenie! Girl, I know you ain't leaving me!"

*Hood2Hood*                    211

I came out the store laughing. "Shut up bitch, calling my name all up in here."

"Bitch you crazy leaving me! Where was you going?"

"To Kingsboro, to see Cookie and True," I said.

"Bitch lies, all lies."

"Word up. I know they chillin with a fat sack by now, it's after twelve."

"Yeah true. You know some dumb ass hollered five–o cuz they man's was fuckin' with some broad in the back and couldn't get none."

I laughed at Trina in disbelief. "Stop playing."

"Yo, that's my word. He did. I figured it out after I came back in from outside. I was talking to this fine ass nigga named Raheem. He one of those older cats, about twenty five."

My eyes got big as Trina went on bragging. "For real what he want with you?"

Trina glared at me annoyed. "Bitch, what you mean what he want with me? To fuck that's what. But it's cool, 'cuz little do he know I'm game. This nigga like a lottery ticket. He drives a black Cherokee and he work for Transit."

"Nigga got a legit job and a ride? You moving up in the world."

"I know. Don't hate the playa, hate the game bitch," she said holding out her fist to give me a pound.

I was jealous. Trina always found niggas that would pay her ass lovely. I always got stuck with the nickel and dime ass niggas. One day I was gonna get me a sugar daddy.

See, that was the goal. Once you got a sugar daddy, you had it made. He would want to fuck, that's a given. And he would do anything to get some young tender pussy. That's when you set shit in motion. Break his ass off and get keys to the whip. Money to keep you looking freshly dipped and shit. I knew mad bitches round the way that hooked up with older cats that always had the latest shit. Most of the time, you could hear them bragging about how their man brought them this and that, took them on shopping sprees. I wanted that type of shit for myself. With Trina teaching me the game, I couldn't lose.

"So we heading to Kingsboro or what?" Trina was asking as we crossed Fulton Street and Ralph Avenue.

"I guess," I shrugged.

"Damn, I wish I would have stayed," Trina said. "I was into that nigga Raheem for real."

"I know. How many numbers you get before we jetted?" I asked.

"One, just Raheem's. He lives out Bushwick, off Broadway."

"A Bushwick nigga? I don't like it out there, Trina."

"I know. But he seems cool. Maybe he got some friends that I can hook you up with," she said.

"Bet," was all I said back. I wasn't down with nobody's rejects. I would find my own man.

When we got to Cookie's house, her man True was still asleep. The apartment smelled like a barrel of weed. Cookie was so high, her eyes looked crossed.

"I hope you got some food up in this motherfucka!" Trina yelled as soon as Cookie let us in.

"This ain't no soup kitchen bitch. Where y'all broke ass hoes coming from?" Cookie said.

"Spot on Ralph and Decatur," Trina said.

"Pookie's spot?" she asked.

"Yeah?" I said.

"I heard they got raided. That true?" she asked.

"Yep," Trina said sticking her head in the fridge pulling out a box of cheesecake from Junior's restaurant and eating it.

"Bitch, I know you not eating my cheesecake," Cookie

said running over to Trina trying to pry it from her hands.

True came from the back bedroom wearing just his black boxer shorts and white T-shirt. He was tall and coffee brown with a bomb ass body. He did a bid upstate in Albany for armed robbery and he had just gotten out a few months ago. Ever since he got out, he's had Cookie stuck in the house like a housewife and shit. She couldn't even hangout no more and shit, 'cuz True was crazy jealous and shit like that. He didn't even like me and Trina coming over to hang out and shit. But because of Cookie, he put up with us.

"So school out today, kids?" True said wiping sleep outta his eyes.

"Shut up, damn high school dropout," Cookie told True shoving cheesecake inside his mouth and mushing him upside his head.

"So…I'm just saying 'cuz I didn't finish, I am trying to school these young girls on what they *need* to do to become productive members of society," he said laughing at his own bullshit.

We all laughed at how crazy his ass sounded.

"Who got some La?" Trina asked while pulling Dutchies out her purse.

True rolled us up a blunt a piece, and we took care of business puffing away. I was out of it by the third blunt, and the second shotgun blast. I was more of a drinker than a weed smoker. Before I knew it, I was crashed on Cookie's couch. I didn't hear anybody leave and I was startled to hear that it was quiet. I got up and went to the bathroom to pee, and that's when I heard True call me from the back.

"Queen. You up?" he called from the bedroom.

"Yeah I gotta pee," I said closing the bathroom door behind me.

When I got out True was standing in the doorway of

the bedroom which was across the hall from the bathroom, stroking his dick through his boxers. I tried not to look but I could tell he was packing. He was bone hard and his dick was peaking from his boxers.

"What's up True?" I asked quietly. I was unprepared to handle this situation. I didn't know him *that* well. And I only knew Cookie through Trina. This nigga wanted to fuck. There was no doubt about that and I was scared as shit. He was an older cat, about thirty *and* he did some time. If I said no, would he rape me?

What if I let him and Cookie caught us? There was no way, I can handle this shit.

True was looking at me with lust in his eyes.

"You tell me shorty?" he asked licking his lips and eyeing my tits.

"I don't know True. You Cookie man, I ain't tryin' to hear what you sayin'," I said quietly.

But he stepped closer to me and brushed up against my titties. He had me pinned up against the wall in the hallway. "I'm sayin' that I know you wanna fuck me, Queenie. I seen you eyein' me. We can keep this on the DL."

"True," I began to protest. But it fell on deaf ears. He was tugging on my shorts, my heart was beating fast as shit. He was poking me with his dick through the top of my shorts, which were drawstring and tied up. I could smell the musk from his balls and I wanted to hurl. Sound seemed amplified by a thousand and every thing seemed loud as hell. Where the fuck was Trina and Cookie?

True pulled down my shorts and panties after undoing the draw string. My mind was saying no, but I don't think the words came out. I was too fucking scared to say a word. He was rubbing his dick between my legs which were closed. I could see it and it looked so big. I wanted to scream and run. But where would I go? Trina wasn't here. As if answering my prayers I heard Trina and Cookie coming up the stairs, laughing and talking loudly. True backed away from me, walking back into the room. I pulled my shorts back up and went to the couch to lie down. I was shaking and I knew I was busted.

Closing my eyes, I tried to relax like I was sleep as Trina and Cookie came in the door with Chinese takeout.

"I know y'all still ain't sleep. You are the sleepiest nigga I know!!" Trina said.

I didn't say a fucking word. True was in the back playing sleep 'cuz he ain't say nothing either. I just wanted to blaze by this point. But I was too scared to move.

Cookie went to the back to take the food to True as Trina passed me some beef and broccoli to me.

"Hooker, wake up and eat," she said.

I rubbed my eyes sleepily pretending to just wake up. I'm not sure if Trina bought my fake ass sleep act, but she didn't act like she knew what was up, so I took the food and shoveled it in my mouth so I wouldn't have to talk. The next thing I knew, Trina and I heard the bed squeaking so we knew Cookie and True were fucking.

"Damn niggas can't wait till we leave at least?" Trina asked disgusted.

I didn't say a word. I was too busy wondering if while true was fucking Cookie, he thinking about me.

## CHAPTER TWO

The next day we skipped school all together. Trina wanted me to go meet Raheem and his homeboy Red. At first I didn't want to go, but I didn't really want to go to school either, so what the fuck?

"You cool with meeting Raheem's boy right? Trina asked.

I shrugged. "Yeah. I hope he ain't no ugly nigga," I said.

"Nah, Rah told me he was legit. Plus if he wanna get some pussy, he better not be lying to me."

I sighed. She had nothing to worry about. Her shit was legit already. I still had some work to do finding me a sugar daddy to trick. "So you gonna fuck this nigga or what?" I asked.

Trina looked at me like I was crazy. "Bitch you crazy, if you think I ain't. I am gonna make this one my sugar daddy."

I was quiet as I thought about what she was saying. If Trina taught me anything it was to use what you got to get what you want. And Trina learned from the best, her sister Adele, may she rest in peace. Adele was found murdered in an abandoned building on Atlantic Avenue raped and beaten to death. Her downfall was that she was fucking some Italian guy from Canarsie supposed to be linked to John Gotti, so rumor has it. Adele was telling everybody in the hood about her man Vinnie this and that, and he had a wife. Once, Adele and Vinnie's wife got into it on Fulton Street. The chick threatened to kill her if she didn't stay away from her husband and the next thing you know Adele was found dead. Trina vowed to never wind up like her, but sometimes I wasn't so sure. There were worse scenes than death. Some niggas could put you out on a stroll or get you strung out on crack and shit. Death was easy. Living in the ghetto in Brooklyn was hard as shit.

Trina advised me to wear something that would show off

my assets, so I put on my tight ass red leather skirt and red stripped shirt that clung to my breasts and made them stand out. I was looking cute as hell. I needed Trina to hook me up further so that we would look older. We had this Raheem cat thinking we were like eighteen. So after our outfits and makeup, we were gonna be set. Trina knew how to hook shit up so fucking good that she was always able to get us into the Sound Factory.

We went to the train station at Nostrand Avenue and Fulton Street to catch the A   train going to Broadway Junction. Raheem lived on Kosciusko Street and Bushwick Avenue, which was one block from the J train stop. Like I told Trina I wasn't really feeling Bushwick, but it got me out of the Stuy, which was cool 'cuz I knew my peeps hardly knew anybody out this way.

Trina was working her baby blue Tommy jean outfit with her sneakers. She had on her sneakers because she said you never knew when a bitch had to make a run for it. Today was Raheem's day off and he wanted to spend some time with Trina to get to know her. I just hoped I wouldn't be bored. The train ride was short and before we knew it, we were at our stop.

I didn't know where I was going, so I increased my pace to catch up with Trina. Raheem lived one block up from the train station in a three-story brick house that looked well kept. You could tell that back in the day Bushwick was a real nice part of Brooklyn, but now it was so run down in some parts, it was hard to tell it was even in Brooklyn sometimes.

Trina paused for a hot second, looking in the side view mirror of a parked car to check her reflection before walking up the steps and ringing the doorbell. She stepped back and waited for Raheem to answer it.

He answered the door in a T-shirt and sweatpants and looked as if he had just awakened. He also looked surprised to see us, but he quickly recovered by kissing Trina and looking her up and down with approval.

"Where you coming from looking all cute?" he asked smiling.

Trina styled and profiled for him, liking the attention.

"This is my homegirl, Queenie," Trina introduced me as I waved like an idiot. Raheem nodded in my direction and stepped back from the door to let us in. He lived in the back on the first floor. I could tell it was one of those places where he had to share the bathroom. My cousin Noonie lived in a place like that. He had a one bedroom kitchenette though. I always hated visiting him because his pervert neighbor always had to take a leak when I came over.

Raheem's crib was nice, he had all kinds of African art and shit on the walls and he had a large collection of CDs on a wall rack system. He walked in and offered us something to drink. We both said no, so he sat sown on the futon and offered us a seat. Trina sat beside him and I sat on the chair across from them taking in the scenery.

"So what brings you to see me shorty?" he asked Trina.

She looked offended and sucked her teeth in frustration. "Remember you told me to come see you on your day off?"

Raheem sat there frowning trying to think back. "Yeah, but I didn't think it was gonna be today."

"Why you playing Ra? I asked you yesterday on the phone when we talked."

"I don't remember Trina, for real. I'm sorry."

Trina began to pout as if she was upset. I watched knowing that this was all apart of her game to make him feel bad. Watching Trina in action was always cool, because she always got her way. Niggas was just gullible like that.

"Aww...don't be like that Trina. I'm glad to see you. It's just that I was surprised to see you today. You know my mind is bad and I am getting old?" he winked at me and laughed.

Trina flashed a smile at me as she hugged Raheem. She knew she was in the house.

"Listen, I don't have much to entertain with, so you mind going to the store to get some stuff?" he said looking at Trina, but she was busy looking at me, giving me the eye.

This was the part where I'm supposed to jet and give them some privacy. I hated this part. I wish that this Red nigga was here, so at least I would have somebody to flirt with. I was looking all cute for nothing. Raheem gave me a twenty and told me to get some snacks for the both of us, whatever we wanted. I knew the deal. I had to stay gone twenty minutes. I wasn't sure where the store was but in Brooklyn it wasn't too hard to find a local store or a bodega on the corner.

I heard a lot of catcalls and whistles, but I ignored them. It made me feel good though. Walking into the store, I saw two Spanish cats behind the counter and they both said hello to me. I went to the back of the store and got some coolers that I knew Trina liked to drink, and some snacks to munch on, after we smoked some weed. I went up to the counter and paid for the stuff after checking the time. It had only been ten minutes since I left, and I knew Trina always wanted me to give her twenty minutes just in case. Sighing, I really didn't know what to do to kill more time. Fuck it. I guess I would just have to just bust up in the spot and cock block. Older dudes are so excited to get some young pussy that they nutted quick anyway, so ten minutes should be long enough.

I rolled up to the crib after ten minutes and was surprised to see Trina ready to go.

"Yo. You got all you need Queen?" she asked looking at me with a wild look in her eyes.

"Yeah I guess," I said confused.

Raheem was in the back I guessed. Trina seemed preoccupied with combing her hair into a ponytail so I wasn't sure what was up with her. She just seemed ready to go.

"Rah. We gonna leave boo, aiight?" she called to him as I heard the shower turn on from the back bathroom.

"Aiight. Call me later shorty," he called from the back.

Trina pushed me towards the door, bag in hand. I was still confused as hell. I thought we were gonna chill for a minute?

Trina was practically dragging me down the steps outside the stoop hollering and squealing like crazy, "Girl, that nigga packing like nine inches, word life!!!"

"Stop playing!"

"Word on the strength. He large as fuck! I was crying and shit trying to take it."

"So y'all didn't fuck?"

"Well he tried, but my shit was too tight. So I just sucked his dick," Trina said all nonchalantly, digging into her bag, grabbing a Twinkie.

" Eww. That shit is nasty. I can't believe you did that shit," I said.

Trina stopped dead in her tracks and looked at me like I was crazy. "Bitch believe this," she said as she reached inside her Luis Vuiton bag and pulled out a wad of hundreds.

"How much?"

"It's a grip. He just got paid. Payday is my day baby. I had that nigga's eyes rolling in the back of his head and shit, cuz I am all that. You need to watch and learn Queen. I'm gonna show you how to get paid in full. Now let's go shopping bitch."

"Whatever. I still ain't sucking no dick." I was stunned. Trina had hit the big time with this sugar daddy. All the other's was nickel and dime cats compared to Raheem.

He was the man. No doubt.

Fast Girls

## CHAPTER THREE

We arrived at A&S ready to cop the latest gear. The next stop after this was Macy's on 34th Street. I wanted Trina to take me to Dapper Dan's Uptown to get us some custom made Gucci outfits next, but she didn't want to go. We shopped all around A&S buying up leather skirts and spandex shit to rock at the next Avenue party. There was this saleslady that kept following us around, but once we got to the counter and Trina pulled out a knot of cash, Miss Whitey was all on our shit then.

It was all that and I was having so much fun. Trina decided that we should go to grab some eats, so we went to Juniors on Flatbush next to grab some cheesecake. Trina liked to eat her cheesecake with cappuccino now, ever since some cat named Elwood turned her on to it. On the way to the ladies room once inside, I noticed I had some crumbs on my shirt, so I looked down to wipe it off when I bumped into a tall dark dude wearing an expensive suit and tie. I nearly fell over, but luckily he caught me before I could fall.

"Excuse me miss, I'm sorry" he said checking to make sure I was OK.

"It's all good. I'm cool," I said staring at him. He smiled at me.

"So what's your name beautiful?" he asked.

"Queen," I said waiting for what I knew would come next. People always asked me why my momma named me some shit like that. I would always say because she wanted me to grow up like royalty. In reality, I had no clue why.

"Hello, my name is Michael. You can call me Mike."

"OK. Mike."

"Hi."

"So you here with somebody? If not, can we talk over by

the booth?" he asked.

"Oh, I'm here with my girl Trina," I said pointing to the table where Trina was flirting with a guy at the counter.

"So can I call you sometime? Maybe take you out? That way we can get to know each other?" he asked smiling at me. He was a cute ass older guy. I wondered how old he thought I was as he reached into his pocket and handed me a card.

"What is this for?" I asked staring at a gold embossed card with his name on it. Damn this guy was forward, but I liked that in a guy. Nobody wants a punk ass man.

"Call me when you get a chance and then you can give me your number OK?" he said. His card had Citibank, his name and pager number on it. Shit, I just may have found my sugar daddy.

I gave him a look up and down. Damn, this nigga was bow legged, too. And everyone knows that means. Don't front. Big dick, ya heard?

Michael winked at me and I walked back to where Trina was. I had forgotten all about going to the bathroom, my thoughts were all on this fine ass older man. He wasn't *that* old from what I could tell. I looked out Junior's window, and watched him pull off in his BMW. He honked the horn as he passed me by.

Trina looked at me waving at Michael and nudged me in the side. "Girl, who is that? You done bagged you a baller, huh?"

"I don't know, but I got the number."

"You gonna call him?"

"Sho you right."

We gave each other fives and laughed. Things were looking up for the Queen.

I called Michael up, I was lonely as hell. Trina was up at Raheem's crib as usual and I was left alone to do for self.

Trina kept promising to hook me up with Raheem's friend Red, but so far that hasn't happened. Desperate for attention and craving male companionship, I called Mike to see if he was down for an episode.

"Hello beautiful," Michael said, making me feel all warm and tingly from the sound of his deep baritone voice.

"Hi. What are you doin'?"

"Nothing. Just thinking about you."

Smooth operator, this one.

"So what you wanna do? Want to see me tonight?" I asked hopeful he would say yes.

"Aww…boo. Tonight is not a good time. I have to go to my son's school for a game. He goes to Erasmus Hall."

"Oh. You have a son in high school," I say trying to play it off.

"Yeah. He lives with his mother in Flatbush."

"By the way, Mike, how old are you?"

"I'm thirty five. I had my son young in case you are wondering."

"Oh."

"And if you don't mind me, asking how old are you?"

"I'm eighteen," I lied taking a deep breath. I usually said eighteen. I hoped he believed me.

"I guessed that much. You carry yourself a lot older though. You can pass for twenty."

"People tell me that a lot"

"I can't wait until you are twenty-one, then you'll really be legal."

I laughed nervously. *If you only knew buddy.* "I'm legal now. I can vote and buy cigarettes, right?"

"True. I was just playing. So what you got up for Friday night?"

"Umm…nothing why?"

"How about I take you to a special spot I like to go in Harlem?

I think you'll like it."

"Cool. That's OK with me. I'm down."

"Great. Can I pick you up?" he asked.

I panicked. If he picked me up from around the way, these trifling niggas would blow up my spot.

*Think Queenie, think.*

"Umm. I can come to your house. Still live with my moms, and she be trippin'."

"OK. I live in Clinton Hill, near Fort Greene Park. Do you know where Brooklyn Tech High School is?"

"Yeah."

"I live on Fort Greene Place, across the street from the school, OK? My address is building 32, on the first floor brownstone apartment."

"Got it," I said committing his directions to memory. I couldn't wait to see him. I was gonna need Trina's help with makeup and what to wear.

"Listen, I have to go Queen, but I will call you when I get back if it's not too late.

I don't want to disrespect your mother."

"Don't you have to work tomorrow?"

"No not tomorrow. What do you have to do tomorrow young lady?"

"Nothing. I go to John Jay."

"Really? What's your major?" Damn I hadn't thought out my lies so I had to be quick on my feet. I needed Trina. She was good at this type of shit.

"Criminal Justice. I am not sure if I want to be a lawyer, yet, though."

"That sounds good, real good," I said. "Well, I will talk to you later Mike."

"Later Queen."

The way he said my name made me feel good from my head down to my toes. I could tell that this guy really liked me. We had been talking on the phone now for at least two weeks. I was anxious to go out, so I could put it on him. The sooner the better.

I called Trina's house to see if she was home yet. Her brother answered the phone and told me she wasn't there so I figured she was still with Raheem. He had given her a Skytel pager, so I paged her with my code 411 which meant what's up?

Sitting in my room I gave her about five minutes to answer me back.

My moms was out and about somewhere, and I was stuck in the crib like a herb with no where to go. After a few minutes I realized that Trina was not gonna call me back so I decided to head outside to see what was going on on my block. It was a cool Indian summer night. Breezy, but still warm. Nobody was outside at first, so I headed for the spot on Nostrand Avenue and Pacific Street to see if my nigga Ginsu was around.

Ginsu was my nigga on the side, I was supposed to be talking to him exclusively but as my girl Trina said, "Why limit yourself?" Ginsu was a thug nigga from around the way. He was down with the Pacific Street crew and with the Decepticons in Brooklyn. He was a big nigga too, not fat but solid, and he had cute dimples. I knew I could get my flirt on with him at least to kill some time. When I got to the corner of Nostrand and Pacific, there was a crew of niggas on the corner like ten deep. I didn't see Ginsu at first, but I spotted his boy Shadow and asked if he had seen him around.

Shadow looked at me and shook his head. He was smoking a spliff.

"Nah, shorty. Last I heard he was up at the crib with some bitch, I don't know if you wanna go up there Queen. He know you was coming through?" he asked.

"Nah, it's cool. Tell him I will get up with him later," I said as I began to walk towards St. Marks. I was hungry now so it was off to the Jamaican spot for a Roti.

See, the average chick would have went off about what went down just now, but me and Ginsu had an understanding and I knew how to play my position like Trina taught me. I didn't have any claim on Ginsu anyway. We hadn't even fucked yet. The nigga acted like he was scared to hit it actually.

So we was cool. We would hang out, I would hug up all on him, flirt and shit smoke some weed, hit him up for some cash and be out. He always showed me mad love and respect. I guess he really liked me cause the average bitch ain't getting what I am without giving up the skins and that's a fact. So in reality, I would walk up on him with another broad and I wouldn't trip. I would just say hi all sexy and shit to make that bitch all mad and shit. 'Cuz eventually he would get tired of her ass and be checking for me. All I had to do was wait.

The Roti spot was mad crowded and I was debating if I should go in or just say fuck it and go to the Chinese place and get some chicken wings. As I stood there thinking, I felt someone come up from behind me laughing.

"Run your shit bitch," a voice said from behind me poking me in the side with a finger.

"Nah B I cant do that," I said turning around to see my friend Tati grinning at me. Tati used to live in Herkimer projects with Trina and me back in the day in grade school. Tati got pregnant when we were in the seventh grade by this big time baller named G Money from East New York. After Tati dropped out of school and went to a pregnant alternative school, her moms sent her to live out in Corona, Queens with her aunt. Tati always managed to come back around the way to see us though. She couldn't stand Queens 'cuz she didn't know nobody out there.

"So what's up bitch? What's up with you?" she asked.

"Still scheming and shit as always. What's up with you?"

"Nothing I'm waiting on a friend to take me to this party in Brownsville. Wanna go?"

I stood there thinking. Hell, I didn't have anything else planned. So why not? "Fuck yeah. Let's roll."

I walked with her towards her friend's crib on Eastern Parkway and Franklin Avenue. Tati pulled out a spliff from her pocket and sparked it. She was walking and puffing as she passed me the blunt. I took a toke just to get nice. I didn't want to be too high going to East New York. I didn't really know a soul out that way, so I was depending on Tati to hold me down. She was a wild girl. She had a scar on her neck from where a bitch tried to shank her in Spofford when she was sixteen. Tati was a bad bitch, bottom line. I remember one time we was at the bus stop waiting for the B54 when a bitch tried to take Tati's bamboo doorknocker earrings and run. Tati chased the bitch down and commenced to whipping her ass so bad we couldn't see her face it was so bloody. Tati had stomped her so hard that a Timberland imprint from her boot was across the girl's forehead.

We started towards Eastern Parkway igging the heads making comments and trying to get at us as we passed. One nigga even tried to snatch the L that Tati was puffing. The look in her eyes made them back up. Tati was one crazy bitch once she got started and she wouldn't hesitate to take on someone in a heartbeat. Ask anybody on Nostrand and they knew what was up. So by the time we reached Eastern Parkway and Franklin Avenue, we were buzzed and had the munchies. I decide to stop in the corner store and cop us some chips and snacks so we can be ready to drink when we get to Euclid.

Tati went to the payphone to call her homegirl so that we can bounce afterwards and go get on the train. In the store, I see some girls that I know from Prospect Heights that are eyeballing me and whispering and shit. They know I am from Nostrand Avenue 'cuz they seen me from around the way. I sense beef and I'm hoping that Tati come in the store so that shit can get squashed 'cuz I am not in the mood to rumble tonight. One girl, the biggest of the crew, walks up to the potato chip aisle to get pass me and damn near knocks me over. I smell it in the air. This is the shit that will set other shit in motion. Based on my reaction, these bitches will be ready to jump on me any second. Heart pounding I stand my ground watching and making eye contact as she approaches me with a smirk on her face.

*C'mon Tati* I'm thinking to myself as the girl gets right up to me and knocks me on the shoulder. Now it's time to set shit off.

"Watch where you going bitch," she snarls looking back from over her shoulder. Before I can respond Tati hits her over the head with a forty ounce bottle of Old English beer. BAM!

"Now what bitch? Who want it up in this muthafucka?" Tati screamed, her eyes blazing.

*Aww shit.* They done set her off now. Shit is about to get crazy though 'cuz it's just us and they six deep in the store and ain't no telling how they rolling. But I'm no punk bitch and I got Tati holding me down, so I play my position. I grab another bottle and get ready to swing too.

"What? What?" I ask looking at the chick holding her bleeding head.

By this time, the Arab store owner is talking shit and a crowd has gathered around and outside the store. As always in Brooklyn, niggas is nosy. The store owner is cussing us out, threatening to call the cops and cussing us in his native tongue. I know he is calling us all kinds of bitches and niggas in his native tongue but fuck it. The girls are talking shit too, but backing up grabbing their friend who is holding her bloody gushing head. She gonna need stitches, I know but fuck it. Tati is laughing as we leave out the store and go by rushing around the corner.

"Damn. I can't leave yo ass alone for a minute without bringing some heat," she laughed.

"Nah see what happened was…" I start as she drags me along.

"Save the drama, Queen. Bring your ass on."

"Aiight," I said as we bounce to the train station to catch the number 3.

We're headed towards Da Ville now. Niggas is ruthless out in Brownsville/East New York. So I was uneasy to say the least. But Tati was in her element. Another good thing about rolling with her was she knew somebody, every fucking where in Brooklyn. So I really had no worries. We got off the train at Junius Ave and walked up to Van Dyke projects. We had to walk from the station, which was dark as shit. There was a bridge that separated Brownsville from East New York when you got off the train then you had to walk up to Livonia Avenue. Crackheads, prostitutes, and drug dealers all lurked in the shadows under that bridge and many a dead body had been found in the street or in the creek of water underneath. I was scared as shit, but Tati didn't seem fazed. See if Trina was here, at least I had someone repping for NA Rock, but it was just me and Tati so I had to hold it down for dolo.

Brownsville East New York chicks get down differently then we do in the Stuy. A posse of two ain't shit against a mob of about ten deep, ya' mean? I decided not to sweat it. I always had a razor in the roof of my mouth and a rusty box cutter in my pocket. Wasn't no telling what Tati was holding 'cuz she always wore baggy jeans and tight shirts to hug her little boobies. In her pants could be anything from a machete to a fuckin' semi-auto. Tati was motioning me to follow her to the store across the street from the projects to get some drinks. I'm low on cash and we ain't old enough to get no beer or any liquor so I wonder what her plan is. Tati is and looks older than me, so she goes in this time as I stand by the payphone pretending to make a call. Hoping nobody detects that I'm not from around here. I attempt to chill.

Then all of a sudden, Tati is running out of the store with two forties in her hand and a Spanish guy is yelling at her cursing as she sprints across the street as if she is weightless. I pause contemplating what to do next then I turn my back to dude so he won't notice we together. I wait count to thirty, then walk/run across the street spotting Tati in the courtyard. Walking swiftly, my eyes moving everywhere checking for Tati when I see a group of niggas sparking some La in a cipher, bobbing their heads to some reggae. In the middle is Tati getting her flirt on with some dark skinned cat passing him one of the forties and taking a swig from the other.

"Bitch is you crazy?" I shriek at her as I approach the circle. All eyes are on me, then back at Tati as I snatch the forty and take a swig. She just laughs at me and points. "Aww...was you scared? I do this shit all the time," she laughed.

The guys look at both of us assuming that all is cool and go back to their smoke fest and drinking. Tati hugs me and tells me to follow her to the party which is on the tenth floor of one of the high rises. We walk all ten flights 'cuz for those of you who know ain't no way in hell we riding in the elevator. Tati reaches the tenth floor and we hear music coming from behind the door. I start to get uneasy again as I realize I am at a party ten floors up where I don't know a soul. Plus I always made it a rule not to go to parties where it was always one way in/one way out. I'm scared of closed spaces.

Tati looked over at me as we knocked on the door to the

crib and smiled like everything was all good. We knocked twice and a big ass nigga answered the door as a crowd of people came out at the same time. This shit was crazy. Mad weed smoke was coming out the door, and it was packed with wall to wall people. If five-o rolled up we would all be fucked. Tati didn't seem fazed as the big nigga patted us down and let us in. We walked in and attempted to walk to the middle of the room. The whole apartment had no furniture in it.

The DJ was playing "Pirates" by Chaka Demus and I found myself singing along. "Dem a call us pirates dem a call us illegal broadcasters."

Tati was making her way through the crowd, guys were passing her blunts and she was passing it back to me. Trying to be cool I puff, unsure if I am smoking pure weed or a mixture of weed and coke. Some niggas be trying to slip shit in a blunt quick so it is hard to tell. Tati speaks to the DJ who she seems to know and he puts on the next jam, Shelly Thunder's Kuff and a guy from the crowd asks me to dance. I am no slouch when it comes to dancing, so I oblige. I throw my ass to his dick and work it. He is beginning to get hard I can feel it through his pants as I allow him to turn me around and I grind him face to face my titties rubbing on his chest. Tati is behind me in the crowd shouting "Work it Bitch" as some people make room for me to really show my skills on the dance floor. I am so into what I am doing that I don't see Tati swing on this one chick for advancing towards me like she was about to rock my knot, nor did I know that I was grinding her man. I am totally oblivious to the commotion going on around me until the music stops and guys start to shout into the crowd "Fight!"

Everything stops and as if in slow motion I snap out of my fog to check for Tati. She is stomping the hell out of a bitch on the floor and I don't know whether to stop her or cheer. Tati is kicking her in the ribs, jumping on her back and spitting on her while cursing at her and talking shit. The crowd is moving to the outside as sirens are heard in the background. A lot of niggas got drugs and burners on them so they don't want to get popped. I follow the crowd out but don't see Tati so I walk with a group of chicks that are all riled up talking about killing a bitch.

"That's my word. When I see that bitch come out, I got something for her ass."

"Who the fuck she think she is?"

"She betta recognize where the fuck she at!"

"Word she stomped the shit outta Peaches but I got something for her ass though and poppy and they cant save her ass this time. They know what's up!"

I realize that they are talking about Tati. The tallest one in the group is reaching into her bag, at first I can't see what she has until we step in front of the housing project. That's when I see it. In her hand is a baby .380...*Shit is about to get thick.*

I search for Tati and she is nowhere to be found. The crowd is dispersing slowly and the girls are off to the left still within the crowd, but not easily seen. Praying that we make it to at least the train, without incident, if possible. I realize that I am scared shitless. These bitches are playing for keeps and I don't know how to hold them off. Then I see the dude that Tati was talking to when we first rolled up in the courtyard. This was the same dude that was deejaying in the crib. Then Tati comes from behind him looking crazy ass hell. I hope she is strapped 'cuz a gunfight is the only way out of the Ville tonight it seems. I see her scoping the crowd and I know that she is looking for me. I try to give her eye contact without drawing attention to myself, but before I can do that the broad who is strapped spots her and her posse is advancing.

SHIT.

Tati sees them too and to my surprise she pulls from her

waist a glock nine millimeter semi auto that is her special gun that she calls *Pablo.*

"Now who want it?" she screams, popping off into the crowd. People is screaming and flying everywhere. The crew of girls started to run, but not before shooting back at Tati from the .380 in return. Tati is walking calmly towards the bullets not away from them as if in slow motion. Amazingly none of them are touching her, not even grazing her ass!

I start to run in the direction of the train station away from the bullets, fuck all this crazy mess. It's after midnight so the station is pretty deserted. My heart is beating like crazy, as me, two dudes and another chick scramble back up Livonia Avenue heading for the direction of the bridge. I still hear gunshots in the background so I don't dare look back. A few more feet and I will be at Junius station. A crackhead pops out of the bush and asks me for a dollar scaring the shit out of me.

"Nah. I don't have no fucking money!" I snap at him. I guess it's at him because whoever it is, dirty and funky looking. Its eyes are all bugged and shit. This fiend is on a mission so I scurry pass and let it get on its merry way. The girl dips left and two dudes run pass me headed for the East New York side of the bridge. The only way you could tell one side from the other was it was divided by the bridge and a sign that said Brownsville/East New York.

I needed to stay on the Brownsville side to get to the subway. I started to hear cop cars in the distance and I suddenly thought of Tati. I hope she is not mad that I left her ass, but I ain't taking a bullet for nobody. I arrive at the station trying to be cool as a fan. I don't know when the next train is coming but I feel relatively safe on the platform alone. The 3 train pulls up and I get on walking to the middle of the car. The doors close and I breathe a sigh of relief. I punked on my girl, but I had to look out for self.

Wait until I tell Trina all this shit!

I get home about two in the morning and I am tired as shit. My mom's still at work. Herkimer projects is quiet and I don't want to go inside my house alone. I tap and throw pebbles at Trina's bedroom window. After three tries, I am about to give up when the window opens. It's Trina's brother Rob.

He looks pissed as he asks who it is.

"It's me. Is Trina home?" I ask shyly. I always secretly had a crush on Rob. He was tall, brown skin and fine as shit.

"Yeah, she's in the living room come up, so she can let you in."

I knew when shit was tight, I always had Trina's place to crash if nothing else.

That was why she was my homegirl, my road dawg till the mothafuckin' end. I go inside and Trina let's me in. She's on the phone talking to Raheem all lovey dovey, so I don't interrupt. I slide over to the recliner and curl up waiting to talk to my homegirl. I gotta tell her about tonight and Tati.

But before I know it the sandman is tap dancing on my head and within minutes I am fast asleep.

## CHAPTER FOUR

My moms and me have a real strange relationship. To outsiders it may seem like we are more like friends or some other shit than mother and daughter. But that is not the case at all, really it's just that my mother is a hard chick to get along with when she's home. My mother works a lot and she ain't hardly home, working mad overtime for Transit so when she home, she call herself trying to punish me or some shit. It's crazy 'cuz I am like if you ain't here, how you know? I stay over at Trina's so much with her moms, Ms. Earlene that you might as well say they my family. It's all lovely.

And its not like I don't have love for my mother, she tries her best. See, it's not like I got a father to look out for me. And my grandmother in Queens could only do but so much. I love my grandma Jane. She's my mother's mom and she can be the sweetest lady on the planet. My mother is the only girl and her two brothers, my uncles, stay locked up so mama the only one who take care of Nana when they not in jail. Anyway last night, my mother knew I was over at Trina's so she didn't sweat me which was good. But in the morning she came looking for me, which made me wonder if something was wrong.

It was eight thirty, too damn early for my moms to come by on a Saturday especially since she usually had to work. Ms. Earlene is tapping on Trina's door telling me to get up and get dressed that my moms is here. I get up and walk out to the living room in my Smurf pj's to see what's up.

"Queenie. We need to go home get your stuff. Tell Trina you will see her later." My mother's tone was abrupt and she didn't look at me. I could tell she was serious so I decided not to play with her. She still had her work uniform on which meant she had come straight off shift to get me. I was suddenly scared.

"OK. Lemme get my stuff. I will be right back," I said rushing back to the room to get my few pieces from Trina to leave. After I got my shit said my goodbyes to Trina and the Fam, we was out. Me and my moms go to our crib, which was on the first floor in the back apartment, 1D. My mother opened up the door to let us in and I put my stuff in the room waiting for my mom to let me know what's up.

See I could always tell when some heavy shit was about to go down. She would play with her hair and puff on a cigarette like she was all aggie and mad stressed. She was doing exactly that when she approached the doorway of my room pacing back and forth like she was debating on whether to tell me what was on her mind. So I decided to speed up the process of my mother talking by talking myself.

"What's up Ma?" I asked.

"Queen, it's about your grandma Jane," she said looking at me with a straight face. I get scared now 'cuz more than anything, I don't want a thing to happen to my grandma. She is all the family I got. My mother shakes her head, runs her fingers through her hair and pulls out a cigarette to smoke. I hate it when she smokes in the house but what can I do?

"Grandma Jane is sick Queen and I gotta decide if I need to be with her to take care of her or have someone else do it."

"Who else would take care of grandma but us?" I said knowing that it's true. Uncle Henry stayed in an out of jail and Uncle Earl was God knows where.

"I know but I cant possibly raise you and take care of Ma. I work extra now on my route, so it's crazy. I didn't want to say this but I was saving to get us a house out on Long Island."

I just looked at my mother like she was crazy. She was coming at me with a lot at once. "Well, Ma what's wrong with grandma though?"

"They say she got Alzheimer's."

I didn't know what to say to that.

"Either way, it's up to us to take care of her Queen. We are all she has. The rest of the family, she can't depend on."

Didn't I know that. Grandma Jane held our family together when she was better.

"I am going to see her tomorrow and I need you to come with me," she said taking a pull from her cigarette before walking out the room. The phone started ringing before I can say anything else, my mother leaves me alone. I figure she will answer it, but by the third ring I get the picture. My mother is in one of her moods where she doesn't want to be bothered. She's probably in her room locked away. I pick up the phone annoyed having to answer only to realize it's Trina.

" Yo, Queen what you doin? You wanna go to Raheem's?"

I paused and thought about her offer. What else did I have to do? I needed to get from under my mother and her self pity.

"Cool. Give me like twenty minutes, aiight?" I asked before Trina hung up the phone in my ear. I took that as my cue to hurry the fuck up because it was one thing I knew, Trina was impatient.

I met her in the hallway at the bottom of the steps leading to the front of our apartment building. She looked mad stressed as we started walking towards the A-train stop on Nostrand Avenue.

"Yo, T. What's up? Why you look stressed?"

"Queen. I think that nigga Raheem cheating on me," she said looking at me as if she was about to cry. I didn't react at first because I couldn't believe Trina was trippin over this nigga who she was supposed to be gaming. She was breaking the first rule of the code that she had taught to me early in the game which was: *Never Let Them You See Sweat*

"I swear if he is, that's my word, I will slit his fucking throat," she hissed mad as hell.

I could tell she was serious and Trina was a chick of her word. She had sliced many a nigga before, and Raheem wouldn't be the first or the last to meet his match when it came to Trina's blade. I didn't know what to say to her. After that Trina was in a zone and I had only seen her like this once before. A while ago, when her ex-man Theo tried to play her out at a party. Theo had told Trina to wait for him while he delivered a package uptown. He was a small-time hustler on the avenue and was down with the Gates Avenue crew which consisted of a bunch of niggas with tinted vintage '79 Cadillacs with booming systems. Anyway, Trina wanted to go to a party at a club on Utica Avenue and Eastern Parkway but Theo wasn't having it.

"Just chill until I get back T, then we can go wherever you want OK?" he said

Trina agreed, but I knew better.

Trina waited until Theo was off the block and we dipped out the back entrance of the projects and over the fence that led to Atlantic Avenue. Walking to Atlantic towards St. Johns Hospital, we were almost positive we wouldn't be seen by anybody that Theo knew. We was off to the party, shit was sweet. We were both looking like ghetto superstars with gold galore and our matching pink and purple shearling coats. Niggas was all over us. I was getting my mack on when all of a sudden shit stopped like a scratched record. Theo and his crew had stepped into the party on the way back to Nostrand Avenue. He spotted Trina winding to Rockers with some cat from Pacific and Franklin. This was the ultimate diss to Theo, who after spotting her walked over and yanked her off old boy. The music was still playing but everyone had stopped knowing that shit was about to pop off any minute.

"What the fuck did I tell you T?" he asked.

Trina faced him with a mad expression on her face. "Nigga you done lost your mind?" she asked hot like fire and embarrassed.

Trina was not one to just sit and take shit. She was a broad who gave as good as he got.

"Let's go now!" Theo shouted flexing for his boys who by this time was enjoying the show.

"Nigga, I ain't ready to go, so back the fuck up off me," Trina spat at him. The guy that she was dancing with a cat named Asiatic was smirking at Theo, ready to spark beef over Trina on GP due to the fact that Nostrand Ave and Franklin Ave had longstanding beef.

"Yo, sweetheart you ain't gotta go nowhere. I got you boo," Asiatic said eyeing Theo like: *Now What Nigga?*

Theo was itching for the word from his boys. He was not one to easily back down, he was laughing and looked at Trina waiting for the final word. I was scared that any minute there was gonna be an all out war. But Trina, true to form, was enjoying the power play, knowing full well the ball was in her court.

"Look, I will leave when I am good and ready," Trina said, but Theo was looking at her like she was crazy. He was not about to let Trina punk him in front of his boys. Without another word Theo pulled her away from Asiatic and towards the door of the club, while Trina cursed him out the whole way. Asiatic, the Gates Avenue crew and I followed behind anxious to see how the rest of the scene was gonna play outside the door.

Trina set shit off by slapping the shit out of Theo in the face. Theo caught her next swing mid strike and punched her in the jaw. Trina went down momentarily, then back up again. She was not even fazed catching Theo in the jaw with a wicked right. Stunned Theo went down and then Trina moved in for the ultimate kill. Spitting a razor blade from underneath her tongue, she sliced his neck just barely missing a major artery.

"You fucking bitch!" he shrieked as his boys held him

back.

"Take that *Maricon*," she spat at him laughing. "You ain't shit nigga, fuck you!" she continued to yell, holding her middle finger up.

I was shocked. Trina was one crazy bitch.

"I better not see you around the way," Theo threatened holding his bleeding neck as his boys lead him to his ride. I couldn't believe what I was seeing. Had that been me, Trina would have been one dead chick. Word. This shit was too good to be true. Trina was laughing as I began to pull her away in a different direction. Asiatic looked amused and impressed by Trina's skills and walked over to us offering a ride in his jeep Cherokee.

We accepted and after that night, Trina and Asiatic kicked it for a while. Long enough for her to trick him into buying her a pair of Jordan's with a matching velour Nike suit and two ruby bangle bracelets. That's my girl Trina. As for Theo, all that shit he popped weeks after the incident, he still came by and brought Trina a stereo system for her room. Trina's brothers were major players on the Ave so Theo knew better than to try them. Trina just had it like that.

Raheem and Trina had only been two weeks strong, so I didn't really know why she was tripping so damn hard. This wasn't like her at all.

"I called his crib and I swear to God another bitch answered his phone, Queen. Word!"

"Say Word?"

"Queen, that nigga don't know who he playing with!" Trina had that glazed look in her eyes like she was already plotting her revenge as we boarded the upstairs platform to Raheem's house. Trina was quiet as we got on the train and I was hoping that her silence meant that she was calming down a bit. It was wishful thinking because I knew better. Trina was plotting how to kick this niggas ass.

"Trina, maybe we should just chill. Raheem ain't worth getting into no shit over. You be pulling all kinds of niggas all over the Stuy. Why you sweating this Bushwick nigga?" I was asking trying to reason with her.

"I can't Queen. I love this nigga," Trina said sadly.

I was shocked. Trina whipped? Hell no!

"I just can't believe that he would play me out like this," she whispered tearfully.

She was gone and I had no way to reach her. I knew that depending on what we saw, when we got to Raheem's house, would depend on how she was gonna react. I prayed he was gone. The train pulled into the Broadway-Junction stop before I knew it and we got off the train and headed for Raheem's. Trina seemed to gain momentum as we reached Kosciusko Street. I was shitting bricks by the time we reached his brownstone. The front door to the building was cracked, so we didn't need to ring the bell to get in. Trina raced up the steps ahead of me screaming all the way to his apartment.

"Raheem open this fucking door! I know you got another bitch up in there!"

I flinched and closed my eyes waiting for what might happen when Raheem opened up the door. Trina had never got into it with Raheem before. There was no way to tell just what type of reaction he would have for her theatrics. If I had to bet money on it, when he opened the door he most likely was gonna flip out.

Raheem finally opened the door after a few minutes passed with Trina ranting and raving like a lunatic and his neighbors threatening to call the cops. He looked pissed off but said nothing as Trina stormed passed him almost knocking him down to get inside his crib.

"Where that bitch at Rah? I know she here!" Trina was yelling looking around the room trying to see if she saw anyone.

"Fuck is you talking about shorty? Ain't nobody up in here but me," Raheem answered in a quiet but angry tone.

"Raheem just show her man, so she can calm the fuck down," I said finally saying something. I had enough of Trina's drama for one day. I was secretly hoping Raheem would beat Trina's ass. Raheem laughed and grabbed Trina by the elbow. Reluctantly, she let him lead her to the back bedroom where he closed the door behind them. On my tip toes, I went to the back room put my ear to the door and listened.

"Why you trying to disrespect me Rah?" Trina was asking.

"I haven't done anything to you ma, why you trippin? " Raheem answered.

"I know you got some other bitch up in here. Where she at huh? Huh?" Trina was about to start up again. I could feel it. Raheem was either a patient man or an idiot to put up with all of Trina's drama.

Raheem was cool, calm and collected as he whispered in Trina's ear.

It seemed that they had forgotten that I was here. Then I heard sniffles from Trina and Raheem saying it was gonna be OK. For Trina to cry was a big deal because Trina hated to cry unless it was being used as a ploy to get her way. To cry for Trina, was for punk bitches and Trina was a far cry from *a punk bitch*.

"Baby, it's all about me and you boo. You are my baby," Raheem said before kissing her. It was quiet again and then I heard a soft moan from Trina. I backed away from the door, then because I couldn't believe that Trina had given in so easily. Maybe she had a plan up her sleeve that she hadn't hipped me too. Or else she was just weak for that nigga's dick.

I walked back to living room scanning my surroundings

and looking for something to do. I started to hear the squeak of the bed and I knew that they were fucking. Sighing, I grabbed the remote and prepared for a long wait. After a half an hour to an hour and several MTV videos later, she emerged from the room wearing Raheem's shirt and looking a shitty mess. Trina was all smiles and glowing from multiple orgasms when she approached me. I was pissed and she knew I was, so she tried to butter me up.

"Sorry Queen, but you know how it is sometimes," Trina said rubbing my shoulder softly. I yanked away from her grasp and sucked in my breath with attitude.

"Nah, I can't say that I do know how it is. You always pull this shit Trina."

"Queen come on. Don't be like that. I'll make it up too you boo," she said.

I shook my head in disbelief. She ranted and raved and threw a tantrum just to get laid? All this shit just for some attention? Trina was my homegirl but I hate to say it, but this bitch crazy. "Well now that you set him straight," I said sarcastically, "are you ready to go?"

Trina paused and looked at me.

"Aww fuck no! You staying!"

Trina looked at her nails and pretended to search for dirt.

"You playing yourself if you stay T," I said.

"Queen look to make it up, Raheem is gonna call you a cab so don't be mad," she said. "I'll call Black Jane."

"Whatever T. I'm out," I said getting up and walking to the door.

Trina followed me handing me a twenty from the pocket of Raheem's shirt that he was wearing. I opened the door and stopped to snatch the twenty.

"Call me when you get to the crib," she said mouthing the words *I'm sorry.*

I glared at Trina on my way out the door. I couldn't believe that Trina was sending me home from Bushwick by myself.

"Queen, please don't be mad," Trina called after me. I didn't answer. Inside I was laughing. Trina and I couldn't stay mad at each other for long. I was gonna forgive her. After all Trina was my homegirl. But as I walked to the corner of Bushwick Avenue to hail my gypsy cab, I couldn't help but think of all Trina had taught me about the game and how to game niggas. I guess even for a major playa like Trina, you had at least one loss coming to you. Game recognizes game. Trina had finally met her match. His name was Raheem.

## CHAPTER FIVE

Trina had taught me all that I know today in the art of gaming niggas. The first victim was Darryl, this lame ass nigga from Fort Greene projects who worked for UPS. I jerked him off, let him nut on my titties and I got a pair of jumbo doorknocker earrings, a name ring and a purple shearling. Next came Scott, a Jamaican cat with a big dick but a two minute brother when it came to stroking. He claimed my pussy was just that good that's why he came so damn quick. Uh huh.. *whatever nigga.* Scott sponsored my 40 below boots, and my fur trimmed leather trench which I paid half price for haggling with the Jews on Delancey Street in Manhattan.

The first two I had to fuck before I could master what Trina referred to as the Art of Mind Fucking. Now to all those who don't know what's up, let me put you on. Mind Fucking as Trina explained it, was the art of getting what you wanted without actually fucking a nigga. Still confused? It was getting what you wanted on the *promise of pussy later.* Like a Coochie coupon. Mind fucks were especially for the gullible and lame. You could only take it so far before a nigga would catch on. Then it was give up the ass or roll out. So far with Trina's successful coaching, I had three mind fucks under my belt. I hide my stash at Trina's so my mom's wouldn't find out. She was always working hard so shit was sweet. Plus she gave me dough and brought me shit to make up for the time she couldn't spend with me.

I hadn't decided if I wanted to make Michael my mind fuck or my sugar daddy. Sugar daddies were different. They had to be the main niggas getting the ass 'cuz they always broke you off with the dough. Rule number one for sugar daddies though, was *never get caught up.* Catching feelings was a No

JOSIE N. BRADLEY

No. but it was hard to keep that rule because sometimes you had niggas that would give you the world.

Trina had this one cat Rodney from Queens, he worked under the big time niggas out in Southside Jamaica. He took Trina to the Bahamas, Florida Keys and Cali. Brought Trina's peeps a floor model TV and a Nintendo to keep them from asking Rodney too many questions. Whatever Trina wanted, she got. They even talked about marriage once Trina got legal age. Rodney knew Trina's real age which she had lied about so much sometimes that I think that she even forgot. This went on for a year then Rodney got killed. Some Dominicans slit his throat while he was parked outside a club. Trina was devastated.

After that, Trina made sure that she kept her business and pleasure separate. Seemed like she was breaking the rules again for Raheem. I just hoped that this time she knew what she was doing.

I got home from Bushwick in half an hour. It didn't take long to get a cab. The fare was only six bucks but I gave the driver ten and kept the change. I was hungry so I walked to the Chinese spot on Fulton and Marcy. It was either that or Burger King. As I started to walk across the street to the spot, I heard a car honk the horn just as I stepped off the curb. Being nosy I looked into the car a black BMW with tinted windows as the driver let the window down on the passenger side.

"Need a ride?"

I took a good look at the driver and broke out into a grin.

It was Michael.

"Do you always pick up strangers?" I asked as I opened the door to get in.

"Only beautiful ones," he replied pulling off and heading straight up Fulton Street.

"Oh brother. Are you always this corny?" I replied laughing

*Hood₂Hood*     247

anyway.

"Where were you off to?" Michael asked.

"Just to grab some grub."

"Oh yeah, like what?"

"Just some beef and broccoli," I said.

Michael smiled as he turned onto Throop Avenue. "You still in the mood for Chinese? I can take you to a spot to eat at in downtown Brooklyn."

"Cool," I sat back and enjoyed the plushness of his BMW and its new car smell. *This nigga is a baller* I was thinking to myself as the soft sound of jazz flowed throughout the car's stereo system.

"Is this boring you? Would you rather listen to Hot 97or something?" he asked.

I laughed. "So 'cuz, I am younger than you, I gotta wanna listen to Run DMC all the time?"

He blushed.

"No ,I didn't mean to offend you I just want you to be comfortable."

"Nah it's cool. I like Najee too you know."

Michael looked pleased that I knew who was playing. "What you know about Najee?" he asked.

"I know that he is playing the instrumental version of Stevie Wonder's song *A Ribbon in the Sky*. And I know that *A Ribbon in the Sky* was on Stevie Wonder's album A Key of Life."

"I am impressed. Are you a Stevie Wonder fan?" he asked.

"Shit who isn't? My favorite song is *Living for the City*," I answered with confidence. I was a young girl, but I was far from dumb.

"Wow. Who turned you on to Stevie?"

"My moms she used to sing to me all the time, especially *You Are the Sunshine Of My Life* when I was little."

"Oh," Michael answered and then we both were quiet.

In the silence I stared at the city lights from buildings and the clock tower that was on the bank in downtown Brooklyn. It was the tallest building in downtown and the clock's face glowed in red looking like a ghetto version of London's Big Ben clock.

Michael headed towards Livingston Street by the court buildings and made a left. I had no idea where he was taking me, but I was thrilled at the surprise. I glanced slyly at the side mirror to check my appearance. I was looking bummy compared to usual. Michael had on slacks and a nice Benetton shirt. He was clean shaven and nicely trimmed. He smelled nice too. Like Cool Water. I had on some tight jeans and a tank top.

My hair was pulled back into a short ponytail since my hair was growing out of my short cut and I had on my Reeboks. I hoped that Michael didn't think I looked like this all the time.

"Is this place fancy? Do I look OK?" I asked unsure.

"You look good. C'mon," he replied getting out of the car. Before I could open the door, Michael had locked me in with the automatic locks and ran over to the other side to let me out.

Opening the door, Michael scolded me gently. "A gentlemen always opens the door for a lady," he said letting me out and taking my hand. Michael locked the door with his car alarm as we walked to the entrance. He held my hand and I felt all warm and tingly inside. The Chinese restaurant had lanterns and red dragons painted on the walls. The hostess was dressed in a white top and black skirt her hair was pulled back into a bun.

"Hello, would you like smoking or not?" she as we walked into the foyer of the restaurant.

"Non-smoking please," Michael answered.

The hostess said nothing. She was smiles as she led us to a

quiet table in the middle of the restaurant. It was a small table for two. She sat two menus in front of us and asked what kind of beverages we wanted.

"I'll have a Long Island iced tea," Michael said smiling at me.

"Just iced tea for me," I said. The hostess walked away and left us alone.

"So where were you headed when I ran into you?" I asked.

"I had just stopped to see a friend on Franklin Avenue. Before I saw you, I was just driving through the neighborhood."

"I see, on the prowl huh?" I teased.

"Not hardly. It was just dumb luck that I ran into you," Michael answered. He was smiling with his sexy chocolate self, looking at me as if I were the only one in the room. The restaurant was crowded, but I felt like it was only me and him.

"I'll buy that."

The hostess came back with our drinks and asked if we were ready to order. We both said no and she nodded, taking off again.

"So order what you like Queen."

"I think I will be adventurous today. What are you having?"

"I think I will have the duck in orange sauce."

I made a face and Michael laughed at me. "You never had duck?" he asked.

"Maybe, not knowingly. Don't they have any chicken up in here?"

Michael laughed his ass off at me and I was embarrassed that my age was showing. In my head I could hear Trina's voice saying *Slow your roll and play your position chick.*

"Sure they do Queen. But duck is like chicken. Try it. You will like it, I'm sure."

I shook my head. "No thanks. You order it and I will taste it off your plate, OK?"

"OK," Michael said, signaling the waitress over to take

our orders.

"Are you ready to order now?" she asked

"Yes, we are. I will have the duck in orange sauce and the lady will have…" he paused looking at me. "Queen have you decided yet?"

"Ahh, yes. I will have chicken lo mein with steamed rice and vegetables."

The waitress took our menus and nodded placing chopsticks and conventional silverware next to our napkins. I picked up my chopsticks and nervously played with it as Michael stared at me intently.

"I feel like I met you before," Michael said squinting at me as if trying to place where he knew me from.

My heart raced in panic. *Shit Queen he can't make you before you at least hit this nigga up for some dough* I was thinking to myself.

"I hear that a lot," I answered anxious to change the subject. "It will come to me. Anyway, do you have any plans after you finish John Jay?" he asked.

"Umm…" I stalled trying to think.

"Still undecided, huh?"

Here comes the waitress placing our drinks in front of us and I welcomed the distraction, instantly gulping down my iced tea before he can ask me something else. I just couldn't figure this shit out. I was never nervous with cats I was tricking on before, what made Michael so different?

"Actually the only reason I am undecided is because I am trying to get pass my freshman courses," I answered satisfied with my response. *Hopefully he won't ask me shit else about school until I could get my lies together.*

Michael nodded seeming satisfied with my answer as he reached across the table to touch my hand. His hands felt so soft and warm and I noticed that they were manicured and nicely done.

"Do I make you nervous Queen?"

I blushed.

"Ahh…not really, maybe a little."

"Aww, lil ole me? I'm harmless," he said smiling at me.

Michael's order came first and he excused himself to say grace and offered me a sample of his duck. *What the hell you only live once.*

I took a bite and surprisingly liked the sweet taste of it. The orange sauce tasted like duck sauce that I used on my wings all the time.

"So do you like it?"

"Yeah it's OK," I said blushing again. *What's with the blushing?*

Michael laughed and sipped water while waiting for my food.

"So tell me about yourself Queen. What makes a young lady like yourself tick?"

"I feel like I'm on a interview Mike. What's up with that?" I asked defensively.

"Sorry. I just want to get to know you better, that's all."

"It's cool. I'm sorry if I was tripping. What do you want to know?"

"Whatever you want to tell me."

"I'm an only child, on my mom's side anyway. I think my dad has some more kids but I don't talk to him."

"Oh I am the baby boy out of five," Michael said.

"Really?"

"Yep," Michael said stuffing his mouth with duck. My food finally arrived and I was hungry so I dug in taking a moment to figure out just how much of the truth I was ready to tell him and how much game he was gonna get.

"I'll tell you something else, too."

"Yeah?" I asked.

"I am originally a country boy from South Carolina."

I started laughing.

"What's so funny."

"I could tell kinda. You still have a slow drawl."

"Well, I've been in NYC since I was eighteen. I moved up here with my sister."

"Cool," was all I said in response.

"And you?"

"Born, bred in Bed-Stuy."

"Do or Die."

"And you know this," I said.

We laughed together enjoying our food. I found myself relaxing with Michael and feeling like getting to know him better. In this crazy world you never have too many friends. Michael seemed harmless. I began to let my guard down and we talked until the restaurant closed. We could feel the staff giving us the "get the fuck out" look. Michael paid for dinner, and we walked to the parking spot where he had parked his BMW. Opening the door for me to get in on the passenger side, made me feel like a princess. Michael was definitely a nigga with class. I just hoped that I could keep up my charade without getting caught up.

"Where do you live again?" he asked pulling off the curb.

*Oh shit. I couldn't let him drive me to the hood. Somebody's nosy ass would spot me and blow my cover. C'mon Queen. Snap out of it and get your shit together!*

"Oh take me to my friend's house. I am spending the night over there."

"Girl or guy friend?" he joked.

I rolled my eyes in an attempt to be angry. He smiled and turned on the radio. The Quiet Storm was playing on WBLS and the Force MDs *Tender Love* played in the background. I loved listening to slow R&B songs at night.

"Is this OK? If not I can put in a tape. I have Public Enemy," he joked.

I groaned at his corniness. "This is cool. You don't have to try so hard Mike. You good peoples. We'll listen to PE another time OK?"

"OK," he answered.

"T lives off Herkimer and New York Avenue before you get to Atlantic Avenue."

"Bet. I know where that is at." Michael drove us the rest of the way in silence until we reached Fulton Street and began, "So Queen, when can I see you again?"

I paused thinking to myself.

"Umm...lemme check my schedule. With my class load and everything. You know…"

He nodded and squeezed my knee gently. "I enjoyed your company and hope to see you soon Queen."

I felt my face grow hot from his touch. I was in un-chartered territory, but I was determined to handle my business. Michael was a challenge. If I could pull this trick off, get him to believe I was an eighteen-year-old college student then I was the master! A true *Trick Mami* as Trina would say.

"I like you too Mike. Tonight was cool. I can't wait to hook up again either," I replied sincerely .

Michael reached over to kiss me and I let him. His lips were soft and at first, it was a peck then gently he probed his tongue between my lips into my mouth. I responded back with all the skill my fifteen-year-old self could give and when we pulled away, I felt weak.

Michael looked at me with sleepy eyes. "This is your stop lady."

"Yeah," was all I could say back. *Damn.* My young curious mind began to wonder if he had bedroom skills. *Slow it down girl.* My mind was made up.

Michael was gonna be my *Sugar Daddy.*

I let myself out before Michael could open the door for me. "I'll call you tomorrow OK?" I told him walking towards the entrance of the projects.

"OK, I'll be waiting," Michael said pulling off and driving up New York Avenue.

I stopped briefly trying to get my heart to stop beating so fast as I watched him drive up the street. I had to make sure that no one saw me get out of Michael's Benz.

The block was dead. It was after ten o' clock. *Shit my moms might be home!* I looked at my living room window which could be seen from the south side of the building.

Lights were on! Dammit!

I needed Trina as a cover. More than likely Trina was still at Raheem's. Thinking of plan B, I walked into the building through the back way and ran upstairs to the second floor where Trina's apartment was. After knocking on the door like a maniac somebody finally answered after the fifth knock.

"Who the Fuck is it?"

"Queen." I heard latches and locks unlock before the door finally cracked open. Trina's dad answered the door with an attitude.

"Yo momma been here looking for you. You need to call downstairs before you go home," He said rolling his eyes.

"Why?"

Trina's dad just looked at me like I'm crazy. "Ask your mother. What the fuck am I, a messenger service? Where the fuck is Trina anyway?"

I looked down and slid pass him inside closing the door behind me as he steps to the side. I had to think quickly, so I say the first thing that comes to mind. "She's at the store and she's on her way now," I lie. The shit sound lame as hell even to me but it was the best I could do on short notice. Trina's dad grunts and mumbles under his breath as he walks into his room closing the door behind him. Trina's mother Earlene, grandma Gertie and Uncle Jack were all in the living room on the couch watching syndicated reruns of Jenny Jones.

I said "hi" to everyone as I passed. They all grunted but paid no attention to me as I went into Trina's room. It had a lock but I knew how to pick it. Trina had a phone installed in her room, so I called my mom from there to see what was up.

"Hello?"

"Queen, is that you?"

"Yeah ma"

"Where have you been?"

"I was with Trina. I'm upstairs in her house now. Mr. Joe told me you wanted me to call you." I heard a male voice in the background and instantly I had an attitude.

"Ah yeah hold on a minute," my mother put the phone down and I heard her laughing and the music in the background playing the Stylistics song *Betcha by Golly Wow.*

"I have company Queen so spend the night at Trina's. School closed tomorrow, right?"

"Yeah Ma. Jew holiday."

"Right. Tomorrow I have to work overtime at the station, so stay at Trina to eat dinner, then be home by ten. Tell Ms. Earlene I will pay her by Friday OK?"

"Un huh," I was half listening.

"Queen, you even listening to me?" she was asking.

"Yeah Ma."

"OK. I will talk to you tomorrow baby," she said giggling. I could hear the guy saying something in the background as she hung up on me. I was pissed. My mother always made me stay at Trina's when she had male company. I began to wonder what this guy's name was. My mother never introduced me to her male suitors unless it was serious. I didn't understand when I was younger. I thought she was ashamed of me. But then I began to realize that if it was just a booty call, why bother to introduce me?

I was bored. Trina wasn't coming home until the A.M. and nobody inside Trina's house was worth talking to so I decided to call Michael.

"Hello?"

"May I speak to Mike?" I asked unsure if the male voice on the other line was him.

"Hi. This is Mike."

"Were you asleep? This is Queen"

"No, not at all I just got out the shower."

I began to imagine him undressed and instantly my nipples got hard. "Want me to call you back?"

"Nah, I can talk. Lemme just put on my robe. Hold on." Michael put me on hold for a minute and then returned back to the phone sounding happy to hear from me.

I heard Luther Vandross playing in the background as he began to speak. "So what's on your mind pretty lady?"

"I don't know. I just wanted to call and let you know I had a good time tonight." *No harm in that right?*

"Me too. I would like to do it again soon Queen."

I was blushing again and glad I was on the phone so that he couldn't see me.

"Me too."

There was a short pause of silence as I listened to Luther sing *A House is Not a Home.*

"There has to be something on your mind. Were you thinking about me?" Mike asked.

I rolled my eyes. Niggas are always so full of themselves. I decided to play along and bring my strongest game just as Trina had taught me. "Yeah . I was thinking about you."

"Really? What were you thinking about?"

"What it would be like to make love to you."

Silence.

*Got 'em.*

He probably didn't think I would come on that strong.

"Ahem. Are you trying to seduce me Ms. Thang?" he asked.

*Of course.* "Are you resisting? I mean c'mon Mike. I am too old to play around. I want you, you want me. Let's make this happen," I said full of confidence and teenage bravado. He laughed and at first I was pissed. How dare this nigga laugh at me! I was serious.

"Queen. There is nothing more sexy than a woman who knows what she wants. Believe me," he said trying to control his laughter.

"That's what I'm talking about."

"But I am not a man to rush 'getting the skins' as you youngsters say," he said.

*What the fuck?!* "Excuse me?" I asked

I know he wasn't turning down no pussy. Unless this guy was an in-the-closet faggot. Exactly what type of game was this nigga running?

"I am saying that I want to get to know you. Everything about you. I believe in making love to your mind first, before getting intimate with you," Mike answered seriously. He paused waiting for his words to sink in.

This niggas game was so weak. Old heads were so fuckin' corny. No wonder why he didn't have no woman! This guy had no game!

"I must say Mike. I ain't never heard of a man turning down sex."

"You're young, so you have a lot to learn."

"Just what is that supposed to mean?" I snapped defensively.

"Whoa. I didn't mean to upset you. I meant that you are probably used to brothers that are pressed to get some ass— excuse me for being so blunt, but I am not a pressed man. I believe that good things come to those who wait and I am willing to wait for the experience of making love to you."

I was quiet as I listened to what he was saying, taking it all in. *Was he serious? Or* did he just have more game than me? I needed Trina's input on this cat. Despite it all, I couldn't front, this guy was turning me on. I saw his game as a challenge and I never walked away from a challenge. Ever.

"Do you agree?" he was asking.

"I see where you are coming from Mike, and I must say I like your style. I was testing to see if you were just some guy on the take. But I can see that you are down a to earth brother. I am looking forward to seeing where this goes," I said as I waited for his response.

*Game recognizes Game nigga.* Bring it.

"Me too," he said.

All of a sudden a knock at the door startled me.

"Mike hold on a minute OK?" I put the phone down and pressed the mute button so he wouldn't hear any background noise. I got up and opened Trina's bedroom door to see her brother Rob standing before me with just a towel on.

"What up kid? I am looking for my Nike sweat suit. You seen it?"

"Nah," I said admiring the view of his chest and tight abs. This nigga's body was the bomb.

"I didn't mean to interrupt. I know that broad got my shit somewhere," he said looking around the room.

"OK," I answered going back to my comfortable spot to talk to Mike. "I'm back. Did you miss me?"

Rob made a face at me as he picked up his sweat suit from under Trina's bed.

"Yeah I did. What took you so long? I was beginning to wonder if you forgot about me or something."

Walking out the door Rob winked at me closing the door behind him. "Never that Mike."

We talked into the wee hours of the morning until I started

to see daylight peek from the curtains.

"Mike?"

"Yeah babe?"

"What time is it?"

"It's…oh shit it's five am baby."

"Don't you have to go baby?" I ask.

"Yep. Work is gonna be real interesting today."

I laughed. "Too bad you don't get a Jew holiday off, too."

"I know."

"Well, call me later OK?"

"Bet. Have a good day I will be thinking about you."

"Me too."

I hung up the phone and rolled over in the bed to get comfortable on the big ass Queen-sized bed. It was soft as shit with the big comforter laid across it. Maybe I could get some z's before noon. After all, I was tired as hell. It didn't take long for me too find sleep dreaming of Mike and how I was gonna enjoy playing his ass for all his paper.

## CHAPTER SIX

Trina got home a couple of hours later bragging about her night with Raheem. She apparently gamed his ass for a shopping trip. Trina had stacks of Macy's bags with Liz Claiborne, Tommy Hilfiger, Polo, Guess, and Nautica gear. She also had a pair of Jordan's and a pair of jumbo shell doorknocker earrings with her name across it in script. I was jealous as shit but refused to show it. I kept a poker face as I asked her about her loot.

"Damn bitch. You scored like a bandit."

Trina was all smiles as she modeled her yellow and white Polo jacket in my face. "Don't hate. You could have this too. I'm gonna hook you up with his friend Red. He got his own business and everything."

That sounded like what was up. I could hold out longer with Michael on giving up some pussy if I had another nigga on the side. *Queen you are a genius.* "Hook me up T."

"Bet. But first help me hide all this shit from my nosy ass brothers and my uncles," Trina said.

We put all her bags in the trunks she had with a lock and a hidden combination under her bed and in her closet. I didn't even know the combo to any of them, so I hoped that nothing ever happened 'cuz then she would be screwed on getting access.

After helping her with all that I decided it was time for me to take my bum ass home to change clothes. Since it was Friday, it was time for me and Trina to hang out. Usually we go out to the clubs on Friday. I hadn't decided if I wanted to go out to the club tonight or not. But I headed back to my crib and told T, I would hook up with her later.

When I got home, the house was quiet. My moms was

gone and the place looked messy from last night. Burnt incense sticks were on the coffee table and Tina Marie was still playing in the tape deck singing *Portuguese Love*. Our apartment was small for a two bedroom. We lived on the first floor. It was a cool place, had a modest sized kitchen, small living room one bathroom and a large hall closet. My mother's room was the smallest of the two rooms located in the front of the apartment, right by the door. I hated that. She always knew when I came in when she was home. So I would creep in through the patio screen sometimes.

My room was bright I painted. It was a pretty light yellow and I designed it with posters. I have all kinds on my wall from when I was small to now. Salt–n-Pepa to Big Daddy Kane to Public Enemy. I even had Storm from the X-men. That was the shit. When I was a little kid I was a comic book head. I loved Marvel comics. I used to even read DC comics and be a fan of Wonder Woman that was before shit got bad and we moved to Herkimer projects.

My mom was a teacher's aide at a church daycare before I was born. Her dad and my dad still kicked it off and on, and then he bounced before I turned two. We had no place to go and no worthy relatives to stay with, so my mother and I went to a homeless shelter system in Manhattan. She stayed nine months working during the day and saving money. In 1980 she was placed on the wait list for a new apartment complex in Bed–Stuy. It was called Halston Court houses but we all knew it as Herkimer projects because of the street it was built on. I had just turned two when we officially moved in.

The first apartment was a one bedroom on the third floor. My mother got pregnant again in 1982 and we moved into a two bedroom downstairs on the first floor before my brother was born. On August 12, 1982 my brother Xavier was born. Two weeks later he was found dead in his crib. He had died of

SIDS. My mother never talked about Xavier or his father. I do know that she keeps his baby picture along with his birth and death certificates in her bottom drawer. Sometimes I look at it and wonder what it would be like to have had a baby brother. Maybe then I wouldn't be so lonely with my mother gone all the time. I mean I had Trina and her family, but that shit ain't the same. The only good thing that came out of Xavier's death was that grandma Jane and my mom rebuilt their relationship. We started visiting her out in Queens and I started getting to know her more and more.

I turned off the tape deck and put the radio on as I went into the kitchen to clean up. I had the dishes done, swept the floor and mopped by five o'clock. Suddenly I was hungry and decided to make a grilled cheese sandwich to hold me until later on. If it was one thing I could do, it was cook a little. I was good at following recipes too. At I.S. 117, I took a home economics class and learned how to make all kinds of shit like spaghetti, chicken, and meatloaf. Shit, if I was ever gonna survive living with moms, I was gonna have to learn how to go for self. Word.

Trina called to check on me around seven. "Sup bitch. You gonna be ready by nine or what?"

"Why so early? The club ain't poppin' until around twelve."

"I gotta go get some money from Rah."

I sucked my teeth. "C'mon T, you know once we go to Bushwick you ain't gonna want to go!"

"Stop fucking whining. We going. I just need some dough that's all."

"Whatever."

"Whatever nothing! Your broke ass ain't got no ends so you can't say shit."

"Forget what I said then damn."

"What you wearing anyway?" Trina asked trying to

change the subject.

That was a good ass question. Unlike Trina I had no new gear to rock.

"I got that suede skirt from A&S I could rock."

"No way. Wear that spandex with your acid wash jeans."

"I don't have any."

"Bleach a pair of Levi's. Don't you have a pair you got from VIM's last week?"

"The one that I got with the jacket that I tagged from the 45 Kings at the mall?"

"Yeah with Jessica Rabbit on it."

"Cool."

That jacket was fly as shit. It had a black version of Jessica Rabbit of *Who Framed Roger Rabbit?* on it, drawn by the 45 Kings who were some Bronx graffiti artists who tagged clothes and shit out at the Coliseum in Queens.

"I can wear my shit to match. We can stop in Bushwick and be in Flatbush by twelve," Trina said.

"OK. Peace."

"Peace."

I hung up the phone and decided to shower. I had to iron, curl my hair, and decide what jewelry to rock. En Vogue's *Hold On* was playing on the radio as I walked into the bathroom to shower. Just as I was about to hop in, the phone starts to ring. I hesitated and debated as to whether I was going to answer or not, the phone rang loudly and consistently as if it was pissed off. I knew I had better answer it because it was probably my moms.

"Hello"

"Queenie?"

"Yeah, Ma"

"You ain't hear the damn phone ringing off the damn hook?"

"Yes, I was in the shower at first though"

"For what. Where the fuck is you going now?"

"Nowhere except back to Trina's house. I been cleaning all day. I smell like Pine Sol and bleach." *Ungrateful old bitch.*

"You mopped the kitchen and bathroom too?"

"Yes. I just gotta get the laundry."

"Good," my mother's tone softened now that she had no more reason to fuss at me.

"Listen I won't be home tonight I will be out, so I want you to stay at Ms. Earlene's."

"You gotta work?" I asked.

"Mind your business," my mother snapped. "No…"

Silence.

I waited for an answer.

"I will be at Vincent's"

"Who is that?"

"My new man."

*Whatever* I'm thinking *let's see how long this shit lasts….*

"So when *will* you be home?" I snap.

"Who the mother, who the child here?" My mother asks

I roll my eyes. I was glad we were on the phone though 'cuz had we been in person my mother would have slapped the shit out of me.

"I will be home on Sunday. I want your fast ass over at Ms. Earlene's."

"Yes, Ma."

"Oh, and Call your grandma Jane she's in the hospital."

"Where?"

"St. John's. The number is 718-555-3214. Room 281. We are going to go visit her soon. OK?"

"Aiight."

"You heard me?"

"Yeah Ma!" I snap. Damn she gets on my nerves. My mother is a trip.

"You better call your grandmother and I better find your

ass over at Trina's," she said as we finally hang up from each other.

I was irritated and horny as hell. The radio was on and the Rap Mix was playing Almond Joy's *Doin It* that song was nasty as hell but I loved it. I began to gyrate and sway to the song imagining that I was Almond Joy talking to Michael. Facing the mirror on my wall in my room, I began to strip tease taking off my clothes piece by piece until I stood naked in front of the mirror . Once naked I lay across the bed to get comfortable. I was so damn horny. I began to tweak my nipples until they rose at attention. Then I caressed my breasts in a slow rhythm as Almond Joy sang about what she was gonna do to her man.

I began to slowly go downward with my hands until they were at the meeting of my thighs just at the top of my neatly trimmed bush. I had not touched myself in a while, instantly I felt my heat surging from between my legs, hot with anticipation of what I was about to do.

Gently, I put one, then two fingers inside myself, parting my lips which were so very wet.

"It felt so great and oh so good," Almond Joy sang. I imagined Michael's head between my legs licking my pussy like he was hungry. I closed my eyes as I probed deeper inside my pussy, rubbing my clit with my thumb.

"Oh , shit…" I moaned despite myself. Two fingers wasn't doing it so I put another in stretching my walls, pretending that it was Michael's big fat dick thrusting in and out of me. I was on the edge and I felt a warm feeling rush over me. Heart racing breathing hard, sweat beginning to form as I struggled with my nut. I was almost there…

"He tried to front but I heard a sound…"

In my mind I heard Michael on top of me pounding my pussy like a nigga fresh out of jail. In, out, in, out…I could imagine the look on his face as he came inside me…

Oh God that did it…

"Yes! Yes!" I moaned. Finally I released my nut leaving my fingers wet and sticky with my own juices.

Sometimes touching yourself is better than sex with any nigga. Word.

By eight o'clock I was ready to head to Trina's crib. My gear was crisp and I had on my new Jordan's. All I needed was a touch of makeup to make it complete. After locking the door behind me, I was off to Trina's for a new episode. Trina's brother Rob opened the door when I got there. He didn't even speak to me like he usually did, and the house was unusually quiet when I got there. I walked to the back where Trina's room was since Rob seemed to have an attitude and shit. Trina's bedroom door was cracked and I heard soft voices coming from behind the door. A creepy feeling came from over me and instead of making my presence known something told me to wait. Since curiosity was getting the better of me, I paused at the door taking a peak through the cracks being careful so that no one would hear me.

I wished I wasn't being so nosy, I wished I never looked. As I peeked through the crack in the door, I was shocked at what I saw. It was Trina. She was down on her knees giving her Uncle Jay some head! Her eyes were closed and she seemed to enjoy taking his dick in her mouth. From what I could tell, he wasn't that big in width or length. Her uncle was her father's youngest brother. I felt sick to my stomach, but I was unable to walk away despite myself. I started to force myself to back up before I got caught.

I backed up just in time as Trina got off her knees and got on the bed. She was totally naked but her uncle had on clothes. He stepped out of his pants and was naked from the waist down. He got on top of Trina and inserted his dick inside her and he began to fuck her with her legs on his shoulders as she made noises. I was frozen with fear of getting caught staring at them. My mind refused to believe what I was seeing!

How could Trina let her uncle fuck her? It didn't take long for him to cum and all of a sudden it was over. Her uncle got off Trina, wiping his dick with his T-shirt as he reached for his pants. I backed up slowly into the bathroom which was next to her room. I heard Trina speak as I stood in the bathroom doorway.

"You got what I asked for?" she asked.

"Yeah, damn. You worst than a Trick?"

"You a fucking trick motherfucker. This pussy ain't free nigga. You gotta pay to lay," Trina snapped.

From the corner of where I am standing I see her sitting in the bed naked, titties swinging mad as hell.

"Here," he said pulling a wad of cash from his pants pocket. It looks like at least a hundred. I can't tell.

"It better all be here too," Trina says counting it.

"Next time pay on time or Daddy will find out what kind of sick ass brother he got," Trina threatens.

"You think he don't know you a hoe? Who gonna believe your hoe ass?" Jay laughed.

"If you wanna chance that go ahead. I betcha Rob would love to get his hands on you."

Her uncle got quiet.

"Bitch," her murmured. As he opened the door to let himself out, I froze a hot second then closed the bathroom door with my heart racing. *Oh shit, oh shit, oh shit.* I just knew he saw me.

I heard Trina's door close and lock, and then the front door open and close. I decided to wait it out. If her uncle saw me I was sure he would call me on it. I wanted to let Trina know I was here but if I went in the room now, I would smell sex. I wanted to vomit. Trina was fucking her uncle and bribing his ass for money. Ain't that a bitch? What type of fucked up shit was this family into?

A knock at the door startled me as I rushed to act like I was using it. I turned on the water pretending to wash my hands. "Who is it?"

"Trina. Who is it in there?'

"Ah it's me Queenie. I will be out in a minute."

"OK. Hurry up I gotta douche right quick," Trina said walking away from the door.

*I bet you do* I think to myself turning off the water in disgust. I walk out the door walking pass Trina without looking at her.

"Who let you in?"

"Rob," I answered walking into her room.

"Oh, I didn't think anybody was home."

"Ah yeah. He left after he let me in," I said still not looking at her.

Trina was staring at me even though I did my best not to look her in the face. I could lie with the best of them but Trina knew me like a book. "You was in the bathroom the whole time then?"

"Yeah, I think I got the runs. I had some nasty left over Chinese at the crib before I came over," I lied again glancing over at her quickly to see if she bought it.

Trina's face gave away nothing. "Whatever. Lemme just get fresh real quick. I will be right out so I can do your makeup."

"Cool." I sat down in her room on the other twin bed that I slept in facing the wall. All I could do was stare at the sheets as I recalled what I had seen. I could never admit what I had saw. I would take that to my fucking grave…

# Meet the Authors

## Kia DuPree

Kia DuPree, a native of Washington, D.C., received the Fiction Honor Book Award from the Black Caucus of the American Library Association for her debut novel *Robbing Peter* in 2005.

She also holds degrees from Hampton University, Old Dominion University and New York University. She lives in Brooklyn, New York where she is currently working on her next novel.

### Also by Kia…
*Robbing Peter*

www.kiadupree.com

## Gena Garrison

Gena L. Garrison a native of Greenville, South Carolina, began writing as a teen-ager. She attended SC State University in Orangeburg, SC majoring in music. Gena has a well rounded love of the arts including singing and writing.

Baring it All, a love story between a sinner and a saint, Gena's first published novel was released in May 2005 by Publish America. She was voted Best New Author and Best New Book Club discussion by Mahogany Media.

Gena currently resides in Greer, SC with her son and pet Pekingese.

genalgarrison@yahoo.com
www.genagarrison.com

## Michael A. Gonzales

Michael A. Gonzales has written cover stories for XXL, The Source, Vibe and Uptown. His short fiction has appeared in Brown Sugar: A Collection of Erotic Black Fiction, Bronx Biannual and the forthcoming The Darker Mask. Originally from Harlem, he currently resides in Brooklyn.

blog: http://blackadelicpop.blogspot.com
ww.myspace.com/blackadelicpop

## Da'Neen Hale

I was born and raised in Cleveland, Ohio. While being an avid reader of Urban fiction and Street Lit I always longed to pen my own tales. After taking my share of bumps and bruises of trying to enter the writing world I was offered the opportunity of a life time by Mr. Shannon Holmes. Please look forward to my debut novel "Possession" coming soon under Shannon Holmes Communications Media.

Jus4Neen@hotmail.com.

## Dwayne O. Byfield

Born in Kingston Jamaica, Dwayne came to America with his mother at the age of 5. It was while living in Long Island that he excelled in many art forms, from drawing to music, and fell in love with the sport basketball. He used basketball as a tool to get out of public school, into a private education, and later to a University.

After traveling the world with a ball in hand and receiving his Bachelors' in Business Management, Dwayne found comfort in something he never thought he would—his writing. Writing was therapeutic to him and today he still uses it to council himself. Some of his work can be found online at the following sites.

dwayne.byfield@gmail.com
http://myspace.com/alookinside2008
http://www.facebook.com/profile.php?id=1040087166
http://www.thoughts.com/alookinside2008/blog
http://alookinside08.livejournal.com/

# Nicole "Jahzara" Bradley

Jahzara is a native of Gary, Indiana. She attended West Side High School where she graduated with honors. She is also a graduate of Indiana University Bloomington. Jahzara is a member of Zeta Phi Beta Sorority and Author 4 Charity. She also is the owner of Tranquil Moments LLC, her very own therapeutic massage business and publishing company. Her community involvement includes facilitating fundraisers for organizations geared to children and those in need, facilitated a "Massage Therapy 4 Charity" event for a homeless shelter, hosted a pampering session for battered women. In her spare time, Jahzara enjoys hosting pamper parties, being pampered, traveling, reading, and spending time with family, friends, her husband, and last but certainly not least her two pretty princesses.

## Also by Nicole
*Contradictions*
*"A Life of Trials—A Testimony of Faith"*
found in
*My Soul Looks Back and Wonders: How Faith Pulled Me Through*

## Coming soon...
*Luv Don't Live Here Anymore*
*Luv U 4 Life.*
*DA Test: Is He Date-able?*
*Real Talk: A Heart to Heart Among Sisters* (DVD Format)

jahzara2007-book@yahoo.com
Jahzara@jahzarawrites.com
www.jahzarawrites.com
www.myspace.com/iluvjahzara

# Russell Little

After being laid off, feeling betrayed, armed with an unemployment check and two handwritten notebooks, he created A Little Publications. Russell Little's enthusiasm to continually innovate and push the literary envelope drives him, and he currently resides in Philadelphia where he is completing his second novel, Freddy Shanks (West-Philly ripper) and follow up to "Hell to the no" part 2. Drawing upon his abilities as a hustler, his experiences as a social worker, along with his business savvy, Russell Little has gone on to teach, publish and release his first novel, Hell to the NO!

## Also by Russell
*"Hell to the no!"*

## Coming soon...
*"Hell to the no!" Part II,*
*Freddy Shanks (West-Philly ripper)*

rsl@alittlepublications.com
www.ALittlepublications.com
www.myspace.com/rslittle1169
alittlepublications-subscribe@yahoogroups.com

# Rhonica Wesley

Rhonica Wesley began to write at the young age of seven years old. While her peers got toys for Christmas Rhonica wanted writing tools. Gaining a love for quiet corners and still afternoons Rhonica began her lenghty love affair with writing. Today, Ms Wesley resides in Shreveport, Louisiana and is the mother of two beautiful children. Aside from writing, she also manages her graphic design business.

## Also by Rhonica
*"Live for thyself"* (novella)

## Currently working on first novel...

rhonicawesley@yahoo.com
www.rhonicawrites.com
www.myspace.com/doubledigits713

# Angel Mitchell

New author, Angel Mitchell is looking to make waves in the literary world with her debut novel, *Another Woman's Husband*.

Angel's passion for writing keeps storylines and characters constantly running through her mind, and her fingertips continuously pecking on the keyboard. Her goal is to become a full-time author.

Originally from Florida, Angel resides in Virginia with her

two children. She is currently working on several projects, while anticipating the release of her debut novel under Shannon Holmes Communications Media, Spring 2008.

## Coming soon…

*Another Woman's Husband*

www.myspace.com/writeordiechic
angelmechelle@hotmail.com

# *Eric White*

Born in the Northeast section of the Bronx, Eric has always found an escape from the everyday stress of life by burying himself in a good urban novel. After reading countless stories from an array of talented authors he decided to put his thoughts and experiences on paper feeling that the realities he'd seen or lived would make for good reading. When Shannon Holmes offered him an opportunity to participate in an anthology, he immediately accepted. Over the past three years, he has been working on multiple manuscripts that he is hoping to have published in the very near future.

## Coming soon…

*"Under The "L"* (the novel)
*"What's Sweet is Sour"*…
*"Un-Named Urban Fiction" Tale*

EWhite3349@aol.com
www.myspace.com/Bookpaper

# *Josie N. Bradley*

Josie N. Bradley has been writing since the age of ten. She is a single mom of three children ages 12, 14, and16. Josie is very grateful for the opportunity to be published being given to her by Mr. Shannon Holmes. Without his support she would not be this far in her writing career.

Josie is excited about being a part of this anthology and is looking forward to her upcoming novel, Trick Mami. Ms Bradley has other stories in the works as well, including a yet to be titled love story.

## Coming soon...

*Trick Mami*

Josienikkidaauthor@yahoo.com
www.myspace.com/daauthor

# Tony Black
### Clothing Co. 2004

*Struggle*  *T-Shirt*

**SHIP TO:**

Name:_____ _____
              (First)                                           (Last)

Street Address:_____ Apt #_____

City:_____ State:_____ Zip:_____

| Size | Color | Quantity | Price Ea | Total Price |
|------|-------|----------|----------|-------------|
| 1X | Blue | 2 | $15.00 | $30.00 |
|  |  |  |  |  |
|  |  |  |  |  |
|  |  |  |  |  |
|  |  |  |  |  |
|  |  |  |  |  |
|  |  |  |  |  |
|  |  |  |  |  |
|  |  | Merchandise Total |  |  |
| (Allow 2 wks for delivery) Shipping & Handling |  |  |  | FREE |

**NO CASH REFUND, EXCHANGE OF SIZE OR COLOR ONLY**

Colors: Black, White, Grey, Tan, Royal Blue
Sizes:   Large – 3X

Make Check or Money Order
Payable To:
Tony Black Clothing Co.
P.O. Box 1297
Bronx, NY 10451-1297

Contact Info: TonyBlackApparel@yahoo.com • (917) 428-7144

# NEW LIFE HAIR

## CHESHIRE PLAZA SHOPPING CENTER